Inked Up

INKED UP

TERRI THAYER

WHEELER
CHIVERS

This Large Print edition is published by Wheeler Publishing, Waterville, Maine, USA and by BBC Audiobooks Ltd, Bath, England.
Wheeler Publishing, a part of Gale, Cengage Learning.
Copyright © 2009 by Terri Thayer.
The moral right of the author has been asserted.
A Stamping Sisters Mystery.

The text of this Large Print edition is unabridged.
Other aspects of the book may vary from the original edition.
Set in 16 pt. Plantin.
Printed on permanent paper.

LIBRARY OF CONGRESS CATALOGING-IN-PUBLICATION DATA

Thayer, Terri.
  Inked up / by Terri Thayer.
    p. cm. — (A Stamping Sisters mystery) (Wheeler Publishing large print cozy mystery)
  ISBN-13: 978-1-4104-2162-3 (softcover : alk. paper)
  ISBN-10: 1-4104-2162-7 (softcover : alk. paper)
  1. Women artisans—Fiction. 2. Murder—Investigation—Fiction. 3. Halloween—Fiction. 4. City and town life—Pennsylvania—Fiction. 5. Large type books. I. Title.
  PS3620.H393I65 2010
  813'.6—dc22   2009038001

BRITISH LIBRARY CATALOGUING-IN-PUBLICATION DATA AVAILABLE
Published in 2010 in the U.S. by arrangement with The Berkley Publishing Group, a member of Penguin Group (USA) Inc.
Published in 2010 in the U.K. by arrangement with The Berkley Publishing Group, a member of Penguin Group (USA) Inc.

U.K. Hardcover: 978 1 408 47786 1 (Chivers Large Print)
U.K. Softcover: 978 1 408 47787 8 (Camden Large Print)

Printed in the United States of America
1 2 3 4 5 6 7 14 13 12 11 10

ACKNOWLEDGMENTS

Thanks to my ever-ready critique group, Beth Proudfoot and Becky Levine. They always know what I need to move my story forward.

Thanks to Sandy Harding and the various editors at Berkley Prime Crime, who make my work better with their insights.

CHAPTER 1

"Mother Goose, tell us a story," April said.

Mary Lou, dressed in a white puffy-sleeve blouse and very short skirt, struck a pose, licking her finger dramatically as though she were turning a page in a giant storybook.

"You look more like the St. Pauli girl than Mother Goose anyhow," Rocky said, snapping the top of her thigh-highs. "All you need is a bowl full of pretzels."

"Danke," Mary Lou said, dropping into a curtsy and pretending to scowl at Rocky. "What do you think?" she asked, directing her remark at April. "Too slutty?"

Uh-oh. April Buchert meant to be diplomatic, but the wine that Rocky had been liberally pouring had stripped her of her usual filters, so she found herself blurting out, "That vest is working like a push-up bra, giving you Dolly Parton boobs. But with the right accessories . . ."

April's voice petered out as she saw the

look on Mary Lou's face. Ever since her daughter had given birth to twins, Mary Lou had been fighting dressing her age. She was afraid people would assume she was old just because she was a grandmother.

"Where's Suzi, anyhow?" April asked. "It's her party."

When Rocky had offered her aunt Barbara Harcourt's collection of Halloween costumes to the group for their upcoming stint helping Suzi at her nursery's inaugural corn maze, April had pictured them in a dank basement or musty attic, pawing through trunks of vintage clothing.

Instead, the five of them were in Rocky's studio, which took up the top floor of her long ranch house that overlooked the valley. A professional rack of clothes had been installed along one wall. The floor was littered with red bras and tulle skirts and see-through tops. Aunt Barbara — Mrs. H., as April knew her — had a thing for sexy Halloween costumes. TMI. April was helping in the restoration of Mrs. H.'s mansion every day. She really didn't need to know this about the woman she was working for.

Rocky had put out a spread of smoked salmon, veggies and cheese. And poured the Dolcetto. Good thing April had ridden over with Deana. The wine was going down too smoothly.

April, Deana, Mary Lou, Rocky and Suzi were all rubber stampers. They got together each week to craft, usually without imbibing. Sometimes they made projects from the Stamping Sisters line of stamps Deana sold, but just as often they worked on creating their own designs.

Rocky was a mixed-media artist, earning her living by selling her collages at tourist spots in the Poconos and Bucks County. The shelves and wooden library drawers of her studio contained the photos, paint, fabric, found objects and stamps she used. The walls were covered with works in progress, giving the place an inspiring air.

Mary Lou was a realtor, and like Suzi, she stamped for stress relief. April was a home restoration expert, using stamps to fill the walls of her clients' homes.

"Ta-da!"

April and Deana turned to see Rocky striking a pose. She'd finished getting into her Liza-Minnelli-in-Cabaret getup with miles and miles of leg. She looked great. The black bodysuit emphasized her small waist and the black felt bowler perching on her usual fall of hair emphasized its smoky darkness.

The door opened and Suzi, the owner of

Dowling Nursery, huffed in, lugging a big cardboard box.

Suzi was aghast. "No way."

Rocky cocked her head at the newcomer. "Not scary enough? I could put a scar on my neck and do dripping blood . . ." Rocky checked herself out in the mirror over the dresser, craning her neck, using her red fingernails to illustrate her point.

Suzi was shaking her head. "We're not doing sexy. Or scary."

Rocky stopped making come-hither looks at the mirror and faced Suzi. "You said we were working the Halloween corn maze. Old chum."

"You are. I need you guys to work the admittance table and the make 'n' take project for the children. Kids, get it, kids."

"I want to be Mother Goose," Mary Lou said, coming out of the bathroom.

"You're not going like that?" Suzi said, her voice squawking with disbelief.

Rocky and Mary Lou exchanged a glance. "We look good," Rocky said.

"Hot," Mary Lou agreed, returning to the bathroom mirror to make sure.

Suzi shook her head. "That would be great if we were going to the club's Halloween ball. The Pumpkin Express is a strictly PG affair. I had to sign an affidavit."

Rocky balanced on one foot, strapping on one red stiletto. "Well, that doesn't sound like much fun."

Suzi said, "What can I tell you? This is tame. The Pumpkin Express is in the daytime, and my A.maz.ing Corn Maze is supposed to be fun, not earth-shatteringly scary. Definitely not sexy."

The Pumpkin Express, or "PE" as it was called by the locals, had been started a few years ago by seven Aldenville businesses. On the Saturday before Halloween, each turned their place into a Halloween destination. They challenged the customers to visit every business and take part in their festivities. In one day. At each venue, the customer would collect a stamp on their PE Passport. People who completed the route, with a stamp from each location, were eligible for prizes.

After last year when the Popper Petting Zoo had dropped out, Dowling Nursery was voted in. Though she had been featuring a fall corn maze for the last few years, this was the first year Suzi's place would be an official stop on the Pumpkin Express. That meant thousands of people would be going through her corn maze, maybe spending money in the gift shop, and hopefully returning to the nursery in the spring for their annuals. It was a great opportunity for Suzi.

But there were rules to be followed.

"That sucks," Rocky said. She put on the heels anyway and strutted around the room. April heard her humming strains of "Life is a Cabaret." Rocky switched to "Puttin' on the Ritz" as she joined Mary Lou in the bathroom. She complained loudly about not being allowed to scare little children.

Suzi sighed and dumped the contents of the box she'd been carrying onto the bed. Costumes spilled out.

"These are not sexy," April said. She pulled out two hats: a Sherlock Holmes deer hunter and a pirate's trefoil, complete with fake parrot.

"Good," Deana said. "Maybe I can find something to wear."

As the owner of the local funeral home, Deana's costume options were limited. No Grim Reaper or Casper the Friendly Ghost for her. Even Snow White brought up reminders of the coffin the fairy tale princess had spent her coma in. Deana couldn't afford to alienate any potential clients.

"I'll help you find something more appropriate," Suzi said.

"Where's Mitch, April?" Rocky said, joining them and pawing through the clothes.

"My brother needs a costume, too. Maybe you two could use the Sonny and Cher outfits my parents wore in 1978."

Eww. April didn't fancy dressing like Mitch's parents or washed-up rock stars.

Deana shot her a sympathetic look. She knew April was keeping her relationship with Mitch quiet, letting it grow slowly, out of the very public eye of the small town they lived in.

"I don't know where Mitch is," April said. That was literally true. Not at this exact moment, anyhow.

"Are you going to see him later?" Rocky asked.

Mitch came over to April's most nights, after their long workdays were over, for a few hours.

"Probably not," April answered. "I have an appointment with Xenia Villarreal."

Rocky popped her head through the green shift that Suzi had dropped over her.

"Kind of late for an appointment, isn't it?" She used air quotes around the word "appointment" and looked significantly at the clock. "It's nearly nine now. And on a school night," she said.

"Xenia is the mom of the family that won Mitch's lottery?" Deana asked.

April knew Deana was trying to shift

Rocky out of her nosy sister mode. Rocky was always fishing for more information. April thought it was up to Mitch to talk to his sister, not her. "That's right, Dee. Mitch's first Winchester Home for Hope."

Rocky buckled the patent leather black belt severely over the green shift. Adding a felt hat, she looked like she had stepped straight out of Sherwood Forest. "This is what my brother should be wearing. He's the real Robin Hood, robbing the rich and giving to the poor."

"He's not really robbing anyone," April said, wondering if that meant she was his Marian.

"You know what I mean. Aunt Barbara's land, some money donations, and suddenly my brother is building homes for the down-trodden."

Deana said, "It's a wonderful thing Mitch is doing. He saw a need for low-income housing and he's stepped up."

Rocky smiled. "No argument from me. My brother is quite a guy."

April said, "Anyhow, Xenia is coming after her kids are all in bed. We're going over paint choices for the house."

"Is the house that far along?" Suzi asked. "That was fast."

The stampers had all been at the ground-breaking ceremony for Mitch's Winchester Homes for Hope two months earlier.

"Prefab housing can go up very quickly," Rocky said. "He used a kit house for the shell."

"And lots of volunteers," April added. "The drywall mud is going up this week, and the well is being dug. We'll be ready to paint the interior after Halloween."

"Mark and I will help," Deana said.

"How about this, April?" Rocky said. She'd returned to the pile of costumes. She pulled out a calico dress. Empire waist and floor length, it looked like something a hippie chick had taken off at Woodstock just before jumping naked into a muddy pond.

Rocky said, "I remember my mother wearing this one year with a headband and granny glasses."

"Lovely," April said. So not flattering.

"How about this?" Rocky pulled out a cheerleader outfit.

"I'm not really the rah-rah type."

As they were looking for something suitable for April, Deana changed into a colonial woman's dress. The strings of the sheer batiste bonnet dangled near her chin. Rimless reading glasses perched on the end of her nose. She looked old enough to be Benjamin Franklin's wife, but she was fine with that.

Mary Lou came out of the bathroom. She'd taken a cuticle scissor to the skirt hem. The fabric now reached well below her knees.

"How's this? Now I look like I'm wearing a burka. It's either this or looking like an over-the-hill beer-peddling, customer-diddling fraulein."

"You don't have to," April said. "Just cover up a little and everyone will recognize you as a hip Mother Goose."

Mary Lou smiled at April and flopped on the bed. Deana followed her and promised to fix the skirt to a suitable length. Mary Lou agreed to downplaying the cleavage with a piece of lace. She and Deana put their heads together to plan their strategy.

Suzi drifted over to the rack of costumes Rocky's aunt had sent over. Something shiny and sequined was hanging behind the cheerleader outfit.

"I want this," Suzi said, her eyes wide with lust. *This* was a surprise.

April had figured Suzi would wear her usual denim overalls and call herself Mr. Greenjeans. This red sparkly thing was a Wonder Woman jumpsuit. Suzi perched the gold crown on her forehead. She held up the short red, white and blue costume to her and looked in the mirror. "Shazam!" she said, twirling the lasso attached to the shorts.

She turned to the group at large. "I'm wearing this," she said in a tone that broached no discussion. Just as well, they all seemed to be struck dumb anyhow.

April snuck a glance at Deana. The costume was so unlike Suzi, who usually dressed in a man's T-shirt and jeans. Her only departure was the khakis and dress shirt she wore to church each Sunday.

April knew if she started giggling, Deana would lose it. She gulped, hoping a large breath would stymie any laughter wanting to escape. Rocky nudged April with her elbow and grinned wickedly. Deana covered her mouth.

"Wonder Woman?" Mary Lou asked finally. "Really?"

"Why not?" Suzi said. "I just finished readying the nursery for the Pumpkin Express. We had to build the corn maze, put up all the Halloween decorations, stock the gift store. In less than two weeks. You bet I'm Wonder Woman."

Rocky grabbed her wineglass to toast her. "Here, here," she said. "Here's to letting your inner action hero come out and play."

17

CHAPTER 2

Back at her home, April thought about Mitch's project as she waited for Xenia. Mitch had always been inspired by Jimmy Carter and had even spent a summer building Habitat homes in Guatemala. After his aunt Barbara gave him a piece of land, he decided to use his talents and build his own version of the Habitat for Humanity homes. He split the plot into four pieces and set up his own foundation, the Winchester Homes for Hope. He built a website, calling for needy families to apply for the first of the houses. He had a long list of restrictions. Income was the major one. Out of the forty people that had applied, the Villarreals had fit all the criteria the best, and last month, had been declared the recipients of the first Homes for Hope house.

April hadn't met any of the family, except for the father, Pedro, who worked in the country club kitchen with Bonnie. She didn't know what to expect from Xenia, but she was excited to finally meet her. Mitch had spent all his spare time on this project, and she wanted to meet the lucky woman who'd be moving in soon.

When she heard the knock on the kitchen door April figured it was Xenia and was pleased that she'd bypassed the giant barn doors, finding instead the entrance that family and friends used. Though it was after ten, Xenia was brimming with energy.

"Sorry to come so late," she said. "I have to wait for my children to get to bed before I get any time to myself. My husband is at work. My oldest is watching the others."

"Oh, is that okay?" April asked.

"Vanesa's fourteen now," Xenia clarified, "so it's fine."

"Sorry, it's just that you don't look old enough to have a teenager."

"I'm thirty-six," Xenia said. She was a pretty woman with soft dark brown hair that curled around her face. Having five children had not had much effect on her compact, athletic body. With her youthful looks, people probably assumed she'd been a child bride, pregnant in high school. April was a little ashamed to realize she'd been thinking along those lines herself.

Still, curious, April heard herself ask,

"How old are your other children?"

"Tomas is eleven, Greg, nine, Jonathan is eight and baby Erika is five," Xenia replied proudly.

"Good for you," April said. She had no idea what it meant to want kids, never mind nearly a half dozen. But she admired someone who knew what they wanted and made their dreams come true.

Xenia laid an envelope on the table.

"Is Mitch coming, too? I stopped at the house to remeasure the kitchen windows. I'm heading to Wal-Mart tomorrow, and I want to buy some fabric for curtains. When I went in, I found this slipped under the door."

Mitch's name was lettered on the front of the envelope, using an alphabet stamp. April had the same set, little round pegs with the stamps affixed to the front. It had to be from Rocky. Was she so desperate to talk to her brother she was leaving him notes at the house? His Homes for Hope project had left him little time for much else and he spent any spare time with her. It was tough but April figured Rocky would just have to learn to let go of her brother a little.

"He'll be along soon," April said. "I'll give it to him. Shall we get to work? Let me show you what Mitch sent over," April said, pulling out a chair at the kitchen table for Xenia to sit in. Pushing her stamping supplies and sketchbook over to one side, April sat down across from her and spread out the paint chips Mitch had supplied.

She expected Xenia to look at the samples. Instead, Xenia grabbed April's sketchbook and turned the pages slowly. A wide grin filled her face. "You do this, too?" she said, pointing to a section of the book that was filled with glossy pictures ripped from magazines and catalogs.

April nodded, a little embarrassed. She didn't let anyone look at her sketchbooks. She had at least two dozen, going back to her first year in college. It was the one place she didn't censor herself as she drew, wrote, stamped and pasted pictures that appealed to her. The images in that book were very personal. No one had seen them. Not even her estranged husband, Ken. Least of all, Ken.

She took the book from Xenia gently, not wanting to hurt her feelings. Seemingly unaffected, Xenia reached into the big purse she had brought and pulled out a cheap spiral notebook, stuffed to three times its normal limit. The edges were uneven with pieces of paper sticking out of most of the pages. A rubber band held everything to-gether.

"Me, too," she said, opening the book carefully and putting the rubber band on her wrist. "I call this Suneo, my wish book. I've been cutting out pictures of the house I want ever since I got married. Furniture, rugs, artwork. Even landscaping ideas."

She handed the book to April, who turned the pages and saw notations dating back fifteen years.

"I want you to see something," Xenia said, wetting her forefinger and reaching over to flip through the book. "Here." She pointed to a picture of smartly dressed people crowded onto a midnight blue sofa. They were all looking at a woman, dressed in red, who'd draped herself over a zebra-print chaise.

April only had to glance at the photo. "I've got the same chaise in my book."

"I saw it," Xenia said, satisfied. She leaned back in her chair.

"You have good taste." April laughed.

Xenia looked around the barn with a questioning expression. The space was still mostly empty. April's lowly futon was the only seating in the living room.

April laughed again. "Don't look at this place. I haven't had the time to do what I want to do in here yet." Or the money.

Picking colors for Xenia's walls was easy once April had gone through her wish book. It became obvious that she liked earth tones, with punches of red. They settled on varying shades of warm golds and greens for the dining room, living room and kitchen. Xenia said she'd make some red throw pillows.

April prepared a pot of tea as they discussed the bedrooms. The sketchbook had revealed a lot about Xenia. She was a person with hopes and dreams and aspirations. Like April.

"I have some ideas on how we can divide up the kids' space," April said. She laid out the blueprints Mitch had given her. The one-story house was a modest one, only about twelve hundred square feet. Every inch had to be well utilized.

There were three bedrooms, one for Xenia and her husband, Pedro, one for the two girls and one for the three boys. Mitch had pressed a local furniture dealer to donate unfinished beds, desks and dressers to the project, and Pedro and Xenia were going to stain and paint them. They were bringing their own dining room set and living room furniture from their rental home.

"We've got a set of bunk beds for the older

boys," April said.

"Tomas and Greg," Xenia said. April made a mental note. She still didn't have all their names down.

April stood up and gathered several clear storage boxes of stamps, stacking them on the big kitchen table. She opened the top one and took out several of her home décor stamps. They were larger than her craft stamps, made of heavy-duty rubber glued to wooden blocks. "I suggest we paint the beds white and stamp on the side," she said. "For the little guy, we can go with animals or trucks, but the older ones need something more sophisticated."

She laid out several stamps that she thought might work on the beds — a rock guitar, surfboards, a paisley, a checkerboard border. Xenia examined each one carefully.

April said, "Don't tell Mitch I'm advocating stamping on the furniture. That, to him, is the epitome of horror."

Xenia opened a stamp pad and stamped the image of an ocean wave in her notebook. "From what I've seen, *you* can't do much wrong in his book."

April's head snapped up from the bin where she'd been looking for a spiral. Xenia was grinning at her coyly. "He's always quoting you." She let her voice go gruff, imitating Mitch's tone. "April says gray walls are the latest trend. April says dark hardwood is the only way to go."

"I know he admires my work," April said slowly. "We have a good professional relationship."

Xenia wasn't buying what April was trying to sell. Her eyes twinkled. "If that's what you want to call it," she said, smiling. "From where I'm sitting, the boy has a mad crush. On you."

April steered the conversation back to stamping and paints. By eleven o'clock, she and Xenia had bonded over the inks, embossing and stamp pads. Xenia had sketched out some ideas that she thought her boys would like and agreed to come over again and watch while April carved the stamps.

As they were cleaning up, Xenia said, "I need to find a place for a desk for myself. I have a business. I sell cosmetics."

"Door to door?" April had a vague memory of her mother, Bonnie, buying lipstick and perfume from a friend over coffee.

"Sort of. I work with Queen Trishelle Enterprises."

April brightened. It was a small world. "My friend Deana works with Trishelle, too. She sells the Stamping Sisters line."

Xenia shook her head. "I don't work with that line. I'm strictly beauty products."

"How do you like working with Trish?" April asked. "I'm going to have a meeting with her on Monday. I'm thinking of selling some of my original stamping designs to her. I'm a little nervous."

Xenia waved her hand. "She's not as tough as she thinks she is. Just stand up to her. She likes people who know what they want."

April felt a flurry of anxiety in her stomach. Did she know what she wanted?

"Hey, it's two of my favorite girls," Mitch said. He came in the back door carrying sample boards of kitchen hardware. He kissed April's cheek and she rubbed her hand along his chin. His day had started many hours earlier and his face was rough. She liked the feel.

Xenia smiled at them. "Those my choices?" she said as she took the boards from Mitch.

"Yup," he said. "I need an answer tonight, so I can get them ordered."

"Okay. Vanesa and I can install them. It'll be a good job for her." Xenia rubbed her fingers along a chrome drawer pull. It was cupped, and looked like something found in an old farmhouse. "This one."

"That's what I like. A woman who can make decisions," Mitch said, catching April in his gaze.

"Was that directed at me?" April said, teasingly. She looked at Xenia. "He thought I took too long this morning deciding between buckwheat pancakes or honey-walnut waffles."

"That's a tough one," Xenia said.

"See?" April crowed.

"All I said was I only had a half-hour to eat." Mitch was laughing.

April rolled her eyes at Xenia.

"Listen, girl," Xenia said. "A bit of advice. Never let them get too comfortable. You've got to keep them guessing."

"Oh no. Girl talk," Mitch said, holding his hands over his ears. "I'm not supposed to hear this stuff."

Xenia stood up, laughing. "It's late. You two have to get up early. Aren't you working at the Pumpkin Express?"

"We are."

"My sister and I are bringing the kids to the corn maze tomorrow afternoon."

"April's afraid of corn mazes," Mitch said, with a twinkle in his eye.

"I am not," April said, delivering a glancing blow to Mitch's upper arm.

Xenia's eyes danced, following the two.

She was clearly enjoying their teasing.

Mitch said, "You said you don't want to go in the maze with me."

"They're creepy," April said. She enlisted Xenia in her argument. "Don't you think they're nasty?"

Xenia shook her head. "This one is going to be tame compared to some I've been to."

After she left, April gathered up her sketchbook and the paint cards that were littering the table top, revealing the envelope addressed to Mitch. April picked it up.

Mitch was at the kitchen counter opening a bottle of wine, his back to her.

"Hey," she said. "Xenia found a note for you at the house."

She saw his shoulders stiffen. His hands stopped twisting. "Okay. I'll get it before I leave."

She was curious, but Mitch would tell her when he was ready. "Okay, I just don't want you to forget it."

He laid down the corkscrew and turned, wiping his damp hands on the towel hanging nearby. "I'd better skip the wine and get going."

It was late, but that was their usual pattern. Something else was going on.

"Tired?" April asked. She searched his face for an answer, but his eyes avoided hers.

"Long day. The cabinet install didn't go as smoothly as I'd hoped."

But there was more. April could read Mitch well enough by now to know he was not telling her everything. His eyes strayed to the envelope, still on the table where Xenia'd left it.

"Is this from your sister?" April said, handing him the envelope. "She was grousing earlier."

"Rocky?" Mitch picked up the envelope. "No, no, not her."

April waited for him to explain, but he pushed himself away from the counter, pulling his keys from his pocket.

"I *am* tired," Mitch said. "All of a sudden. It just hit me."

He was hiding something. If Rocky was being a pill, she needed to know. "Let me see the letter," April said, hand outstretched.

Mitch leaned in for a kiss. "I'll see you in the morning . . . hey."

April had the letter out before Mitch had unpuckered. She tossed the envelope on the table and opened up the folded paper. April recognized the alphabet stamp set used in the note. It was called Ransom. For good reason.

Stamped out were two sentences, one atop the other. Not many words, but enough to

29

send a chill down April's spine.

"Stop work on the house. Now."

She looked up to see Mitch watching her carefully. His face was blank as though awaiting her reaction.

"Mitch, this is a threat."

He waved her off, reaching for the letter. "It's harmless. Someone doesn't have enough balls to write a letter to the editor. I'm not going to play along."

"Harmless? How can you know that?"

"Look, this is the third one of these in a month, and nothing's happened . . ." Mitch trailed off as the weakness of his argument was apparent to both of them.

"Three? Mitch, tell me you told the police."

"Who? Yost? Or his chief who's just waiting out his retirement? What would they do? Don't worry, I'll handle it."

"How?"

"In my own way, April."

CHAPTER 3

"Be Afraid."

"Ghost Crossing."

"Ghouls Just Want to Have Fun."

One after the other, Burma-Shave–style, hand-painted signs along the road welcomed guests to the Fifth Annual Pumpkin Express at the Dowling Nursery.

April turned through the open steel gate. Deana was beside her in the passenger seat, and the two friends eagerly viewed the fall decorations. Bales of hay bracketed the road for the last quarter of a mile. On the right, close to the road was the red farmhouse that Suzi had inherited when her parents moved to Arizona. She'd had to pay off several siblings, but the farm, nursery and house were all hers now. And so was the debt load.

Beyond the nursery were the stone silo that served as Suzi's studio, the gift shop, and the corn maze that was the main attraction today. Several brightly striped shade structures had been set up around the grounds. Scarecrows of various shapes and sizes lounged on the hay bales. Pots of orange, yellow and brick-colored mums were everywhere. Pumpkins lined the driveway, leading people onto the property.

One of Suzi's employees, dressed as a bee, motioned to April to roll down her window. She complied.

"Working today?" the bee asked, her antenna bobbing.

April and Deana answered together in the affirmative.

"Park behind the green houses."

They passed others walking from their cars, unrecognizable in their getups. There was a Cookie Monster walking with a pirate who carried a real parrot on his shoulder. He squawked "Kill the cheerleader," as they drove by.

"Look at this place," April said. "I was just here two weeks ago, buying some daffodils and tulips to plant around the barn. That day the place looked sort of forlorn. Now it's completely transformed."

All the spring and summer flowers were gone, the local fruit picked and sold and eaten. Today the space was filled with fall harvest color.

Deana said, "It is amazing. Her parents

used to only have a tiny U-pick pumpkin patch in the fall. Look at it now."

Deana brushed away a hair that had escaped from her sheer colonial bonnet. Her hairline was moist with sweat. Despite it being October, Aldenville was in a heat wave, and the forecasted high was over ninety degrees. Welcome to global warming.

April's costume was a bit more whimsical than Deana's, and not as warm. She'd settled on being a fairy princess. Her tulle skirt was light and airy, and she'd left her legs bare.

"Good, you're here," Suzi said, appearing next to Deana as she loaded Stamping Sisters boxes onto a hand truck. "Where is everyone else?"

April pulled her in for a hug, noticing that Suzi's Wonder Woman boots made her much taller.

"I need to get this party started." Suzi watched a BMW convertible pull in, wincing as it parked too close to her display of gourd topiaries. She pulled on the door handle, revealing Rocky at the wheel.

"Good morning! What's the haps?" Rocky said. She was dressed all in black, with a pointy witch's hat balanced on her lush hair, which chicly obscured one eye, as usual.

"What happened to the Robin Hood

costume?" Suzi asked.

Mary Lou climbed out of the passenger seat, smoothing her apron.

"I wasn't in the mood to rob the rich," Rocky said.

That was ironic. Rocky *was* the rich. Or at least her family was. The Winchesters had once owned the local bank. It wasn't clear how much family money was left, but they still seemed to live well.

Together the women started toward the midway, where orange and black flags colorfully marked the area though they hung still in the windless air.

April turned to see Rocky staring at her. "What are you supposed to be?" Rocky asked, her tone unbelieving and querulous at the same time. She smiled at April to take away the sting, but it didn't quite work. "I don't remember seeing that costume."

"I'm a fairy princess."

The pressure to be something smart and funny for Halloween was immense this year. In her old life in San Francisco, April had rarely dressed up. She'd been able to walk through the Castro and admire the headgear and outrageous outfits without feeling the need to compete. But she'd volunteered to help Suzi at the A.maz.ing Maze at the Pumpkin Express before she'd realized it would mean dressing up.

When Mitch had found out that she and the other stampers were raiding his aunt's Halloween outfits, he offered to go as Sonny to her Cher or Caesar to her Cleopatra. But she didn't want to flaunt their burgeoning relationship by dressing as a pair, so she had resorted to being a traditional fairy princess.

"Okay then, everyone know what they're supposed to be doing?" Suzi hadn't managed to get the dirt out from under her fingernails, so her Wonder Woman costume looked more incongruous than all-powerful. Still, her dark brown eyes seemed backlit by the unexpected glittering red headband that was keeping her short hair under control.

"April, you and Rocky will be manning the admittance table."

Rocky gave her a cheesy thumbs-up.

"The charge for the A.maz.ing Maze is ten dollars. Make sure every person has their hand stamped. No one gets through without that. April designed a very special stamp, by the way."

Suzi stamped out the image of the pumpkin coach and held it up for all to admire.

April felt Rocky shift her feet. She'd submitted a design, too, but a contest had been held at the nursery throughout September and customers had voted April's design as their favorite. It was going to be a long day sitting next to Rocky. Suzi had moved over to a black-and-white striped shade structure.

"Deana, you'll be under the tent right here. Mary Lou will help you with the make 'n' take project for the kids' corner. I've had my people give you four tables and plenty of chairs. You'll be able to have a dozen kids at a time working on your Halloween bag project."

"Thanks," Deana said, wheeling the hand truck, fully loaded with Stamping Sisters boxes, over to the tables.

"What the heck?" Mary Lou said. "Who is that?"

The stampers turned and looked to see who Mary Lou was pointing at.

A nun was making her way from the back parking lot.

Suzi squinted, and Mary Lou modestly covered the bodice of her Mother Goose costume as though her boobs were still on display and not covered by the handkerchief Deana had inserted the day before.

The gait of the nun was uneven on the gravel drive, and April could see she was wearing construction boots. As the nun got closer, April was reminded of the San

Francisco group, the Sisters of Perpetual Indulgence, but there was no evidence of glitter anywhere.

Rocky started to laugh, and April looked back at her in surprise.

"If it isn't Sister Full of Crap," Rocky said.

"Hello, ladies," the nun said. The voice was familiar, but the face was nearly covered with the old-fashioned wimple. The wings on each side of the head had to be a foot and a half long. Only a pinched forehead, cheeks and a chin were visible.

Cheeks that weren't quite smoothly shaved and a chin with a major cleft.

"Mitch?" April said. Rocky was slapping her knee, snorting with laughter.

"I didn't think you'd do it, brother," she said.

"You dared me," he said. Mitch did a turn, then twirled his rope belt.

No one was more shocked than April. Last night he'd said he would be reprising his Axl Rose imitation, coming dressed as a rock star.

"What do you think?" Mitch asked her. "I'm all about raising as much awareness as I can for the Winchester Homes for Hope. People will have a hard time saying 'Don't bother me' to a nun, don't you think?"

"All you have to do is open your mouth

37

and the surprise will be over," Rocky said, wiping tears out of her eyes. "But it was worth it, just seeing you walk across that parking lot. I wish Mom and Dad could see you. Where's my camera?"

Rocky took a few pictures with her cell phone as Mitch posed.

Suzi was checking a list she had in her hand. "Now that we're all here, let's go over the specifics," she said.

The stampers moved closer. Mitch took April's hand and pulled it back through a slit in the habit. She felt herself redden and looked to see if anyone noticed, but all eyes were on Suzi.

She let herself enjoy the heat from his hand, rubbing the callous on his thumb. His hands had a lot of character, the hands of a man who worked hard.

Suzi held up a small booklet made from several pages of orange paper folded in half and stapled together. A black-and-white logo of a train going through the grin of a jack-o'-lantern adorned the front.

"This is a Pumpkin Express passport. Each person will get one of these at any of the seven locations: the Apple Cider Barn, the Parkinson's Auto Sales Haunted Train Ride, the Cramer's Donuts Tunnel of Love, and the rest. The customer will collect a stamp from each place."

To illustrate her point, Suzi opened to the page that said "A.maz.ing Maze" and stamped April's pumpkin coach image on the page.

Suzi continued. "The customer goes to each of the locations today and gets their passport stamped. Each stop has a unique mark. The passenger has until the end of today to collect a stamp from each place. In any order. We don't care where they start or end."

She passed the booklet to Mary Lou, who studied it and handed it to Deana.

"When a customer has collected all the stamps, they turn in their completed passports to get in the drawing for the prizes. The last place they hit takes their passports. If that's us we hang on to them until the Pumpkin Express meeting on Wednesday. The PE vendors will randomly pick the winners from the finishers."

The stampers passed the book around and back to Suzi.

Suzi shifted. Her face was grave. "Thanks, you guys, for volunteering your time. If I had to pay for the extra help, I wouldn't be able to turn a profit. I hope you know what it means for my business to be a part of the Pumpkin Express. Last year they had one thousand people take part, and they're expecting more this year. So I really appreciate what you're doing. It's a big boon to my business."

"Of course," Rocky said. "Who would miss a chance to dress up as a witch and stamp people's hands all day?"

Suzi smiled through the tears that had been building. She wiped her eyes hard. Then she laughed and said, "The grand prize is a trip for two to the Pocono Lodge."

"I heard they brought back the round beds with the satin sheets and fur bedspread," Rocky whispered.

"Did they dig up Dean Martin, too?" Mitch countered.

Rocky sneered. "Yeah. Dead, he still looks better than Jerry Lewis alive."

Suzi continued. "Also, in the prize package, thanks to the generosity of the Stamping Sisters line of products, we've got a complete starter set of Halloween stamps with papers and postcards."

"Nice donation, Dee," April said.

Deana shook her head. "It's not from me. My boss, Trish Taylor, donated it. She's actually giving us a boatload of stuff. This season's, too, not last year's line."

"Impressive." April's stomach did a little flip at the mention of Trish. Monday was right around the corner, and she had work to do before her presentation was ready.

"Mitch, you're doing purely informational, right?" Suzi said. "I've given you a table, and you can set up wherever you want."

He nodded. "I've got a box of flyers and other info in my car. I'll go get it and then put myself somewhere between the admittance table and the kids' table. I want to be able to talk to people when they come in. If their kids are occupied, that's even better for me."

Mitch continued. "I may have to duck out for a time in the afternoon. Lupo Brothers is digging our well. Yesterday they'd gone down two hundred feet without hitting water. Keep your fingers crossed they get there today. Each additional ten feet costs me a hundred bucks."

"You can't afford for them to go much deeper, can you?" April asked, her voice tinged with concern.

His sister leaned forward, the hairs on her arm electric as she murmured, "It's all about getting deeper, is it?"

April blushed. Rocky loved to wind her up, as her mother's boyfriend, Clive, would say. She tried not to fall into Rocky's trap. After all, there was nothing untoward or salacious about her relationship with Mitch, and she wouldn't let Rocky pretend there was.

"Your brother's worried about the finances," April said.

"As usual," Rocky replied.

"Doors open in a half hour. Get yourselves set up," Suzi said.

Deana set out the kits she'd made up for the kids. With Mary Lou and Rocky helping, she didn't need April, so after April laid out the stamp and pad and cash box on the admittance table, she wandered over to Mitch's table. He had tacked up pictures of smiling people on the poles, along with his mission statement. His goal was to enable families to use home ownership as a springboard out of poverty.

Mitch stripped off his habit. The headgear had left him with a red ring around his face and he scrubbed his hands over it. "It's too damn hot for the Mother Teresa getup. We're supposed to set a record."

"Attendance?" April said.

"No," Mitch said. "Temperature."

"It's October twenty-fourth, for crying out loud," April said. "Where's the snap in the air? The pumpkins are going to rot on the vine in the hot sun." She fanned herself with a brochure that contained an application to

42

be a Winchester house owner. Mitch took it away from her, smoothing the edges and placing it on the pile with the others. She felt bad. He'd spent a lot of money on his marketing materials.

"Enjoy the warm weather while you can," Mitch reminded her. "You'll be singing a different tune about the middle of February when the snow is up to your waist and you haven't seen the sun for sixteen consecutive weeks."

April *had* forgotten what the winters were like here in northeast Pennsylvania, but she'd been really looking forward to fall. At home in California, she'd often dreamed about the smell of wood smoke, the variety of red colors and the crunch of dry leaves under her feet. She missed the sense of purpose and activity that came with the onset of fall. The feeling that you had to hurry, get your house in order because winter was coming. The urgency.

This year, however, September and October had been hot and humid. The leaves had been green one week, slightly reddish the next, and then knocked down by a three-day rainstorm fed by Hurricane Jesse that lingered over the Atlantic.

So much for the four-season lifestyle so envied by her California friends.

"Hey, bro," Rocky called. Mitch turned to hear what came next. "No flirting with the hired help," she said, indicating April.

Nice, April thought. *Now I'm the hired help.*

"We were exchanging information about the weather," Mitch said.

"Boring-est pick-up line ever," Rocky said.

Mitch replied, "That because it wasn't a line. It was *conversation* — a pleasant verbal exchange that involves two people, not just one sparring partner."

Rocky made a face at her brother.

"Are you sure you're not the Wicked Witch or Elvira?" Mitch asked. "It's hard to tell the difference."

Suzi walked over to where they were standing. "Come with me. We have a few moments before opening. I have coffee and breakfast for you."

They walked back to the stone silo next to the gift shop. Inside coffee, fruit and bagels had been laid out.

The silo hadn't been used for storage for years, but April was sure she could still smell the yeasty grain. The inside was cool and dark until Suzi switched on the lights.

The round room had been fitted with tables that echoed the curve of the building. When April saw Mitch run his hand along the maple top, she suspected. When she bent down to look at the joins underneath, she knew.

"One of your pieces?" she asked him.

He nodded.

"Very cool," she said. "How did you get the wood to bend to the shape of the walls?"

"It took days of clamping and wetting. Very arduous. Luckily, Suzi wasn't in a hurry."

"That's an amazing feat," April said. She was in awe of Mitch's skills. And for now, he was not only working as a furniture maker but building his homes, too. It was a lot.

"Did you like Xenia?" Mitch asked, spearing a grapefruit section.

"I did," April said, helping herself to the cream cheese. "Turns out she works for Queen Trish, like Deana."

"And you, maybe." He smiled at her. Mitch had encouraged her to sell her line of stamps.

"Maybe, but Xenia doesn't sell the stamping line. Trish is the distributor of Bella cosmetics."

"Oh right," Mitch said. "I remember that from Xenia's financials."

Mitch followed the HUD guidelines for low-income housing and vetted each applicant thoroughly.

"She's so excited about the kids' rooms. Greg is into airplanes, Jonathan loves cars and Tomas is into trains, so I did a stamp for each and showed her how we could do a transportation theme border. She was full of ideas about color. She wants me to teach her how to make stamps. She's going to stamp the walls in the boys' room herself."

"Good," Mitch said. "I can count that toward their sweat equity. Each family has to contribute so many hours to their home, you know."

April hadn't known, but that made sense. People were always more invested in a project that they worked on themselves.

"I'll be happy to get Xenia started and let her do it."

"Great, 'cause I could use you to help me stain the kitchen cabinets."

Suzi cut in. "Mitch, I hear you talking about your houses. Give us an update. The first one is almost done?"

"It is," he said.

"But what did I see in the paper yesterday?" Deana said. "They're calling for you to stop?" she asked.

Mitch looked up from the coffee he was carefully preparing for himself. He'd waited for the women to serve themselves before he'd stepped up. One half packet of raw

46

sugar and enough milk to make it look like warmed over mud puddle.

He said, "As you all know, it's been an uphill battle getting this house built. Because of the low-income component, people assume that the houses are going to Mexican immigrants. Illegals. There was another letter to the editor yesterday calling us un-American."

April hadn't heard about this. He was clearly upset by the newest bump in the road.

"But the Villarreals have lived in the valley for years," she said, outraged. "All their kids were born right here."

"I know. In fact, Pedro and Xenia are second-generation Americans. The only place they immigrated from was the Bronx. And there's nothing illegal about that."

"How can people be against a nice family getting a new house?" Deana said.

Mitch shrugged. "The sad fact is that there are people in our community that don't believe everyone is created equal."

The stampers were quiet. Mitch let that sink in. "I don't care about the politics. I'm just trying to help a few families get a house, and a better life."

Deana gave him a hug. The others lined up. Mitch looked abashed. He knew the stampers were all behind him. He was preaching to the choir.

Suzi said, "Listen up. I've arranged for a surprise, one that I hope will get the community behind your project."

Everyone looked in her direction, hearing the excitement in her voice.

She continued. "You've all heard of Scott Ferguson and his *Highland Fling* show? Well, he's the unofficial host of the Pumpkin Express. He makes an appearance at all the venues. The good news is he's agreed to be here to cut the ribbon to the A.maz.ing Maze. *And* . . ." She drew out the word. "I just heard this morning that the local news will be here to cover the opening."

CHAPTER 4

This was good news. Local news coverage for Suzi's nursery could only help.

"That's great, Suzi," Rocky said. "Looks like they're here."

They walked back outside just as the local news van pulled in. A reporter and a camera guy got out and began to unload equipment. The reporter, a twenty-something woman with a smile planted on her face, started toward them.

"Suddenly, I'm nervous," Suzi said.

"You'll be fine," Deana said.

Suzi met the reporter halfway as the rest of the stampers watched from their spots under the tent. She smiled back at them.

"You should go on TV, bruddha," Rocky said.

"Huh?" he asked, squinting into the sun. "No way."

"I'm telling you. That reporter?" Rocky said. "Jocelyn Jones. She's an up-and-comer. She knows a good story when she sees one. That's what you are."

"That news station hasn't given me the time of day," Mitch said. "I've been trying to get them to do a story on the Hope Homes since day one. Nothing. Nada."

"You've got to go on air, Mitch," Rocky said. "Simple arithmetic. The more people that see you, the better off you're going to be. I'm going to suggest it."

She walked off, leaving Mitch staring after her. He put on a baseball cap, then took it off and ran his fingers through his hair. He succeeded in making it more disheveled, but that just kicked up his sexiness a notch. April caught his gaze and smiled at him.

Suzi pointed at Mitch and waved him over. He took a sip of his coffee and acknowledged her with a tilt of his chin.

"Take one for the team," Rocky said, landing a slap on his butt as she passed him. April stifled a groan.

A red Toyota Highlander hybrid pulled into the drive. Suzi walked over to greet the newcomer, leaving Mitch standing next to the reporter. April felt bad for him. Jocelyn Jones was giving instructions to her people and not paying any attention to Mitch.

Mary Lou pointed her chin at the SUV. "Mr. Scott Ferguson."

The car door opened, and they all got a flash of bare knees. Even from here, April could see they were hairy. Man's legs. A dress shoe topped by knee highs came out next.

April looked at Deana. She was suppressing a giggle, and April followed her eyes back to the man unfolding himself carefully from the back seat of the SUV.

Scott Ferguson was five feet eleven inches tall and two hundred pounds. He had dark, thick hair that was springy and curly, hard to manage. He was dressed in a kilt. His red plaid sport coat matched, and his button-down shirt was a coordinating gold color. A large leather pouch rested below his belly button.

He came out smiling as if he were royalty. Or Sean Connery.

It obviously took a real man to wear a skirt.

Deana was the first one to ask, "What does a guy wear under there?"

Rocky said, "I wouldn't ask him if I were you. He'll probably give you that old line that nothing is worn under the kilt. All the parts are in good working order."

"Eww," Deana said, slapping Rocky on the arm.

"Speaking from personal experience?"

Mary Lou asked. Rocky gave her a dirty look.

"He certainly thinks he looks great," April said. "He's got a Mel Gibson vibe going on."

Scott Ferguson waved in their direction magnanimously and then reached out to envelop Suzi in a hug.

April asked, "Who is this guy?" They returned his wave.

"His *Highland Fling* show is on the local affliate every Saturday night," Mary Lou said. "Not only that but he sponsors dances." Mary Lou ticked off on her fingers. "He's got a travel agency. Didn't you ever notice the Scottish gift shop on Route 309? That's his baby, too. Makes a boatload of money. He's like Jon Bon Jovi to the older generation."

April didn't see the connection but decided there were people in New Jersey who knew what Mary Lou was talking about.

"He's the king around here," Mary Lou continued. "Sort of like Elvis and Joel Osteen put together."

"His show is on that network," Rocky said, indicating the WLUC truck. "That's the real reason they're here. Suzi gets a little airtime; he gets filmed doing a good deed.

Good PR for everyone. Lord know he needs it."

Jocelyn Jones put her microphone up to her mouth and started talking. They couldn't hear her from where they were, so they moved closer. She was still ignoring Mitch, but Ferguson solved that problem.

"Do you know who this is, Jocelyn?" he said. "He's the man."

He took a step toward Mitch and the reporter followed.

"You're the man," Ferguson said, poking Mitch in the chest several times for emphasis. "You the man. The house-building man. Helping the downtrodden man."

Mitch's reaction was guarded. The big man in a kilt had an oversize personality. "I'm glad you approve," he said.

"I do approve. I approve big time," Ferguson said. "I'm just jealous I didn't think of it first."

Ferguson pulled Mitch into him by his shoulders and squared him to the camera. "People like this guy are the ones that will make a difference in our community. You here raising money? Everyone should donate what they can to his project."

Ferguson spread his hands. He looked into the camera. "In fact, this week on the twentieth annual Ferguson Telethon for

Widows and Orphans of Scotland, I will donate one percent of my profits to Winchester Homes for Hope."

"Thank you," Mitch said.

Suzi stepped in, and Mitch gave her a grateful look. "It's time to do the ribbon cutting. Look," she said, pointing.

A line of cars had formed on the road. They were blocked from entering the nursery by the gate Suzi had closed across the driveway. She'd tied a bright orange ribbon on it.

Ferguson waved to the waiting crowd. Suzi gave him a pair of garden loppers instead of traditional scissors. He wielded them like a clabber. The TV camera filmed his clowning, and the crowd, some of them out of their cars, cheered.

People leaned out of their windows to take pictures of Ferguson as he mimed cutting. Suzi grinned as the crowd returned to their idling cars after he finally slashed the ribbon.

April took her position. The cars were filling the parking lot. She and Rocky were going to have a rush of business in about two minutes.

"Do you have corn mazes in California?" Rocky asked, appearing at the admissions table.

Why was she asking about mazes? Had Mitch told her about April's dislike for them? "Will you look at this?" April said, holding up the bag that had held the starting cash, and ignoring Rocky's question for now. "Most people have one with an ugly bank logo. Not Suzi."

The bag was made of white canvas, with a huge blue zipper. The zipper pull was blue sea glass chips alternating with wooden beads. The bag itself had been stamped and painted in Suzi's signature style. The front had a white picket fence with blue lupines crawling up the slats. Behind the fence were rows of flowers, lilies. On the back was a bucolic farm scene, rolling green hills, a silo and a cow. April looked up and saw that the view was Suzi's backyard.

"Suzi would decorate anything and make it beautiful," she said.

Rocky admired it before asking her question again. "Are there mazes on the Left Coast?"

"Of course there are," April said. "I heard there was a great one in Danville."

Any further discussion of California corn mazes was cut off by the customers queuing up to pay admission. Deana enticed some kids to try stamping, and Mitch took his place at his table. Pumpkin Express at

Dowling Nursery had begun.

The morning passed quickly. By lunchtime, business had slowed as the hot and humid weather kept people away, but as soon as an afternoon breeze kicked up, the property was teeming with customers again.

At the kids' table Deana was smiling over her charges, who were stamping their hearts out. The happy noises emanating from her tent were loud and precious as the little kids showed their parents their accomplishments.

But by midafternoon, April badly needed a bathroom break. Rocky had wandered off and was nowhere in sight, so April flagged down one of Suzi's employees. As she ran to the house, she saw Mary Lou in the kitchen, cutting up lemons. On April's way back from the bathroom, Mary Lou handed her a glass of lemonade.

"Great stuff," she said to Mary Lou.

"Secret family recipe," she said. "It refreshes without making you more thirsty."

"What's in it?" April asked.

Mary Lou pushed up her Mother Goose bonnet with the back of her hand, juice dripping down her arm. April had an uncomfortable flashback, remembering her ill-advised cleaning of an historic mural at the Mirabella mansion a few months ago.

"I can't tell you that. If I did, I'd have to kill you."

April laughed. Mary Lou didn't look dangerous at all. She was a middle-aged realtor prone to outfits that showed more cleavage and leg than her age allowed. Her bonnet sat atop a highlights-streaked bob that could be achieved only in New York.

"I'm so glad you could come today," April said. "Since your grandkids have been born, you haven't made it to one stamp meeting."

April knew she sounded whiny, but she'd missed Mary Lou, with her quirky outlook on people and life, always delivered with a caustic wit and an insight gained from working for years selling homes. The once-a-week stamping meetings had been a little tame without Mary Lou there.

"Having twins is definitely not for the weak. Kit has been so exhausted. I've been trying to give her as much of a break as I can."

"But they're darling," April said.

"When they're asleep," Mary Lou said. She straightened and slapped herself on the cheek. "I don't mean that. They're beautiful. Everyone is just a little tired. Me included. I want to come to stamping, I really do. I miss crafting, and I miss you guys."

Now April felt bad. Of course Mary Lou's focus was on her family. "It'll get better," April said, although her experience with babies was limited to watching *Jon & Kate Plus 8.* That woman made having sextuplets look easy.

April finished her lemonade and gave Mary Lou a smile of thanks before returning to her station. Before she knew it, it was five o'clock.

"Great job, everyone," Suzi called out as she closed the gate. "We are finished. The A.maz.ing Maze is officially closed."

CHAPTER 5

"So, you survived your day in the corn maze," Mitch said. They were walking back to the car. Rocky caught up to them.

"She never went near the thing," Rocky said. She exchanged a meaningful look with her brother.

April looked at them askance. She tried to change the subject. "It looks like we took in a good amount of money. I counted three thousand dollars," she told Mitch.

"Are you too chicken to go into the maze?" Rocky said.

Rocky never gave up. She found a weakness and was there to exploit it. Mitch should know better. "Why are you guys ganging up on me?" April finally said. "I read a lot of Stephen King as a kid. *Children of the Corn* freaked me out for years."

"I suppose you have a car phobia, too," Rocky put in. "And dogs. And proms."

"Leave her, Rock," Mitch said. "Not

everyone is like you and likes to be goaded into doing things."

"Thank you," April said, leaving off the *finally* but letting her tone of voice speak for itself.

They got to the silo, where Suzi was directing her crew.

Deana approached April. "Rocky's going to give me a lift home," she said.

April was surprised. She frowned at Deana. "You okay?"

Deana looked baffled and April was reminded that she'd left town for fifteen years. Rocky was now Deana's friend, too.

Deana whispered, "You can get back to the barn that much quicker." Her eyebrows waggled, and April nearly laughed. She'd told Deana of the night she'd planned for Mitch. This was the first time in weeks that she'd have him all to herself for more than a couple of hours at the end of a long work day. She wanted the night to be extra special. She had steaks in the refrigerator and a salad already made.

Deana said loudly, "Rocky's in desperate need of new brayer, and I just got new ones in stock."

"And I'm going to buy some new papers and inks, just to get myself back into the swing of things," Mary Lou said.

"Looks like the Stamping Sisters store is open for business," Deana said.

April leaned in to give Deana a hug, and then Rocky waved good-bye as she, Deana and Mary Lou headed to the parking lot.

"Need any help cleaning up?" April asked Suzi. She was really just being polite. She couldn't wait to get out of her tulle skirt and into normal clothes. Being a fairy princess had its limitations. Besides, Suzi had a passel of teenagers to do her bidding.

"As a matter of fact, could you do me a favor and go through the maze? I got a call that someone is missing their camera," Suzi said.

"Sure we will," Mitch said. He smiled at April, and she wondered if he'd set her up.

"It's going to be dark soon," April said.

"That's why we have to hurry. You're not afraid, are you?"

April looked at him. His green eyes were twinkling, his mouth upturned in a grin. She couldn't let him get away with thinking she was scared.

"Let's go," she said, leading the way as she grabbed his hand. It was broad, powerful, and she could feel the roughness. She liked the feeling of his masculine mitt in hers. He tightened his fingers and she held them until they got to the maze.

At the entrance, Suzi had constructed an arch of white lattice. She'd wound ivy through the slats and placed pots of orange and yellow mums at the base. The phrase "A.maz.ing Corn Maze" was painted on a sign overhead.

April felt her throat constrict. Past the pretty gate, the stalks were tall, and the pathway between them was narrow. "Let's stick together, okay?" she said. Her voice sounded much weaker than she'd intended.

Mitch stopped. He picked up her hand again. "Are you okay? If you're really nervous, we don't have to go in there. I was just teasing."

She broke off her grasp and headed down the path. "I'm fine."

But after a few steps she wasn't so sure. The corn was over her head. Stalks enveloped her immediately, and her heart began to race a bit. She took a big intake of air, smelling the musk of the vegetation, the sweet smell of decay. The wind shifted and the funky smell disappeared. She wished she hadn't let go of Mitch's hand but was feeling too shy to reach for it again.

In front of her the path forked. She looked back at Mitch, who shrugged.

"You pick," he said. "I'm following your lead."

April chose the correct path as they weren't greeted by a hay bale, but they soon came to another intersection. She began to gain a little confidence as each turn she made led to a new path. They laughed when they hit their first dead end and had to backtrack. Mitch moved aside so she could lead again.

The sun was setting and the sky was dusky. It would be totally dark soon. April was beginning to like the feeling of being followed by Mitch. She could hear his steady breathing behind her.

At the next dead end, she changed direction abruptly, bumping into Mitch as she turned. He stood his ground, obviously happy to be chest to chest with her. Her eyes lingered too long on his lips, and she looked away, blushing.

"This is going nowhere," April said, taking a step back.

"This?" Mitch said, the grin back on his face. "You and me, this? Or this path?" His fingers fluttered between them, and then pointed at the maze.

April blushed, and pushed past him. "The maze," she muttered.

" 'Baby, I'm amazed,' " Mitch sang, imitating Paul McCartney.

April groaned. They were deep into the

maze, which was spread out over several acres. Above she could see bats wheeling in the twilight. Several turkey vultures circled. Vultures were a fact of life in this part of Pennsylvania, cleaning up after dead wildlife.

A firefly flitted by, showing itself with its tight lightbulb body.

"We don't have fireflies in California," April said.

"Did you miss them?" Mitch asked, his voice husky. She knew he was asking more. Like did she miss her life in California.

She tried to answer honestly. She did miss the fog, full of the smells of the ocean, and the ding of the cable cars and the sight of huge tankers going under the Golden Gate Bridge. But she was beginning to find a richer life here in Pennsylvania. Richer because of her friends, her family. And him.

"Being here has its advantages," she said mildly.

Mitch pulled her closer. "I can think of one perk," he said, his breath a whisper in her ear.

"And that would be?"

He tilted his head and kissed her gently. "That."

She didn't move, his mouth still on hers. "That it?" she asked, teasingly.

His eyes sparked with amusement. He kissed her again, more deeply. She opened her mouth and felt his tongue explore. She moved closer, letting her body sink into his until he was supporting her with his arm. She felt the softness of the air caress her skin and wanted to take him home to the loft in the barn. Now.

She broke away. "Let's get out of here," she said, her voice quivering.

He squeezed her hand, not letting her pull away this time.

"Where are we?" she said.

She stood on tiptoe, looking above the stalks so she was able to see the gentle humps of Nescopeck Mountain and hear the dim steady hum of cars driving Interstate 80. They seemed to be walking parallel to the highway, so going east-west. She hoped they were past the middle of the maze, about to come out back at the festival.

They started walking. April's frustration grew as they hit three dead ends in a row. It was really dark now and this was not her idea of fun.

"Mitch," she said after the fourth dead end. "Why didn't you bring a flashlight?" She was a little ashamed of how testy she sounded. She wanted out.

"Don't worry," he said. "I know where I'm

going. Follow me."

Before he turned to take the lead, he gave her elbow a squeeze and smiled. April felt a little better.

The first path he took was clear. The second led them to another dead end.

"Damn!" he said.

She looked around. She could see nothing but stalks. Above her. Next to her. On both sides. It was creepy. The stalks rustled, making her wonder about rodents. Crows landed ahead of her on the path, startling her. She screamed. A snake slithered by.

This was definitely not fun anymore. She was okay with scaring herself a little, just enough to get the blood pumping, the adrenalin moving. She didn't mind that. But now she was terrified.

"Get me out of here, Mitch," April said, her voice scratchy and low. Suzi could look for the damn camera tomorrow. The only way they were going to find it now was to trip over it.

"Hey," he said. "It's okay. I know the way out. Really."

He smoothed her hair. A crow cawed noisily, making them both jump.

She laughed. "Sorry, I just freaked myself out."

"It's Halloween. It's supposed to be

creepy. No need to apologize."

He held apart a row of stalks, making an opening for her to go through.

"In there?" she said.

"We'll cut across the maze." He nudged her forward. "I'm right behind you. Just keep going."

They made some progress cutting through the stalks. After a few minutes they came to an area from which April could see Suzi's silo, so she knew they were heading toward the gift shop and the parking lot. Light from Suzi's place was spilling onto the ground in front of them. That was good.

April pushed open the last row of stalks. Something was blocking the way.

"Mitch," she said tentatively.

"No, no. Don't worry," he said, looking skyward. The first star had come out. "We're practically out."

"Mitch, look . . ." she said, finger pointing. Her arm shook.

"We're almost there. Just keep going."

"Mitch!" April yelled, and he finally saw what she was pointing at. Mitch took a step back, his face screwed up as though he didn't believe what he was seeing.

April realized the buzzard noticed what she hadn't. Not the smell of rotting corn, but a rotting body.

CHAPTER 6

The body of a woman, flat on her back, lay on the ground in front of them. Her eyes were open and bright red, her fingers frozen in a clawlike position.

A shadow made April look up. The vultures were right overhead. A violent shiver ran down her back. She looked down again. The black hair was familiar. Oh God, no.

"Mitch, it looks like Xenia," April whispered.

"Xenia?" he said. "Xenia Villarreal?" Mitch stared at the body, but his eyes were unfocused and he seemed not to be seeing anything. April dropped to her knees.

It was darker down here, the light not able to permeate the stalks. She fought back the urge to scream as her fingers brushed Xenia's elbow. There was no reaction.

"Is she okay?" Mitch said.

She thought she heard Xenia breathing. She held her own breath and listened, but quickly realized that was all she'd been hearing.

She put a finger on Xenia's carotid and felt nothing. No pulse. She didn't know if that meant anything. She was no expert. Xenia's body was warm, but the air was still balmy and the day's heat was retained in the cornstalks.

She stood. "I think she's dead, but I don't know. We've got to get help."

"Have you got your phone on you?" Mitch asked.

April shook her head. "It's in my car."

"Mine, too. What was Xenia doing here?"

"I don't know." She had to keep Mitch focused. "We've got to mark the spot," she said. April took off Mitch's Scranton/Wilkes-Barre Yankees cap and threaded it through the cornstalks. The effect was of a makeshift scarecrow. It wouldn't stay there forever, but it would do the trick for now.

"Did you check her in to the Pumpkin Express?" Mitch said.

"I didn't, but I wasn't at the entrance the whole time." April looked to see if she could see a stamp on Xenia's hand. She had to look away. Her hands were too sad.

"Why would she go through the maze without her family? Where are the kids? Why is she over here?"

Mitch looked around as though he expected the rest of the family to materialize out of the stalks. April felt another violent shudder move through her body.

"We need to get out of here," April told Mitch. He didn't answer right away, and she shook him by the arm. It was getting late. They needed to get moving. What if the kids were here somewhere? Were there more dead bodies hidden in the maze? She didn't want to be the one to find them.

"Mitch!" she yelled.

He blinked and looked at her. "Sorry, sorry. I was just thinking about Pedro. He's going to be devastated. He loved her so much. She was his life."

"Get us out of here," April said.

He looked around again and then led her two steps back. He pushed through the stalks, clearing a path with his body. She held onto his belt, unwilling to let go of him. After several minutes of keeping the silo on their left, they came out of the maze into the parking lot.

Mitch ran to his Jeep. He grabbed his phone and called the police. April paced as he called.

What was Xenia doing here? April tried to remember if she'd seen Xenia enter the maze earlier in the day. Rocky might have stamped her hand. Or maybe she came in when April was taking her break with Mary Lou. That had been about three o'clock.

The thought that Xenia had been just feet away from the maze dead — or dying — for hours sent a chill up April's back.

"The paramedics are coming," Mitch said as he finished his call. "And lucky us, Officer Yost is on duty."

April's heart sank. The local cop hated her family and wasn't much kinder to Mitch's. They'd both been present when a skull tumbled out of the fireplace of an abandoned guesthouse several months ago, and Yost had alternated between blaming Mitch's father and April's father for the murder. He'd never apologized when his theories were proven wrong.

Though the air was still warm, April shivered. Mitch noticed and fetched a flannel shirt from his trunk. He laid it on her shoulders, and she breathed in the heady smell of wood, motor oil and Mitch, trying to dislodge the odor of decay that had surrounded them in the maze.

Facing her, Mitch rubbed her upper arms over and over.

Vince Campbell, her father's partner in life and business and a volunteer EMT, was the first on the scene. He slowed his truck across the gravel, parked and jumped out. She ran to him. As a volunteer, he drove his own vehicle.

"April, what are you doing here?" He gathered her in his arms. She hugged him tight, feeling her tension unspool as he rubbed her back. Vince was a bonus, the extra dad she'd come to love as much as her own father, Ed. Right now, she was thrilled to have a guy so different from her father in her life. Ed would fall apart at a time like this.

"There's a body in the maze," she managed to get out.

Vince's forehead furrowed. "Dead?" He looked at Mitch, who nodded solemnly.

"I'll show you," Mitch said, turning to head back down the drive and toward the maze.

Vince held up his hand. "No, we have to wait for my chief. We never go in alone. Besides, he's got the portable defib."

Two other EMTs arrived driving the ambulance. One was a young woman with long braids. Vince quickly introduced Mitch and April to her, Cobie, and then to Gray, the chief. He was a kind looking man with white bushy eyebrows and fleshy jowls. He carried a black-strapped box over his shoulder.

Gray quickly took the lead. "Which one of you is going to take us in there? I'd like someone to stay back and wait for the deputy coroner to get here," he said. "And the Aldenville police."

April exchanged a glance with Mitch. "I don't think I can go back in there."

"I can do it," he said.

April knew that he could, but it would be hard on him. Not finding the way, but finding Xenia again.

"Let's go get her," the chief said to the others.

Mitch set off at a jog with the EMTs. April paced the parking lot, regretting her choice of costume now. Even the added layer of Mitch's flannel shirt wasn't enough to keep her warm in the cooling night air. She wished she'd gone with them.

Maybe she was wrong. Xenia might have been breathing or maybe the defibrillator could bring her back if she hadn't been gone long. The device had saved a lot of lives. Debate over whether the town should purchase a defibrillator had filled the local paper's editorial pages and letters to the editor for months. The town's budget had no room in it for such a pricey piece of equipment, but the efficacy of the defib was undeniable. An unknown benefactor had finally donated the machine to the EMT unit after a young orthodontist dropped dead on the country club's tenth hole.

Yost pulled in just a few minutes after the paramedics had disappeared into the maze. Be careful what you wish for, April thought. She'd rather be alone.

He couldn't keep the surprise off his face. "You?" Yost said. "What's this about? Up to your old tricks?"

"There's a dead woman in the maze, Officer Yost." April was determined to keep this from getting personal. "Mitch Winchester is leading the paramedics there now."

"You two found a body? How sweet, you and Winchester, together again. Good times, huh?" Yost's smirk was more suited to a teenager than a law enforcement officer. Apparently in this town, having a badge meant never having to say you're sorry.

April frowned at him. "You can probably catch up to them if you hurry."

Yost looked toward the maze. The voices of the men carried on the wind, but he made no move toward them. Instead he took out his pad and a pencil, licked the tip and looked at April expectantly.

"Did either of you recognize the person?" he said.

"I think it's Xenia Villarreal," April answered.

Yost stuck his tongue in his cheek as he mulled over this fact. "Should I know that name?"

April explained, "She was the wife and mother of the family that's moving into the Winchester Homes for Hope house."

Yost's eyes widened. "Whoa. I knew that project of Winchester's would come to no good end. Figures. You can take people like that out of the barrio, but you can't keep them from killing each other."

April's eyes flashed. The fact that this buffoon had a badge was so wrong. "Pedro and Xenia did not live in the barrio. They've rented the same house in Butler Township for the past fifteen years. Pedro has worked as a cook at the country club for at least that long. They're good people."

"Well, it sounds like her husband got sick of her essential goodness." He sneered.

April tucked her hands into the sleeves of Mitch's shirt so that she was effectively unable to use them. She grasped her elbows, held on and said, "You have no idea if she's dead or how she died. That's a ridiculous supposition to make."

"Statistics, Miss Buchert, it's all about statistics. Husbands kill their spouses all the time. Do you know where I can find this Pedro character?"

She closed her mouth firmly and shook her head. She didn't have to make his job easier.

"Well, I must notify the next of kin, right?" he said. "Want to play 'Where's Pedro?' "

He laughed at his cute pun. He was so easily amused.

April had to catch her breath. His ignorance was so deep. "I do not know where he is."

"No idea where this rental house you mentioned is?" He made "rental" sound like a dirty word.

A car pulled into the lot, and for a minute April couldn't process why Deana's familiar black SUV was here. Deana got out of the truck, carrying a small bag. She'd changed into black jeans and a white button shirt that glowed blue in the light cast from the parking lot. She nodded to Yost and April and pulled on rubber gloves.

"Coroner Hudock," Yost said, his tone mocking, as though he couldn't believe Deana was the one in charge here.

Deana had been appointed deputy coroner last month. April knew that this was her first call. Unexplained deaths were not the norm in this little town. No doubt Deana had not expected to come back to the nursery this evening.

"Chief Gray called, said there was a dead woman in the maze," Deana said. Yost nodded.

So there was no doubt. Xenia was dead. April felt her hands go clammy. Until that moment, she hadn't realized how much she'd been hoping that this woman who'd been in her barn yesterday, her biggest problem being whether the stamp for the boys' room should be trucks or surfers, wasn't as dead as she'd looked.

Deana crossed the strap of her bag over her chest, leaving her gloved hands free. April put a hand on her. Deana hadn't met Xenia.

"It's Xenia Villarreal. Mitch's pick for the Homes for Hope house."

Deana stopped moving forward. She looked at her friend, her eyes soft with grief. "I'm sorry," she said, her voice low and comforting. April hung on to her words, letting them soothe a hurting place inside her.

"Can you lead the way?" Deana said, her business persona returning.

April nodded. She would get Deana to Xenia. Deana would know what to do.

April led them to the path Mitch had made through the cornstalks and they followed it into the maze. Yost produced a powerful flashlight, and he shone the beam in front of her, which made the shadows dance in eerie ways. Only the sound of Deana's steady breathing kept her feet moving.

When they reached the others, there wasn't much room in the cornstalk cul-de-sac where Xenia lay. The paramedics backed out as Deana took over. Her movements were methodical and businesslike.

April drew back. She'd never seen her old friend at work at her new job before. She and Mitch retreated, being careful to step on the path he'd created. She didn't want to look at what Deana was doing, but she couldn't leave.

Yost shined the flashlight so Deana could see. "It looks like she was dumped here," Yost said.

Mitch said, "Are you suggesting she was murdered?"

Chief Gray said, "I'm not sure she didn't die of a heart attack. If that's true, she could have died here. There are broken stalks consistent with a fall."

"I will determine the cause and manner of death. In my morgue," Deana chided both men. They quieted.

Deana stood. "The state police will be here soon. I need their equipment to continue. For now, I'd like everyone to leave the scene. Except for Chief Gray. He can stay with the flashlight."

Yost protested. "I'm not going anywhere."

"Officer Yost," Deana said with quiet authority, "you need to guard the entrance. There is only one way in and out. Make sure no one gains access."

Yost hesitated, then thought the better of responding. "Move along, folks," he said to April and Mitch, pointing to them as though they were looky-loos at a traffic accident. As they left, April heard Deana and Gray talking softly, and caught the words "petechia" and "ligature."

Vince and the other paramedic followed Mitch and April out of the maze. The dry stalks rustled slightly as though animals raced ahead of them. Stars twinkled overhead. The night should have been a beautiful one, the air warm, the sky full of stars April rarely saw in California. Instead it had turned ugly.

Once they were out of the maze, the paramedics headed back to their trucks.

"Do you want a ride home?" Vince said to April.

"I've got my car. Did she die a natural death?" April asked.

Vince shrugged. "I hate to say. Things

79

might look different in the daylight."

Cobie, the young paramedic, said, "That didn't look like natural to me."

"And how many deaths have you seen?" Vince responded dryly, a hint of warning in his tone.

The light caught the stud in her nose. She took his admonishment in stride. "This is my third," she said defiantly.

Vince wasn't taken in by her bravado. "You'll do well to keep quiet about what you see."

Cobie ignored him, climbing into her pickup and roaring away.

Vince shook his head. "Kids today," he said. "She'll be at the Brass Buckle Inn later bragging about what she saw. That's the kind of lousy help I'm stuck with. No one wants to be a paramedic anymore."

April had heard this complaint over the dinner table. Vince was worried that the quality of the volunteer fire department was heading downhill fast. But was Cobie right? Had Xenia been murdered?

As the questions whirled through April's mind, Suzi came out of the farmhouse, walking quickly to where they were parked. She'd changed out of her costume into sweats and a faded Dowling Nursery T-shirt, and her short hair was wet. "What's going on? I didn't hear anything until just now."

As April told her, Suzi's hand flew to her mouth, and she collapsed on a hay bale. April sat beside her, gathering her close, while the Halloween decorations mocked them, the fake horrors having given way to real ones. Mitch pulled down a dangling skeleton and crushed it in his fist.

"I'm going to find Pedro," Mitch said.

CHAPTER 7

April and Vince looked at him as if he'd just grown another head.

"And do what, tell him his wife is dead?" April asked.

Vince shook his head. "Mitch, it's not up to you to notify him. The police will contact the family."

"There's no way I'm letting Yost tell him. I'll go get him, and bring him here."

"Yost is ready to arrest him," April warned.

"Pedro should be here, with her."

The agony in his voice was a knife in April's side, and she felt tears spring to her eyes.

Vince laid a steadying hand on Mitch's arm. "He won't be able to be with her for a while. Not until they autopsy the body," Vince said softly. "You two already ID'd her so they don't need him for that. It might be harder on him to be here and not be able to go to her."

"He'd want to be close to her," Mitch said, his voice strained. His fists were balled. "I'm telling you, he loved that woman more than anything."

"Let's go get him," April said, making up her mind. "Your little Jeep isn't big enough for three. I'll drive instead."

April followed Mitch's directions, turning left onto Aldenville-Butler Road out of the driveway. They drove for a few minutes in silence, and then suddenly Mitch exploded with rage, punching the dashboard so hard April nearly ran off the road. The tires skidded on the gritty shoulder, and she straightened the car, veering off the roadway. Her heart pounded in her chest.

She stopped the car and turned to look at him. His face was ravaged, his eyes so sad it hurt to look at them.

"Why did this have to happen?" Mitch said. "This is a lovely family."

She had no answer for him. She couldn't blame him for being angry.

Mitch rubbed his eyes. "I can't let this stop me, April. Pedro is going to need a new house more than ever. The kids." His voice cracked.

April put out her hand. Mitch took it. She squeezed but he didn't return her reassurance. She let go and stroked his face.

"Pedro is lucky to have you on his side," April said. "Let's go."

April put the car in drive and got back on the road. A few minutes later, they pulled up to a modest house. There was a trampoline in the front yard, and a worn plastic kid-size picnic table. Assorted bikes and a Big Wheel were scattered about. A jack-o'-lantern sat grinning on the concrete porch. But there was no sign of activity.

Mitch went up to the door while April sat with the car idling. The house was in need of a paint job and didn't look big enough to house seven people. The Villarreals were in dire need of their new home.

A moment later Mitch came back and drummed his fingers on the roof of the car, not looking at April.

"No answer?" she asked finally.

He shook his head, his tapping getting louder and more insistent.

April wanted to get out of here. "How about the club? Is Pedro working today? You want me to swing by?"

He opened the door and leaned in. His eyes were frowning, the pain so deep. "I can't let the police tell him about Xenia."

"Get in. My mother's working today. I'll call her and see if he's there."

Mitch slid into the passenger side and April pulled away as she used her cell to call the country club kitchen where her mother and Pedro worked. The phone rang sixteen times and they were practically to the club's driveway before Bonnie came to the phone. April put the phone on speaker while she drove.

"What?" Bonnie said.

April was used to her mother's total concentration at work. She glanced at the clock. It was nearly seven, the heart of Saturday night dinner, and a busy time for the restaurant. "Sorry, Mom. Mitch and I are looking for Pedro."

"Pedro?" Bonnie asked, mystified.

"Pedro Villarreal?" April had to shout to be heard over the noise behind Bonnie. People were yelling, and she could hear fat splattering and dishes clattering.

"I know Pedro who. He's not here. He hasn't come in yet."

Mitch frowned.

April's heart sank. "Do you think something happened to him, too?" April said to him.

Bonnie hadn't heard her. She said, "If you see him, tell him to get his butt in here. It's not like him, but I don't care what his reason is. The kids are sick, that wife of his

85

has a meeting to attend. I need him."

April pushed the Off button. Mitch was looking out the window.

"Drive by their new house," Mitch said.

"I thought there was no one working this weekend." Mitch had given everyone the weekend off. They'd needed a break.

"Pedro's probably there pulling weeds or something. He can't stay away."

April took a left on Birch Road and cut across the valley. Ten minutes later, she pulled off onto the private road of the Winchester Homes for Hope house. The lot had been graded and leveled. Where there had been a steep embankment was now a gentle slope. Most of the trees remained, hiding the house from the main road. The road curved, then branched into four driveways. The first one on the left had a beat-up VW Rabbit parked in front. The other drives led to empty lots, where stakes with orange plastic ribbons marked the locations for future houses. Houses to be built as soon as Mitch raised enough money to complete them.

"That's his car," Mitch said, scanning the lot and nodding toward the Rabbit. There was no sign of Pedro. There wasn't much of a lawn, just some scrubby grass that grew where the trees let in weak light. "He's probably around back. He wanted to surprise the kids with a swing set. He's been using scrap lumber and salvaged metal to build it."

Mitch didn't move to get out. April sat still, hands resting on the wheel. She looked over at him and saw he was staring out the windshield, his mouth moving as though practicing what he wanted to say.

"We can leave," April said. "He doesn't know we're here. Leave him in peace. Let the cops tell him. At least he won't know his wife is dead. He can be happy for a few minutes longer."

Mitch was quiet for so long, she took his silence for acquiescence and turned the key in the ignition. The car roared to life, but Mitch reached over and stopped her, his hand closing over hers on the gearshift so tightly she gasped.

"We're not going anywhere. I couldn't live with myself if I didn't tell him," he said.

With one explosive move, he was out of the car and running toward the back of the house. April pulled her keys out and followed.

By the time she caught up to him, he had already turned the corner of the house and was in the backyard. The ground was littered with construction debris. The well-drilling truck hulked in the dark.

But the back porch light was on and Pedro was there, sitting on an empty plastic five-gallon joint-compound bucket. His hands dangled in front of him. For a moment, April thought Mitch had told him. Pedro's face was so devastated, so ravaged by pain that he had to know. She could see streaks from tears on his handsome face.

But Mitch hadn't had time. And they weren't looking at each other. They were both facing the back of the small one-story ranch. Four windows ran across the back, which was bisected by a small concrete porch with three steps leading to the back door.

April followed their gaze. Her heart hammered in her chest.

"Wetback, go home" was scrawled in black spray paint across the siding. The lettering was awkward and the paint had dripped, making irregular peaks that looked even more obscene.

"Oh, Mitch," she said.

All of his hard work.

Mitch went to Pedro. He put his hand on the man's shoulder as they faced the ruined façade.

"I'm sorry, man," Pedro said. "I tried to clean it . . ."

A ladder was leaning against the wall, with a bucket of sudsy water underneath. Pedro had tried to wash the siding, but he'd only succeeded in making it wet.

"Shh," Mitch said. "It doesn't matter."

Mitch looked even sadder than he had a few minutes ago. The determination he'd shown in the car was gone, replaced by a resignation that made April hurt. She felt like an interloper in their very private moment.

Then she realized people were missing. "Where are your kids?" April asked, looking into the trees around the property. She didn't want to be surprised by little ones who'd been gathering arrowheads. They didn't need to overhear what Mitch was going to say.

Pedro nodded formally at April. He recognized her from the work she'd done on the house with the Retro Reproductions crew. "Xenia has them. She and her sister were going to the pumpkin festival."

He looked to Mitch. "Isn't that where you were all day? Didn't you see them there? She said she was going to stop by and say hi."

Mitch said no and glanced at April. She shook her head. "I didn't see her or the kids."

89

"They were going out to eat after. Maybe they're at Perkins," he said. "I came over to touch up the drywall in the living room. And this is what I found."

He pointed at the wall. His eyes filled with tears and he turned away. Mitch leaned over him.

"Mitch?" Pedro said. "You look like hell. Oh, sorry," he said to April. "Heck."

Cursing was going to be in order. April looked at Mitch, who didn't seem to be able to get enough saliva in his mouth to form a sound. He swallowed hard.

"It's Xenia," Mitch began. "Something happened to her."

"Happened?" Pedro looked to April for clarification. She felt tears well up in her eyes. She knew her expression was giving her away, but she was incapable of hiding the tragedy in her face.

She closed her lips, pinching them together with effort.

"She's dead, Pedro. I'm sorry," Mitch said.

April's eyes filled as Pedro looked disbelieving from her to Mitch and back again. "What do you mean? Where is she?"

Mitch coughed, a strangled noise that left him panting and unable to speak. April moved to him, rubbing his back as he tried to regain his composure.

April filled in the quiet space. "We found her body in the maze," April said. "It looked like she just collapsed or something."

"Her body?" Pedro was shaking his head from side to side like a big cat.

"Come with us," Mitch said. "We'll take you to her."

April drove quickly back to Suzi's nursery. With Yost at the maze, there was no one to ticket her for exceeding the speed limit, so she hit sixty on the straightaways. Mitch kept his face to the backseat, where Pedro sat. He still carried the sponge he'd been using, and he shifted it from hand to hand.

Glancing at him in the rearview mirror, April could see he hadn't processed what they'd told him. The fact that his wife was dead was not sinking in. He could have been going to pick out a kitchen sink for all the emotion on his face.

April slowed going into the curve before the nursery. She didn't want to slide on the leaves, but it was more than that. She didn't want to get there at all.

Mitch was out of the car, almost before she stopped. She threw the car into park. Mitch opened the back door and pulled Pedro out.

Pedro saw the police cars and the EMT vehicles at the same time and dropped the sponge on the ground. Vince and Chief Gray were sitting on top of a picnic table. They jumped up when they saw April approaching.

Vince came to April and put an arm around her shoulder. She leaned in, again taking comfort in his steadying presence. The chief approached Pedro.

"That her husband?" Vince asked, sotto voce.

April nodded. Mitch was talking to Pedro, urging him forward. "Do you think this is a good idea?" she asked.

"Not my call," Vince said.

"Any word on how she died?" April asked.

"Nothing new. The staties are here, setting up their crime scene. We're just waiting to transport the body when we get the okay."

The chief led Mitch and Pedro toward one of the brightly striped tents. The spiderweb decorations and string of plastic-skull lights mocked their mission.

Before they reached the tent, Yost broke out of the latticework declaring, "Pedro Villarreal, you're under arrest."

CHAPTER 8

Mitch's headlights filled April's rearview mirror as they each turned off the road into the barn's driveway. The return to the barn was nothing like she'd planned, but she was glad he was coming home with her. Neither of them should be alone tonight.

It was just after ten thirty. The police had questioned them and let them go with the caveat that they remain available. The air was still warm, hinting that the unseasonable weather would be with them for another day at least.

An owl hooted. April looked up to see if she could see him, instead catching sight of three bats as they wheeled around the top of a tall pine. She felt her skin crawl.

As they walked around the barn to the kitchen door, motion detection lights came on, lighting their way. The barn belonged to Vince and Ed, who'd restored it into a beautiful living space before moving on to another old home that needed their attention. The outdoor lights were a new addition. They'd insisted on installing them when April moved in over the summer.

She unlocked the door. It led right into the galley kitchen. A small slow cooker sat on the countertop, a steady orange light glowing from the panel indicating the apples and mulling spices April had started hours ago were still cooking.

Mitch took one step inside and involuntarily covered his nose.

Instead of filling the barn with the essence of fall, the cider smelled burnt and cloying. After more than fifteen hours on high, even a slow cooker can overheat.

April unplugged the pot with a yank.

"Sorry," she said. "I thought we'd be here hours ago. Real mulled cider was something I missed living in California."

She flipped on a light switch. She was glad now she hadn't set out the tiny cheese plates with the matching tiny forks. The evening was not going to be the cozy time she'd envisioned for them.

She stepped closer to him, and he opened his arms to embrace her. She laid her head on his shoulder and felt his strong arms draw her in. He nestled his head against hers, and they stood for several minutes without talking, just letting their bodies take comfort from each other.

"Yost was his usual charming self," April said. He'd had to back off arresting Pedro Villarreal, but had encouraged the state police to hold him for questioning.

"Understand that from Yost's point of view, Pedro has a lot that he doesn't have. He's played by the rules as he sees it, and he doesn't have a house as nice as the one I'm building for the Villarreals. It makes him a little nuts."

April wasn't ready to let him off the hook. "Do you think he had aspirations beyond being the number two cop in a town so small the dog catcher lost his job for lack of action?"

Mitch smiled. "Pay for cops in this country isn't much."

"I'm just appalled at the mentality."

"Hey, you've just come from the big city and not only that but San Francisco. I'm sure tolerance is brewed in the coffee out there."

"Well, we can't let Pedro be the victim of this town's ignorance."

Mitch drew her in for another hug.

The refrigerator clicked on, startling them both. April began babbling about the evening she'd planned. "I bought that kielbasa that you like. The venison stuff that Del Hinkey makes. He's nearly out, you know. I got the last batch out of his freezer. Hunting season doesn't start for another month."

"I can't stay," Mitch said, his voice muffled by her hair.

Disappointment made her knees weak. She looked at the fireplace and thought about how long it had taken her to lay the logs in perfect formation.

She broke away, quickly grabbing some pot holders from a hook and then dumping the contents of the cider pot into the sink, splashing the noxious liquid onto the countertop. She grabbed a sponge and began wiping. Anything to keep busy.

She didn't like herself right now. She felt silly, but she didn't want to be alone. Even though the romantic evening was out, she didn't want Mitch to leave.

Mitch grabbed her hand. "Of course I'd rather stay. But I've got to get back to Pedro's house and make sure everything is locked up tight, and I want to be at the State Police barracks when they move him in the morning. Yost told me they do it bright and early. I need a few hours' sleep."

She opened the back door. "You're right. I don't know what I was thinking. You need to be there for Pedro."

"I'll call you tomorrow," he said. He pecked her cheek and left.

April walked around the barn turning on every light, even climbing into the loft and flipping on the reading light over the bed and climbing back down. She didn't want the darkness outside seeping into her place.

The barn was stuffy, and she was sticky from having the day's sweat dry on her again and again. She tried a cold shower, wrapping herself in a short terry robe when she was done and letting her hair dry naturally. Then she sat down at her drafting table. Most of the time, as soon as she put her butt in the chair, she was transported into her imagination. There she'd find peace of mind. She could sit at this table for hours, sketching, stamping and creating. Her bedtime routine started here. It was always the best part of any day.

Not tonight. She felt completely spent but unable to sit still. She pushed away from her desk, leaving her sketchbook unopened. Suddenly, she hated the barn with its wide empty spaces. She was too small to fill it up. She wanted to talk to someone. But who?

Deana wouldn't be home for hours because she was tending to Xenia. Her father had left a message expressing his concern for her. But she didn't have the energy it would take to reassure him she was okay. She'd let Vince do that. Bonnie was working and wouldn't be home until after midnight. Her boyfriend, Clive, was probably at home, but April was still getting to know him. She couldn't just call him up out of the blue and vent.

She had nobody.

April's ire rose. She'd had plenty of friends in California she could have called in the middle of a crisis. Now, none of them would return her calls. One guy, her estranged husband, Ken, was responsible for that.

She called Ken's cell. She would leave him a blistering message about not signing the final divorce papers. To her dismay, he picked up on the third ring.

"Hey, April," he said. She was still in his caller ID, obviously.

"Ken," April said briskly. He'd never been able to accomplish the smallest task without her constant nagging. She was done with that. She would talk to him as though he were a dawdling subcontractor. No coddling.

She said, "You haven't sent me the final

paperwork. What are you waiting for?"

"I thought maybe I'd deliver them in person," he said, his voice taking on the hoarse tone she used to find so seductive. Now she recognized it for what it was — a pitiful ploy for attention. Nothing behind it but empty promises.

"Not necessary," April said, clipping off the words so he understood she wasn't playing. "Just find a post office and mail them to me."

Ken wasn't giving up. "Come on, babe. You know I've always wanted to see Pennsylvania in the fall. I've never seen the leaves turn. I wanna be a leaf peeper this year."

Leaf peeper, my foot, April thought. Loser peckerwood was more like it. She gritted her teeth. Going off on Ken never worked. He just shut down and ignored her words. He needed a mother, but she'd long given up that job.

She put even more bite in her voice. "The leaves are gone, Ken. You're too late, as usual. Not only that, but the temperature is averaging ninety degrees and ninety percent humidity. It's like that twenty-four hours a day. You have no idea what that feels like. I don't want to get out of bed in the morning."

"That sounds good to me," he purred.

April kicked a box she'd emptied earlier. She'd ordered special inks for her work project. A project that she was supposed to have ready to show Trish on Monday morning.

"I'm giving you five days to get that stuff out here. You've got my PO Box number. Do it."

She hung up the phone and leaned against the kitchen counter, shaking. She didn't know how she'd follow through if he didn't send the divorce papers, but she hoped the threat was enough to get some action. Boy did she want to be a free woman.

A light went on outside and she stiffened. Deer didn't usually come close enough to the barn to set off the motion detector. Bears were a possibility, but her garbage was safely locked up in the shed. Then she heard a knock on the kitchen door and looked out to see Bonnie's car in the drive. As she walked through the galley kitchen to the side door, Clive's face appeared pressed against the glass. Behind him Bonnie was smiling at him, tugging at him to move back but giggling at his silliness. This was the new improved mother that April was still getting used to.

Damn. Drop-in visits were a fact of life, living in this town so close to her parents.

Both were guilty of it, although so far they had avoided running into each other at her place. They never crossed paths as long as Bonnie stuck to her usual habit of stopping in late at night on her way home from her job as chef in the country club kitchen.

April opened the door, putting on a too-bright smile. She knew her mother would see it for what it was, false hospitality.

"We saw the lights on," Clive said.

Nice try. The barn lights weren't visible from the road.

He misread her body language. He started to step over the threshold, but Bonnie laid an arm across his chest.

Bonnie stayed outside. "We won't stay. These chicken breasts were going to go to waste. I thought maybe you could use them. Freeze them and make soup."

April couldn't remember the last time she had made soup, but she knew better than to fight with her mother. "Come in," she said. A fog of gnats swarmed around the light fixture.

"How was your day, luv?" Clive asked. As usual, he was grinning from ear to ear. He was always happiest around Bonnie.

April could see his bike in the back of Bonnie's car. He must have ridden over to meet her at work. He hated being home alone. April always pictured him standing in the front window of her mother's ranch house, staring mournfully at every car that drove by, disappointed each time it wasn't her. Many nights he went to the club at quitting time.

From the glow in his eyes, April suspected he had spent the evening at the bar.

Bonnie handed her a foil-covered dish. April caught an undercurrent from Clive. He was almost giddy, more than his usual self. He was rocking back and forth on his heels with a self-satisfied expression on his face. He looked like a dam about to burst.

April looked from her mother to her boyfriend and back again.

"What?" April asked.

Clive's eyebrows were dancing as though they'd come alive as two Disney caterpillars on his forehead. April worried that they might break into song next.

Bonnie jerked Clive back as he took a step closer. "Honey, she's not in the mood for company."

Clive made a strangled sound as he swallowed the words that had begun to come out.

"Did you find Pedro? He never did come to work," Bonnie said.

April frowned. She'd thought the whole

world would know about Xenia by now.

Bonnie saw the pain in April's eyes. She put a hand out and smoothed back her daughter's hair, hooking it behind her ear.

"What's wrong?" Bonnie said. "Did something happen to Pedro?"

April could feel her mother's soft touch, but her body refused to unwind. She swallowed hard. "We were looking for him because his wife was found dead."

Bonnie's eyes darkened. Clive let out an audible sigh as his body went still. April was simply glad he'd finally stopped fidgeting.

"Pedro? The cook?" he asked.

April nodded and said, "Mitch and I found Xenia in the maze. Dead. Then we went looking for Pedro. We found him at the Homes for Hope house. Someone had spray-painted the siding with 'Wetback, go home.' He was trying to clean it off. The people in this town, I swear . . ."

Bonnie said, "Slow down, honey. Folks around here have always stuck to their own kind. You can't change them."

"Just because that's the way it's always been doesn't make it right," April said.

Her mother's eyes flashed. "What happened to Pedro?"

April said, "He's being questioned by the police."

103

"Why?" Bonnie blurted out. "Pedro would never have hurt his wife. He talked about her all the time."

Clive nodded. He found Bonnie's hand and brought it up to his mouth and kissed her palm gently. He was a little guy with a big heart.

Bonnie took April by the shoulders and searched her daughter's face. It wasn't the usual surface scrutiny; she was looking straight into April's soul. April felt the love behind it and drank it in.

"Oh, honey, are you okay?" Bonnie asked.

"I just need to sleep."

Bonnie relaxed a notch. "You go up to bed."

April felt the events of the day bear down on her like a weight. "Okay."

Bonnie seemed reluctant to leave. "Want me to tuck you in?"

April laughed. "Not really. You guys go on home. I'll talk to you tomorrow."

"Don't forget dinner's on Tuesday this week," Clive said.

April give him a mocking thumbs-up. A weekly dinner with her mother and Clive was mandatory, and even if they changed the day once in a while, there was no way April was allowed to miss it.

Clive smiled and guided Bonnie out the

door. April could hear him murmuring, the words incoherent, his voice low and soothing as he opened the car door for her.

April felt a pang of loneliness. Right about now, it would be nice to have someone whispering in her ear.

CHAPTER 9

April was up early the next day. The fact of Xenia's death hung on her like a wet blanket, but she had work to do. She had to carve several more stamps for her portfolio for Stamping Sisters and create a scene using all of the stamps. She wanted to redo the layered Golden Gate Bridge stamp. She wasn't happy with the way the cables had come out.

She fought the urge to call Mitch. He'd call as soon as he knew anything. She poured herself a cup of green tea and sorted through the sketches, trying to concentrate on the phrases she'd come up with to describe her projects.

She needed this gig. It would give her another source of income. Despite the fact that her expenses were low here, money was still tight. There were days when her father had no work for her and she had to take a day off with no pay. And she'd like to be able to give her father and Vince rent for the barn she was living in. They'd been more than generous letting her live here for free, but she knew the rent money would be helpful to them.

She grabbed her X-Acto knife and erasers and sat down to work.

Fifteen minutes later, she knew it was no use. Her mind drifted back time and again to the sight of Xenia's vacant visage. From there, the graffiti on the house took over, the ugly scrawl filling her mind. She stood, cracking her back and twisting, hoping activity would jiggle her mind back to the work at hand. She jogged in place, trying to outrun her worried thoughts.

The slur on the siding disturbed her. She'd been called a few names in her senior year of high school, after Ed had told the family he was gay. Someone had broken into her locker and written "Fag Hag" on her notebook and book covers. She knew from experience that words could, and did, hurt.

She'd like to think that the graffiti might galvanize the right people, the ones who were not threatened by the prospect of low-income homeowners living in their midst. Who understood the value of reaching down and giving a hand to those in need. But she knew it might only add fuel to the flames that the so-called Border Patrol, the anti-immigration folks, were constantly fanning with their righteous indignation and incendiary double-talk.

For the past several years, the local government in Lynwood, the city on the hill five miles up the road, had been blaming an influx of illegals for all their woes — crime, unemployment and deteriorating neighborhoods. As far as April remembered, those problems had always existed, even before Mexican-Americans started settling there rather than merely migrating through.

But the city had passed an anti-immigration bill, one that put landlords and business owners on the front line of the war against illegals. The law violated so many human rights that it was later shot down by the Supreme Court. She'd thought that the vitriol had died down. Seemed as though the bad blood was getting stirred up again.

April's cell rang about four. It was Mitch.

"How's it going over there?" he asked.

"How's Pedro?" April asked.

Mitch's voice was garbled, and she pictured him running his hand over his face. She asked him to start over.

He sighed and repeated himself. "He's being held for questioning in Wilkes-Barre.

108

They're waiting for the coroner's call on the cause of death before they indict. I'm hoping Deana finds something other than murder."

April said, "And their kids?"

"Haven't you heard? Clive and Bonnie took them to her place for the day."

"I didn't hear." She would have if she'd called her mother, but she hadn't done that, either.

"Xenia's sister's in no shape to watch them."

Mitch blew out a breath. April wondered if he was trying not to cry. "Pedro's having a very tough time. The fact that he can't see his children, now, when they need him the most, is really getting to him. Bonnie and Clive planned a busy day to distract them."

"I'll go over there later and see if I can do anything," April said. "Did Pedro say where he was yesterday?" she asked. "Does he have an alibi?"

Mitch had settled back down, the flare of temper gone. Only the frustration remained in his voice. "Not a good one. Xenia and her sister, Lila, and the kids left the house around ten. He worked all day Saturday on the rental house, painting and getting it in shape for the landlord. Alone."

"Where did Xenia and the kids go?"

"Lila said they went to all the Pumpkin Express stops. Xenia had something to give to Mitch so they saved the maze for last. But they split up before they got there, at about two, because Xenia had an appointment. She left and was supposed to meet up with them later — either at the maze or at Perkins for dinner. Lila looked for her in the maze, but when she didn't see her, she assumed Xenia had been delayed and wouldn't meet then until dinner. She was still waiting for Xenia at Perkins when the cops found her and told her her sister was dead."

"Do you remember seeing the A.maz.ing Maze stamp on Xenia's hand?" April asked. She couldn't remember.

Mitch didn't reply, and she wondered whether he was just thinking or if had tuned her out completely.

She continued. "If Xenia went through the regular entrance, she'd have had a stamp on her hand, but I don't remember seeing her hand."

Mitch said slowly, "If she was dumped there, she wouldn't have a stamp. But if she was alive, and just dropped dead, she'd have a stamp."

"Right." Or if someone had followed her into the maze to kill her. April shuddered at

110

the idea that she might have stamped the hand of a murderer.

April shook it off. They didn't know the cause of death yet. It could be that Xenia had a weak heart or an aneurysm.

"I've got to know what happened to her, April."

"I know. Me, too."

This wasn't just about Mitch's Homes for Hope project. This was personal. She could hear the strain in his voice, and she wanted to erase the wrinkle she knew was growing between his eyes. She hated to see him hurting like this.

She would do whatever she could to find out what happened to Xenia.

"Can I come over tonight?" Mitch said quietly.

April's heart thudded in her chest. "Everyone's coming here. I've got stamping tonight. How about I call you when they leave? Will that be too late?"

"I'll wait up," he said.

CHAPTER 10

April went out to get Farmer's iced tea and snacks for the stamping group. All the stampers were watching their weight, but it was too hot to think low fat. Besides, after the weekend they'd had, a little indulgence was in order.

She drove by her dad's to borrow floor fans. Ed was sitting on the porch of the Sears-Roebuck kit house that he and Vince were rehabbing. The only thing finished was their bedroom. Every other room had been gutted down to the lath and plaster, but because of financial setbacks at their company, Retro Reproductions, nothing else had been completed.

The dust and disorder would have gotten to her by now. She couldn't live with such chaos around her.

Ed patted the seat next to him on the red wooden porch swing. He stopped the motion with his boat shoe, and she sat down.

He put an arm around her and hugged her tight. His tan knee-length shorts and T-shirt were covered in drywall dust, and she coughed, flapping her hand to disperse the dust motes his movement had raised.

"It's about time you came over," he said. "I've been worried sick ever since Vince came home last night. A dead body in the maze! When I heard that you were there, I about fainted."

"It was a shock, but I'm okay."

He patted her back several times. She sank into his hand. She relished her dad's affection. Sometimes he pushed a little too hard and she had to shove him back into his own life, but mostly she was enjoying being near him. She'd always found it easier to accept her father's demonstrations of love than her mother's. Maybe it was because the affection seemed to soothe him, too.

Vince's voice cut through the house, echoing in the near-empty rooms. He sounded peeved. The words were unintelligible.

April raised an eyebrow at Ed. "Who's he talking to?"

"His father, who's fairly deaf and extremely stubborn. The combination usually leads to a lot of yelling. That's why I'm out here."

Vince's voice rose again. Ed's eyes followed him as he moved past the windows in the living room.

April could see Ed was completely distracted by what was going on inside. "Is everything okay?"

Ed patted her hand absently. His jaw was tight. "His parents got a foreclosure notice in the mail. I'm sure once Vince goes down to the bank and pays the taxes, everything will be okay. They're getting forgetful."

April could tell Ed was more worried than his words might indicate. Ed's default mode was worry, but in this case, a foreclosure notice was good reason to panic.

"Do you two put up the money for the taxes?" April asked.

Ed sat back in the seat, pushing the swing so it drifted back and forth. He tore his eyes away from the living room window. Vince's voice grew softer, as though he'd moved into the kitchen at the back of the house.

"Gads, no. We don't have that kind of dough. His parents have got plenty of money, they just sometimes neglect to write checks."

Another outburst followed. Ed started. He listened. When no more noise was heard from inside, he relaxed.

"Lucky you," Ed said. "Pretty soon, I'll be

that doddering and you'll be paying my bills."

"And changing your diapers," April said. She dealt with Ed's constant worrying by joking with him.

"At least your mother will have Clive to take care of her in her dotage," Ed said.

"If Clive lives that long," she said. April closed her eyes, lulled by the rocking seat and the warm breeze that was caressing them. The heat of the afternoon got to her. She nearly drifted off.

"Damn, damnation." Vince's voice startled April back to full consciousness. He appeared in the doorway, his broad face creased in worry.

"You okay?" Ed said.

"Are they all right?" April asked. She'd met Vince's parents at Ed's Fourth of July picnic. They were at least eighty, with matching white hair, although most of his dad's fluttered over his eyebrows. April had enjoyed a verbal sparring match with him about minimum wage legislation. Vince's mom had offered to come over and dig out her peonies in the fall. April had liked them both.

Vince's mouth was a straight line. He said, "Too bad Mitch isn't building houses for indigent old folks. My parents' house was sold at auction for back taxes. They didn't tell me until it was too late. Said Ferguson was supposed to help them. But they're out on the street, as of tomorrow."

"Ferguson? The Highland Fling guy?"

Ed said, "They're part of his inner circle. He's offered to help."

"Where are they going to go?" April said. Her cheek twitched. She was living in Ed and Vince's other house, the barn.

Vince and Ed exchanged glances. They'd already discussed their options. "They can't live here. It's in total upheaval," Ed said.

Omigod. They needed their old place back. She tried to imagine where she would go. The barn had become her home in the last four months.

April took a deep breath. She knew what she had to do. "Give them the barn," she said.

Vince sighed. "No, I can't do that to you." He turned up his lips, but the smile never quite reached his eyes.

She looked at her father. His forehead was knotted painfully again. Did he and Vince fight over her staying at their property? She couldn't have that.

She put on a happy face. "It'll be fine. I can bunk with Mom."

"That'll be great for her relationship with

Clive," Ed said dryly. "Mommy and me and April makes three," he trilled.

April's lips went dry. She'd been trying hard to make a home for herself here in Aldenville. She'd gotten used to waking up in the barn each morning. She'd miss the morning light that she sketched by. She'd been looking forward to seeing the cardinals feeding in the snow.

She felt her hard-earned secure life falling into chaos. But Ed and Vince came first.

"Seriously, Vince, you can move your mom and dad in tomorrow. I've never gotten around to getting more furniture. A couple suitcases, I'm good. I only need a few things."

Her stamps. Her inks. Her drafting table.

Vince put a finger on her hand, tapping her gently, stopping her litany of things she could move. "Hold on. You're forgetting one major problem. The only bedroom is in the loft," Vince said. "My parents can't climb that ladder."

April's shoulders came down, and she tried to keep relief from flooding her face, but her father saw it. He smiled at her.

Ed said, "The barn is an impractical place for an elderly couple. Why do you think we moved out?"

Vince chuckled and April felt the tension

in her neck go away.

Vince punched his fist into his palm. "My sister is going to have to take them in. She's got space. My nephew is away at Penn State. She was turning his room into a ceramics studio, but that will just have to wait."

Ed didn't look convinced. "Your sister and your mother sharing the same space," he grunted. "That ought to be good."

"It can't be helped," Vince said. He'd made up his mind.

April glanced at her watch. The stampers were due in less than an hour. She needed to get the fans going so the barn was bearable.

She stood, digging her keys out of her purse. "I need to borrow a couple of fans, okay?" April asked.

"They're already at the barn. I dropped them off," Ed said. "You were out."

They must have just missed each other.

"Dad!" April wasn't used to people anticipating her needs and meeting them. Her father loved to take care of her. "Thank you," she said.

He shrugged, "I plugged them in and opened the windows. It'll cool down fast."

April kissed them both. "By the way, I've got a business meeting first thing tomorrow, so don't expect me at the Mirabella job until the afternoon."

"Okay," Ed said. "But don't be too late. I've got electricians coming, and timing is everything."

Now that she knew the fans were in place dealing with the unseasonable heat, April decided to swing by her mother's and see how Xenia's kids were doing. As she pulled into the driveway and got out of her car, she heard squeals of laughter coming from somewhere.

Her mother's ranch house sat on an acre of land, which stretched out to the woods in back. In front, only a small strip of lawn separated the house from the street. At the end of the driveway was the large detached garage. Ed had built it when April was a toddler, back when he'd been running Buchert Construction from home. The building had three bays, extra long and large enough so that Ed's construction van could be parked inside. A small framed-out room in the back had served as Ed's office and had become his home for a few years after he moved out.

The garage doors were closed up tight so April headed for the backyard. A blur raced by her. She stepped back to avoid being

119

knocked to the ground. Then she came around the corner of the house. The blurs sorted out into small children and noise became the babble of play.

Clive was surrounded by a gang of brown-haired kids. One girl, who looked close to adulthood, stood leaning against the wall of the garage, watching the frivolity with disdain. Her eyes flicked to April without the hope of rescue.

The other kids, except for the tallest boy, were being distracted by Clive's antics.

"What's going on?" April asked.

Clive stopped running and nodded in April's direction. He was too winded to talk. He tried but nothing came out. He panted, leaning on his knees as an older boy swatted Clive on the backside, trying to get him to resume the chase.

"Don't hit, Greg," the girl by the garage said. Her hair was long and straight, parted down the middle. Her lips were full, her eyes round and deep brown. April realized with a physical pang that this was Xenia's oldest daughter, Vanesa.

"My aunt stuck us here," she said.

April's heart hurt. The other children, who were, now climbing over Clive like ants on a cupcake, were Xenia's boys. April felt her stomach clutch as reality hit her. These were motherless children, whose father was in jail.

She sucked in a breath. Even though they'd only met once, Xenia had felt like a friend, or someone who could have become one. April wanted to help her children. Perhaps she could make their life a little easier.

She'd start by smiling.

"I'm April," she said, holding out her hand. The teenager ignored it. April was rocked a little by the rejection, but she decided to persevere. "You're Vanesa, right?" April could see the resemblance, especially around the eyes.

"Do you smoke?" Vanesa said.

April ignored the implicit request. Vanesa pulled out a lip wand and coated her mouth several times.

April touched the girl on the shoulder gently. "I'm sorry about your mother."

Vanesa shifted away slightly, but April saw the move was all bravado. Her knees shook and she looked so unhappy.

April continued. "She told me you baby-sat the little ones so that we could have our meeting the other day. We were planning on stamping the walls in your bedroom with a retro flower theme. She thought you would like that."

Vanesa bit on her lower lip and jammed the wand back into its case, dropping it into her pocket. "You're the interior designer?" she asked. Her eyelashes were tipped with tears, but she was determined not to cry.

"Sort of," April said.

"That's what I'm going to do when I grow up. Not around here. L.A. There's a lot of celebrities that need their houses done," she said bravely as if she were one phone call away from being hired by Paris Hilton or Britney Spears.

"You can help me," April said. "Here. There's a lot to be done at your place."

She saw a small spark of interest in Vanesa's eyes. Life wasn't going to get any easier for Vanesa for a while. Giving her an artistic outlet might help her work out her sadness. Art had the ability to heal; April knew that firsthand. It sounded like a slogan that Trish Taylor might use to promote her products, but April knew it was true. The last few months, she'd been healing her own heart by creating stamps.

"Maybe," Vanesa said.

April felt the thrill of victory. She remembered being a teenager, playing hard to get with the adults, afraid that showing her hand would mean her dreams would be snatched away before they were fully formed.

"Who wants cookies?" Bonnie came out of the house, a plate mounded high in one hand and a small girl clinging to the other.

Erika.

"Hi, April," Bonnie said, putting the cookies down and leaning in for a kiss. April obliged, wanting to cling to her mother herself. Instead she patted the little girl on the head.

She stayed for milk and cookies and helped settle the kids in front of the television. She could see her mother wanted to talk to her, but every time they started a conversation, Bonnie's attention was snatched away by a little one.

April felt a little put out. Ashamed of her selfishness, she kissed her mother and Clive and went back to the barn.

Ordinarily, April looked forward to getting together with the stampers. The girls were smart and funny, and their topics of conversation ranged from politics to reality TV and back again. There were sure to be several sidesplitting moments if Mary Lou came with stories about the twins. April found the companionship was the best part of her week. Tonight she was glad they were coming over, despite the pall cast by Xenia's death.

Rocky arrived first, pulling her leather rolling cart. She'd outfitted a vintage train case of her mother's with wheels, decoupaged the outside with images and installed compartments inside to hold all of her stamps and tools. She was dressed to work. A red bandanna held back the hair that usually swooped over one eye, revealing the scar that marred her otherwise beautiful face.

The barn was cool, just as Ed had promised. Mary Lou and Suzi arrived together, with Deana right behind. April squeezed Mary Lou's arm. She'd made it. The first thing they did each meeting was show their progress on projects they'd worked on during the week. Each person held up her work and the others took turns discussing it.

This week, no one had brought anything. And the talk was all about Xenia.

"Deana, tell us what's going on. Was she murdered?" Suzi asked. Her question was not just prurience. Suzi was devastated. Xenia had died on *her* land.

"The newspaper called it suspicious," Mary Lou said.

"I'm doing an autopsy in the morning," Deana said. She was calmly setting up her working space, bringing out the Thanksgiving cards she'd been making. "You know I can't say more than that."

"Let's not talk about it," Mary Lou said. "There's nothing we can do anyhow."

Suzi looked mournful, and Mary Lou rubbed her shoulder.

"Let's stamp," Rocky said. "We'll all feel better." No one disagreed.

On a good day, stamping was entertaining. On a so-so day, art could pick up your mood. On a bad one, it was a way to lose yourself. A soul strengthener.

They tried to talk of other things, but the conversation started and sputtered out. Gone was their usual chatter. Every topic seemed to lead back to Xenia's death.

The silence was shattered about eight o'clock, just as April was going to suggest that everyone head home.

"Hey, girls." A voice came through the window. Bonnie entered, carrying a cooler. Since Clive had become a part of her life, she'd added a third day off to her schedule. In addition to her usual Tuesday and Wednesday off, she'd stopped working at the club on Sundays. So here she was.

"What are you doing here, Mom?" April said. She wasn't sure she wanted her mother to show up every Sunday.

"I had company today and made too much fruit salad. Thought you might like it."

Company? April thought. Pedro's kids. They'd probably turned their noses up at Bonnie's idea of fruit salad.

Bonnie off-loaded a fruit salad made of canned oranges, fresh pineapple and minimarshmallows. She got out plates, forks and a serving spoon and laid them out on the kitchen counter.

Suzi got up and stretched.

"Perfect timing. I'm ready for a break," Mary Lou said.

"Yum," Deana said, holding out a plate for Bonnie to fill up.

"I've got chips," April said, getting up and heading to the refrigerator for the iced tea. No one took her up on her offer.

"That's too heavy," Mary Lou said. "Ambrosia sounds just right."

She was doomed to eat the entire bag of chips herself.

"Bonnie, when are you going to just give in and start stamping with us?" Rocky asked. "You know you want to." She helped herself to the fruit salad.

"I don't have time for that," she said. "I'm just happy if I get an hour of knitting in while watching Regis in the morning."

"No, she has just enough time to cut up fresh pineapple into uniform-size cubes and make ambrosia salad," April said. She speared a white cube and held it aloft. "Are these homemade marshmallows?" she asked, twisting the marshmallow, inspecting it from all angles.

Bonnie frowned at her daughter. "I don't make fun of you for carving your own stamps, do I?"

April felt ashamed. She'd been trying to be funny, not mean. "Sorry." The others looked away.

Suzi, Deana and Rocky were seated at the big table. April was leaning against the counter, and Mary Lou was refilling her plate.

Bonnie washed the serving spoon, drying it with the special cotton tea towels she'd bought for April. She was the only one who used them. Bonnie put the spoon away and closed the drawer sharply.

Bonnie said, "I've come over to tell you something important." To April, she added, "I tried to tell you last night." She turned to face the group. "I'm getting married."

April inhaled sharply, lodging a piece of pineapple in her throat. She coughed, trying to shake it loose. Deana dropped the fork she'd been using, jumped up and pounded on her back. April felt the fruit go down painfully.

Deana's hand was cocked in case April needed another blow. April took it and exchanged a look with her friend. Deana had been on the receiving end of many long-distance phone calls, patiently listening to April's worries about Bonnie being alone. Deana squeezed her hand and dropped it.

April turned to her mother, but her voice wouldn't come. The pineapple had scratched her throat.

"Married?" Mary Lou said for her. "To Clive?"

"Of course to Clive," Bonnie said.

"But why?" April said, her voice weak from the choking.

Bonnie's eyes flashed. "What's that supposed to mean?"

Bonnie knew exactly what April meant. Her mother had never talked about remarrying. April had always figured she was not willing to open herself up to the possibility of being hurt again. April's recent breakup with Ken reinforced that belief. Her mother had loved Ken and was devastated when her son-in-law turned out to be a liar and a cheat.

April had often heard Bonnie's credo that

128

marriage was for fools and dreamers. Clive or no Clive, April had assumed her mother would never tie the knot again.

"You seemed so . . ." April said, trying to word her protest carefully.

Rocky had no qualms. She said, "What happened to your theory that marriage is a governmental plot to bureaucratize romance and love? Anyone who didn't intend to have children or raise a family had no reason to get married."

April was grateful for the backup, especially from that surprising corner.

"That's a direct quote," Mary Lou said. "I know, because I used it on my daughter, Kit, when she was thinking about not marrying the twins' father."

When it came to marriage, Bonnie was a libertarian through and through.

Bonnie sniffed. "I'm so glad to know you've all been paying attention. I haven't changed my mind about marriage. It *is* a useless institution."

The stampers exchanged a confused look. They were baffled. Bonnie didn't sound like a person in the throes of engaged bliss.

"That's exactly why I'm getting married," she said. "Look, I know the timing is awful, what with Xenia's death and all, but we're in a bit of a crunch. Immigration has discovered Clive's visa is long expired and they're threatening to deport him." She took a breath. "We're getting married in three weeks. I'd like your help sending out the invitations."

Bonnie's manner was all business. No blushing bride here.

She handed each of them a color copy, about one-third the size of a standard sheet of paper. The paper itself was a hideously bright yellow. She'd used her computer to find a fancy font and some clip art of wedding bells. The result looked more like a flyer for Buffalo Wings Night at the Brass Buckle than a wedding invitation. But it was all Bonnie.

Rocky held it out at arm's length as though she might be somehow contaminated by its total lack of artistic merit. She screwed up her face in revulsion. April felt vaguely insulted for her mother even though she agreed.

"For crying out loud," Rocky said, waving the yellow page. She raised her voice. "You're not selling discounted lube jobs. You and Clive are getting *married.* That's a big deal."

Bonnie said, "It's not. Really."

"It is, Bonnie. It truly is," Deana said. She was ready to step in and soothe any ruffled feathers. It was a job she'd performed a lot during April's teen years. She rubbed Bonnie's arm gently. "Who were you giving these to?"

Bonnie shrugged. "Some friends from work. You guys, of course. Clive doesn't have any family on this side of the pond, although his brother is threatening to come. Maybe fifty people total."

Suzi said, "It's too bad it's so late in the year. We could have had an outdoor ceremony at the nursery."

"No, no fuss," Bonnie said. "We'll get married by the justice of the peace in his office, and then everyone will come over to the house for a meal."

"Mom, you can't be thinking you'll cook for your own wedding," April said. "That's nutty."

Her mother was quiet for a moment. Her eyes clouded over with pain. "I *was* planning on asking Pedro to cook, but that's out now."

All the stampers were silent. The real world intruded. Pedro was in jail; Xenia was dead.

April felt the fleeting nature of life. Her mother deserved the best.

April took her mother's hand. She knew her mother's tough exterior covered a mountain of disappointments and hurts. "Mom, let's do this right. You're not going to get married again. Let me throw you a nice party. Here at the barn."

Bonnie's eyebrows shot up. April realized what she'd just offered. Maybe having the wedding at the former home of Bonnie's ex-husband and his boyfriend was not a great idea.

Deana said, "Can't we get the club for a night?" She looked at Rocky, whose family had been on the board of the country club for years. There was a chapel on site, and a number of rooms that would work for the reception.

Rocky read Bonnie's flyer again, checking the date, and shrugged. She brushed the hair off her forehead. "That's a Wednesday, right? There's usually nothing going on at the club on Wednesdays."

Which is exactly why Bonnie had the night off, April thought. She worked the weekends. And holidays. The club members enjoyed their Saturday Soirees and the Friday Night Lights parties because of her mother's hard work and dedication.

They owed her.

"We could make you some pretty invitations," Mary Lou said.

"And decorate the tables," Suzi said. "I'll

make you a bouquet, too."

"Just give us your guest list. We'll take care of the rest," April said.

Bonnie looked skeptical. "I should talk to Clive."

They all knew Clive would do whatever Bonnie told him to do.

"We're throwing a wedding," Deana said, clapping her hands. Suzi fist-bumped her.

"This is just what we need. Something fun to do," Mary Lou said.

"I've got some gorgeous asters coming in and you'll get the last of the roses," Suzi said.

"The twins could be the ring bearers," Mary Lou added.

Bonnie threw up her hands. The idea of two-month-old attendants was too much. "Don't get crazy now. I just want a small ceremony. Nothing fancy."

Rocky said, "We promise to hold our Bridezilla tendencies in check."

Mary Lou quickly shifted into party-planning mode. "Write down who you want to invite." She handed Bonnie a pen and tore off a piece of paper from the pad in her purse. "Now."

As a part of her job, Mary Lou threw parties several times a year. There were never less than a hundred people at her events.

133

She was a good realtor because she truly liked people. Her parties mixed business and friendship seamlessly. Her Christmas brunch was legendary.

"How about I get my list together and give it to April?" Bonnie said.

"We can design the invites in the meantime," Deana said.

Seemingly satisfied, Bonnie said her goodbyes, and April walked her out to the car. The air was still warm. It was so quiet April could hear the gurgling of the creek and the distant hum of cars on the interstate.

"Mom, are you sure you want to do this?" she asked.

"Marry Clive? It's no problem. He needs to be married. I don't mind."

"I don't mind" didn't seem like a great reason to get married, but April knew better than to argue.

"How about if I give you away?" she said.

Bonnie laughed. "Sure, kid."

April watched her drive off. Her mother asked for so little. She wanted Pedro to cook at her wedding. He'd want to, too. April vowed that he'd be free so that could happen.

CHAPTER 11

"Dude," Rocky said in a silly drawl when April came back in. "You're going to be Clive Pierce's stepdaughter."

"The lead singer of the Kickapoos," Suzi said.

Mary Lou and Suzi jumped up, slung their arms around each other and did an awkward but spirited imitation of the Kickapoo Kick before collapsing in their chairs, laughing. You wouldn't know it now, but Clive had been a major pop star in his youth.

"Maybe you'll get your own VH1 special," Rocky said. She lowered her voice, imitating a voiceover. "Behind the music. April Buchert, stamper. Cue scary music."

Even Deana joined in as they sang the chorus of "Never, Never Land," a Kickapoo classic.

April smiled. The kidding felt good, like she was a part of the group.

Mary Lou stopped midkick. "Will they be there? The Kickapoos?"

"Gosh, I had all their records," Suzi said, dreamily.

"They must be all dead by now," Rocky said. "Make it kind of hard to have a reunion."

"Clive's far from dead," April said.

"Well, rock stars often have a shortened life span," Rocky said.

April looked at Deana. Her friend knew that April's focus was not on becoming a daughter of a Kickapoo. It was on Bonnie and Bonnie's shot at happiness.

April poured iced tea as the stampers gathered in the kitchen. Rocky picked a piece of pineapple out of the salad.

"What was her first wedding like?" Mary Lou asked.

April had the pictures of her parents' wedding — a dozen snapshots she'd smuggled out of the house when she left for college, part of a displaced notion that she could trick herself into believing her family had not been torn apart.

She brought them out and passed them around the table. Bonnie and Ed had been married in the early seventies. The wedding had been held at Ed's family farm, with cows grazing in the background. Ed's tuxedo had been pale blue. A heavily ruffled matching shirt was trimmed in navy. He sported bushy sideburns that nearly met in the middle. Bonnie's hair was long and parted in the center. Her wedding dress was simple, with long bell sleeves and a lace bodice. She wore a floppy hat and gloves.

"Whoa," Suzi said. "They look like hippies."

"I was thinking Squeaky Fromme, myself," Rocky said.

"Nah-uh," April said, insulted.

April pulled the picture from Rocky's hand. Her mother did have a scary blank look on her face.

"Whoa," she said. "I'd forgotten that hat."

She found another picture in which the couple smiled at the camera, their grins wide. They clearly had no idea of what was to come.

"This is a better shot," April said.

"I think they look young, and in love," Deana said.

"These are no help," Mary Lou said. "It's Clive and Bonnie we're designing for."

April gathered up the pictures to put them back in the wooden box she'd bought at a Renaissance fair in Marin. Mary Lou was right. That was the past. It was time to move on.

As April set the snapshots in the box, she felt something scratch her fingers. She reached in farther, driven by a faint memory. She pulled out one glove. The white sateen had mellowed with time to an aged chardonnay. The satiny fabric was cold to the touch.

She glanced up at the stampers who had gone back to picking at Bonnie's fruit salad. If she hadn't destroyed all the pictures of her and Ken, the group might have commented that she and Bonnie wore the same gloves. The lacy cuff made it obvious.

She stroked the glove and was immediately taken back to her wedding day.

Bonnie had flown out; her first, and last, cross continental flight. She was not a good flier. The morning of the wedding, in a small winery in Sonoma, Bonnie had given her the gloves. April remembered how tears lingered in her mother's voice as she gave April the gloves she'd worn at her wedding.

Bonnie'd said, "When I see these gloves, I remember how much I loved your father the day of our wedding. I feel again the anticipation, the wonder at the life we were going to create together. We didn't do a great job, but the possibility is always there. I pass these gloves to you as a symbol of our family. You, me, your dad. All of the hurt was worthwhile."

April had saved the gloves in a box with her wedding bouquet for years. When she'd destroyed all the other artifacts from her marriage to Ken, she couldn't bring herself to throw them out and put them in with her parents' wedding photos. She fought the urge to try them on, to feel the hope and love she'd felt for Ken, and for herself, that day.

Instead, she closed the lid, put the box on a shelf in the closet and joined her friends.

Suzi said, "How about if we each stamp something out? Then we can brainstorm."

Bonnie's announcement had given the group new energy. April kept one eye on the clock. She didn't want the meeting to go so late that Mitch wouldn't come over. She'd gotten used to him visiting for an hour or two every night.

After twenty minutes or so, Deana showed her a stamped-out card that had a vine-covered latticework as the border. She'd colored the vines in deep greens and made the lattice dark brown. It was pretty but didn't scream wedding.

Rocky took the card from Deana and with a few strokes added some aqua flowers to the vine.

April looked over her shoulder. "I like

that," she said. April stamped out the design again and softened the hues of the vines, shading gray-greens with lime, and added a shadow to the lattice.

"You're on to something," Mary Lou said. "Keep going."

April stamped out the lattice and the vine on four pieces of stock and gave one to each of the women. They grabbed pastel pencils and chalk and colored the designs. Suzi embossed a heart in the middle of the card.

"What do you think?" Suzi said, holding up the sample. "We can put the vellum printed with the details on top."

"I like it a lot," April said. "The lattice reminds me of the fence outside her house, and she always has clematis growing up the mailbox."

"It's pretty and soft without being weak-assed," Rocky said. "Totally reminds me of your mother."

"I like it," April said again.

They set up an assembly line with Suzi stamping the trellis and then passing the card to Deana, who stamped the vines and passed it on to April and Mary Lou, who filled in colors.

For the final step, Rocky hand-painted flowers. Each card was unique.

April was thrilled with the results. She

held up a finished card for all of them to admire. "This is lovely," she said. "And it suits Bonnie and Clive."

Working in concert, the five finished fifty cards before ten o'clock.

"Get the addresses from your mother, and we'll meet again at my place to address the envelopes," Deana said.

Mary Lou agreed to print out the vellum sheets with the date, time and place. Deana said she had a source for high-quality linen envelopes. Rocky would check the date with the club. They agreed to get together on Wednesday.

Rocky nudged April. "Do you think she'll invite Vince and Ed?" she said.

April tried to imagine it. "You'd have to ask Bonnie . . ."

"They get along, right?" Rocky said. "It's not like they're going to kill each other. No one's going to raise a dramatic scene, right?"

"Of course not," April said, although she wasn't entirely sure. Her mother and father had managed to avoid each other mostly for the last fifteen years while she was gone, even though they lived within three miles of each other.

Deana stilled April with a touch. She caught her eyes. "Do you want Ed there? For you?"

Yes, April realized with a jolt that brought tears to her eyes. She wanted her daddy present when her mother remarried. She wanted all her family around her. While it was bound to be awkward, she needed her father there. This was her family. As oddly configured as it was. A mother and an aging rock star. A father with his male partner. It was not *Father Knows Best;* it wasn't *The Brady Bunch.* Heck, it wasn't even *Married with Children.*

But it was all she had. And she wanted it intact. Bonnie's wedding was as good a place as any to start.

Deana was smiling at her, having watched her make up her mind. Deana knew how April had suffered as a teen when her parents split up. How far April had run away.

April's own attempt at family — Ken — hadn't worked out. She knew now that she'd jumped too early into marriage with the first guy who treated her kindly. She'd outgrown him after two years but spent the next ten trying to make it work. He'd spent that time devolving into a guy who gambled and used up all of their resources. All that she'd accomplished was to trash her own reputation and lose everything.

She had been too passive, letting Ken call

the shots. She had the opportunity now to take an active part in her family.

April wasn't running anymore. She was standing her ground. Staking a claim. Rebuilding her family.

"I'm sure they'll come," April said.

With the invitations complete, the meeting soon broke up.

Deana pulled April aside as the others were leaving.

"I can't go with you to Trish's tomorrow," she said.

"Dee! You can't make me go by myself," April cried. She felt betrayed. She'd been counting on Deana to introduce her to Trish.

"You'll be fine. Trish doesn't bite." She lowered her voice. "I've been assigned Xenia's autopsy. I've got to get on it first thing tomorrow."

April's eyes dropped to the floor. She was ashamed. Of course she could go by herself. This was only a job. She'd been interviewed by hundreds of clients over the years. She'd just been feeling the need for a little support.

Deana reassured her. "Trish's expecting you. I talked to her today, and she's excited."

April was quiet, gathering her wits. Cars pulled out of the driveway, their headlights raking the shrubs. She heard the road noise change as they drove over the little bridge that crossed the creek.

"I know how important this is to you," Deana added softly.

April heard the apology in her friend's voice and felt the need to explain her selfish reaction. "This could be a good career move for me, you know. If I start a line of stamps. There could be national recognition. Getting into the craft stores . . ."

"You could be the Martha Stewart of the stamp world," Deana said.

"Martha Stewart is already in the stamp world," April said.

"Then you could be the Rachael Ray of the stamp world. She's younger and cuter anyhow."

They laughed.

April said, "You know what I mean. This could be a springboard to a home décor line of stamps."

Deana pulled her in for a hug. "I love the way you think big, girl. First things first. Go talk to Trish about your California Dreamin' line."

Later that evening April heard Mitch's Jeep

in the driveway and quickly finished brushing her teeth. She'd just called him and he was here already. So much for freshening up. She ran a quick comb through her hair, straightening out her bangs. He must not have been coming from home. His house was a good fifteen-minute drive out in the country. He'd probably been watching Sunday Night Football at the Brass Buckle Inn.

He walked briskly to the back door she'd opened, and took her in his arms. She rested on his shoulder. He smelled of beer and nachos, and the dampness that the below-ground bar always exuded.

"Everyone gone?" he said, peeking into the barn as though afraid to move forward. The table was still full of stamping supplies.

"Yes," April said, laughing. "Including your sister."

He walked through the kitchen and sat on the futon in the great room. "Good thing. You women make noises only dogs can hear sometimes."

April tossed an empty paper cup at him. He caught it easily and grinned.

"Is that your way of offering me something to drink? I'll pass, thank you."

He shook his head and patted the cushion next to him. April sat and nestled under his arm, content just to feel his warmth next to her. The barn didn't seem so cavernous when he was here.

He'd visited many times but hadn't spent the night. She hadn't felt ready, and he seemed okay with that. They agreed April should be divorced before they moved forward. But they were definitely getting closer. She had strong feelings for Mitch. He made her laugh, he respected her opinions, he appreciated her passion for work and had no problem with her being independent.

But her time with Ken had left her bruised. She wasn't sure she could trust her feelings about men. Still Xenia's death laid bare the idea that life was short. She felt the finality of life, the relentless timekeeper in her gut. One surefire cure would be Mitch's embrace and mind-obliterating sex. If they didn't wake up tomorrow, why not one night of pleasure tonight?

She knew Mitch was sick about Pedro and his family. Concerned about his project. She'd like to erase the worry lines from his forehead, smooth out his frowning mouth and ease the pain of his broken heart.

"Any more word on Pedro?" she asked.

"I'm kind of glad he's in jail for now," Mitch said wearily.

April sat up straight and looked at him.

"I just don't want him to see what's going on. I managed to power wash most of the paint off the house, but it's still faintly visible. To top it off, there's a protest scheduled for tomorrow."

"A protest?"

He rubbed his chin. "The Border Patrol."

"How did you find out?"

"Hector Valdez called me and told me. He heard about the protest and thought I should know. He's got people everywhere."

"Hector Valdez?" April didn't think she'd met the guy.

"He's the head of MAC, the Mexican-American Coalition. Didn't I tell you?"

MAC was the leading fighter against the anti-immigration ordinance passed by the city of Lynwood last year. The group was responsible for getting the legislation before the Supreme Court, where it had been ruled unconstitutional.

April shook her head. "Didn't you contact them when you started your project?"

"I did. And they didn't give me the time of day. Said my fight was not theirs. But now with the graffiti and Xenia's death, Valdez himself is calling me."

"Is that a good thing?"

"I think so. They've got a national platform. It can't hurt."

They sat in silence. April moved closer to Mitch and felt his chest rise and fall. She felt her own breathing match his. Her eyes were ready to close when she remembered her news.

"Hey," she said. "Guess what? Bonnie and Clive are getting married."

Mitch pulled back. "Really?"

"In three weeks. She asked the stamping group to make her invitations."

"Am I invited?" Mitch said playfully.

"Gee," April said, "I don't know."

"Well," he said as he slowly rubbed a circle on her arm. "I do have an in with her daughter."

"You think so?" she said. "Does she want you there?"

He kissed her. "I'll make sure of it."

His mouth was soft and warm. April felt herself sinking into it. His kiss deepened and she went along for the ride.

CHAPTER 12

Trish lived in a planned community called Pine's End about twenty miles south of Aldenville. When April was growing up, the developer had gone bankrupt several times. Plans for a pool and Arnold Palmer golf course had been scrapped, but the homes that had been built on the ski run were some of the biggest and fanciest around. Still, many lots remained empty. The place had an odd vibe, part luxury community, part ghost town.

The drive out here took a good twenty minutes, and April enjoyed it, thinking over her time with Mitch. Stealing a couple of hours late at night was all they could manage right now. She was working hard, days with her dad on the Mirabella restoration, at night creating her stamps. He had his custom furniture business, and now the Homes for Hope. They were busy people.

Still, she loved talking to him. Sometimes

she woke up in the night, her mind spinning with things she'd forgotten to tell him. She made notes in the dark that were impossible to read the next day.

Arriving at the entrance to Pine's End, April gave her name at the gate. "I'm visiting Trish Taylor," she said in answer to the guard in the small wooden hut.

She smiled at the young kid behind the sliding window. Jobs around here tended to be factory or construction jobs. This guy looked too scrawny to work on a crew. She saw he had a pysch textbook in front of him. A college student. She smiled again. She'd worked her way through college and learned to study anywhere, any time, too.

"Do you know where her place is? I'm afraid I might get lost."

"Mrs. Taylor? Sure. She's one of the few year-round residents. Most of our people don't come back until ski season. Her place is about two miles in. Just follow the main road. It twists and turns a few times. Don't be fooled by the side streets. Just stay on Sugarloaf Loop. She's on Shaking Aspen Way, which is the sixth cul-de-sac off the Loop."

April knew she looked confused. The guard had a pained expression on his face, as though he knew his directions weren't getting in.

"You'll be okay, really," he said.

Away from the guardhouse, the road climbed rapidly. April felt the air cooling and rolled down her window. She could smell wood smoke and pitch. Birds warbled. She leaned over the steering wheel, trying to catch glimpses of houses amid the pines. The road curved and switchbacked. April passed A-frames, log cabins, and one concrete-block monstrosity.

It must have been beautiful here a few weeks back. Judging by the number of bare trees, April figured the changing of the leaves from green to autumn shades must have been spectacular. Every once in a while, she spotted a lone bright yellow leaf clinging to an upper branch. She was sorry she'd missed the change. April made a mental note to come back next year.

She counted cul-de-sacs and turned. She watched the address numbers as they got closer to the one on Deana's directions. Trish's house should be coming up soon. April slowed.

Suddenly, Trish's mailbox, an oversize one housed in its own wooden frame, was in front of her. Ironwork across the top glittered in the sunlight. It looked like a crown.

She made a quick turn into the steep

driveway, her car bottoming out with a cringe-inducing scraping noise.

She pulled in front of a huge post-and-beam house, the wood shiny with varnish. The garage was built into the side of a hill, and the house soared up above it.

The garage was massive, big enough for three cars. Above it, the roof peak was another story high. A flagstone walk led April from the car up to the double front door.

The air up here was cool and clear like a mountain brook. The heat and humidity stayed in the valley she'd just left. She heard the rat-a-tat of a woodpecker. April breathed deeply. The trees freshened the air.

It was a great place to be in the summer and fall. The downside would be the winter. The steep drive and the winding streets would make becoming house bound for weeks in mid-January a real possibility.

April shifted her portfolio and the box that held the stamps she'd made. She took a deep breath and rang the doorbell. The chimes were loud, playing the first few notes of "God Bless America."

She glanced at her reflection in the window to the side of the door. She'd chosen her clothes carefully. She'd rather be over-dressed than underdressed, so she'd pulled out one of her old suits and paired it with a silk top that she'd stamped with images of suns. She hoped the combination of the artistic and practical would let Trish know she was creative but not a flake. She could be trusted to deliver the goods on deadline.

Trish opened the door. She was fifty and fighting it. She wore a polo shirt embroidered with a tiara and the name "Queen Trishelle Enterprises," and a pair of expensive name-brand jeans. Her high heels looked to be right out of New York. In her ears were large diamond studs, and around her neck hung a gold necklace with a large diamond in the center. With rings on all of her fingers, it was hard to determine if one was a wedding band. Her tan was fading.

Trish smiled at her and held out her hand for April to shake. "You must be April. I'm so sorry Deana wasn't able to come. I don't get to see enough of her."

"The funeral home keeps her busy," April explained.

"I know, darn it. It's really too bad. I'd love if she would take on more stamping sales. Let's go into my office," Trish said. She led the way up a short staircase. As they walked through the foyer, April caught a glimpse of a well-decorated sitting room dominated by a massive fieldstone fireplace,

153

next to which was an archway into a designer kitchen. She heard gurgling water somewhere. A fountain or water feature was in one of the rooms nearby. This business of Trish's certainly afforded her a luxurious lifestyle.

Trish's office encompassed the massive room over the generous three-stall garage. They entered in the middle of the room. To the left, toward the back of the house, was a round conference table set up with yellow legal pads and pens, and a ceramic pitcher of water with matching glasses. The walls were decorated with posters of Trish's products. In addition to the Stamping Sisters line, April saw the cosmetic line that Suzi had mentioned as a prize for the Pumpkin Express.

April felt a flurry of excitement. If Trish was doing this well, she was the right person to hook up with. April's mind raced with the possibilities. A nationally known line of stamps. Stamping classes. Books on how to use stamps on walls. Maybe Trish had connections to the do-it-yourself shows on television. An appearance on one of those and April would be able to write her own ticket.

"My aerie," Trish said, bringing April back to the present. She was pointing out the back window. April dutifully stepped over and took a look. The view was of a hillside covered in pine trees. April could see how the room felt like a tree house.

At the opposite end of the room a large maple table had been built in under the window to serve as Trish's desk. Banks of filing cabinets were along the west wall. On another wall, shelving held products. Boxes and boxes of products.

There was another large picture window at this end of the room; the view of the mountains was as spectacular as April had imagined. She could see the break in the pine trees where the ski run would be as soon as the temperature dropped low enough to make snow. Trish could sit on her desk and watch folks schussing down the mountain.

"Are you familiar with my business module?" Trish asked.

"Only Deana's experience with the stamping line," April said.

Trish stood by the shelves like Vanna White next to a Q. She was proud of her accomplishment. There were four sets of floor-to-ceiling shelving. A sign attached to the uppermost shelf indicated the product line: Stamping Sisters Stamps, Bella Beauty.

Trish said, "I'm the distributor for these

155

lines of multilevel products. Are you familiar with multilevel marketing?"

April felt like she had suddenly been dropped into a cheesy sales seminar; the ones where you get a free night at a hotel in exchange for listening to a pitch.

At April's shake of the head, she continued. "Do you know how Tupperware products are sold?"

April nodded. She remembered the parties her mother had thrown. After one, a ten-year-old April had thrown all of her mother's paprika in the garbage. The next time her mother went to make goulash, she wasn't happy. Even April's explanation that the Tupperware lady had claimed there were red bugs that were impossible to see in paprika and that you needed her special container to ensure your paprika was bug free didn't mollify Bonnie.

"My marketing module is similar. It's a peer-to-peer experience. Deana is a baroness, which is the lowest level operator. I have operators in all these lines. Some sell one product line, others, both. Depends on how ambitious they are. The Bella line does particularly well. With the right combination of products and a positive attitude, my operators can make a lot of money. I have several that earn in the fifty-thousand-dollar range."

That was impressive. The average salary in this county was probably closer to thirty thousand. Those statistics made April happy. The more people selling her stamps, the better. Everyone wins.

Trish explained further. "Each operator receives a portion of her baronesses' and marquesas' sales."

April's confusion must have shown on her face. Trish pulled down a chart from a roller shade hung on the wall. It was like a family tree, but one with one only parent.

At the top was a picture of Trish, with a sparkly tiara and an even sparklier smile. Beneath her was the line for duchesses.

Branches led off the duchess line. These were the marquesas. The pictures disappeared, replaced by names. Xenia had many, tiny branches. Under that were countesses and finally baronesses.

April touched Xenia's name.

"Poor Xenia," Trish said. "She was one of my brightest stars. You can see she had worked very hard recruiting others. It was just starting to pay off. She was on the brink of being one of my most successful people."

Trish pulled down a large white round wicker basket. "This is a starter kit," she said. "The baroness makes an initial investment. The Stamping Sisters kit, for example, runs $440. In it is everything the baroness needs to get started. Products to sell, an accounting program to keep track, selling tips."

April pictured baronesses selling her stamps. She could get her nest egg back. Pay back her clients in California who Ken had bilked. Give Ed and Vince a check for back rent. Maybe even save money for a new business. It suddenly seemed possible.

Trish started taking items out of the basket. April saw bath salts, lipsticks, glittery eye shadows.

Trish continued, picking up a pretty blue compact. "The Bella line is one I'm really proud of. As you may know, we've had an influx of people from south of the border settling in the area. Those women love their beauty aids, let me tell you."

April cringed at the broad brushstrokes Trish was painting of a whole community. She started to speak out, remembering the graffiti on Pedro's house, but Trish had moved on, explaining further how a baroness moves up to countess by signing others up to sell the products.

April listened politely. She imagined her stamps on Trish's shelf. Her designs going out to hundreds of baronesses and count-esses in the tri-state area. Maybe one of them would find their way to New York, into the hands of an editor from *RubberStamp-Madness* magazine.

From there it would be a short hop to national recognition.

"So tell me about yourself," Trish said, of-fering April a seat at the conference table. Trish sat opposite her, a black notebook computer in front of her.

April laid out her portfolio. "My primary interest is as a home décor stamper. I stamp walls for historical restorations. I have some ideas for craft stamps, however. Deana said you were interested in producing a travel series."

April opened the box and laid out the stamps she'd worked on over the weekend. The pictures were of her California. Red-woods, palms, beaches. She opened to a page in her portfolio that held the collages and cards she'd made. She'd produced a series of pages that used the stamps in a va-riety of projects, progressing from simple to complex. She was especially proud of a landscape she'd done, incorporating all the images into an ode to California.

When she looked up, Trish was checking her e-mail on the computer.

Flustered, April tried to get her attention. She said loudly, "I'm open to designing more lines for you as time goes on. Eventually, however, I'd like to be manufacturing the large stamps I use on walls."

Trish looked up. "Sounds great."

She stood, walked to her product shelves and took down a box, which she carried back to the table and placed in front of April. "This is the Stamping Sisters starter kit. For a limited time, I'm enclosing my DVD, *Peer-to-Peer Is the Wave of the Future.*"

April was confused. "You see my stamps as a part of this line. I understand that."

Trish continued. "If you purchase this starter kit today, you can also get a line of Bella for only $125. And for you, I'll throw in the faux crocodile sample case. Crocodile is the new black," she said.

April stared at the dynamo in front of her. Trish was poised over the table, her sample kit opened for April's examination.

"I'm not —"

"I prefer check or credit card, but I can offer a credit line, too. I have a tie to Home Credit. Ninety days same as cash. That particular program is also available to your clients. I find an easy source of credit helps to get the products into the customers' hands."

"I'm not here to buy one of your sample kits. I don't want to be an operator, a baroness," April protested. "I want you to feature my stamps."

Trish's hand stopped its movement. She frowned at April. "You misunderstand me. I want to do your line of stamps, I really do. But I need some kind of commitment from you."

"Okay," April said. "You won't have to pay me up front for my designs. I'm willing to take a small percentage each time you sell one. I'd be perfectly happy to work on a consignment basis . . ."

Trish's face shuttered. "I'm afraid I don't work that way. You're either in or out of Queen Trishelle Enterprises. And there is only one way in: become a baroness and work your way up to duchess."

April felt herself blush. She'd been totally kidding herself. This woman wasn't interested in her stamps. She just wanted another body to sell her products and fill her coffers.

April pushed away from the table, stood and gathered her portfolio. "I'm sorry to have wasted your time," she said through clenched teeth, thinking about all the hours

she'd spent creating the California Dreamin'
line of stamps. It wasn't Trish's time she
was really sorry about.

Trish waved her away, head back down
into her laptop. "I'm sorry, too. Deana
didn't do either of us any favors."

"I'll let myself out," April said.

She resisted the urge to search out the
gurgling fountain and spit in it on her way
to the front door.

April had just turned the knob on the
front door when Trish came down from her
home office, bearing a large shipping box.
"Do me a favor, will you? Give this to Xenia," she said as though nothing had tran-
spired between them.

April's mouth dropped open. "Xenia is
dead."

Trish frowned. "I know, but her customers are waiting. Her sister has promised me
to get these orders to the right people. The
addresses are all inside. Take it to her, will
you?"

She thrust the box at April and closed the
door behind her.

CHAPTER 13

April tried calling Deana, but her cell phone didn't work in this area. She threw it on the floor of the car in disgust when she got the beeping that indicated there was no service.

She took the switchbacks too quickly on the way out, causing her stomach to roil in protest, and got a glare from the pimply attendant as she blew past him. She was already doing sixty-five when she hit the highway. Before she could really open it up, she was hemmed in by eighteen-wheelers. One in front was slowly climbing a long grade, but when she tried to pass him, there were two others in the next lane, going just as slow.

They wouldn't let her in between. Their maneuver forced her to slow down.

There was no release in doing fifty. She felt tears building, and wiped them away with brute force. One of the truckers misunderstood her gesture and flipped her the bird in return. Frustrated, April gave in and settled in behind him to drive the six miles to her exit.

Pulling into the parking lot of the Hudock Family Funeral Home, April remembered that Deana was performing the autopsy on Xenia's body this morning. Her desire to yell at Deana quickly dissipated. Thinking about the Villarreal situation put things in perspective. The visit to Trish had been a debacle, but she was not lying dead in a cornfield.

Vince and Ed had a nickname for one of their more well-off customers who they'd been working with for years. Sub-zero. She was a woman who, when faced with the hard choice between the ten-thousand-dollar shower stall or the fifteen-thousand-dollar one, threw a hissy fit at the extra money. She'd agonized over the length of their built-in pool — twenty-four feet long or forty? The kitchen drawers had to be lined with velvet so the silver wouldn't tarnish. When some minor detail went awry on one of her jobs, there was hell to pay. The term sub-zero problem entered the family lexicon, used whenever anyone was fussing over a minor issue.

On a scale from one to dead, Trish was a

sub-zero problem in April's life. She still had a job and a roof over her head.

But damn, she was disappointed. She'd really let herself get caught up in the idea of a line of stamps. Was it just ego? The idea of her name, April Buchert, on a stamping series had been a nice daydream. Maybe she should have stopped herself before she started designing her own logo.

April decided to see if Deana was finished with the autopsy. She could at least tell Deana that she and Trish weren't going to be working together anytime soon.

She took the path from the back of the parking lot to the family quarters. The land sloped so that the building had an extra lower level tucked into the back of the funeral home.

Deana was in the window of her kitchen, drinking a glass of water. She moved aside her gingham café curtains and waved April inside.

They exchanged hugs. "How did it go with Trish?"

"Not good. She wanted to me to sell, not design for her."

Deana's face fell. "Oh, I'm sorry. I had no idea."

April waved her off. They could talk about

it later. "What about you? Done with Xenia?"

Deana nodded. She set down the glass. "I just got off the phone with the state police."

"How did she die?" April said. She braced herself on the kitchen counter. No fancy granite for Deana. The countertop was laminate, a pretty yellow color that matched the wall color above the white bead board.

"I can tell you the manner of death was homicide," she said. "She was strangled."

"Strangled? I didn't see any marks on her neck," April said.

Deana frowned at her. "Not that you were looking or anything, Quincy."

April stuck her tongue out at her friend. They'd watched reruns of the medical examiner show regularly as impressionable preteens.

Deana looked out the window. From here, they could see the tops of the willows that sat around the pond in the middle of the Memorial Garden. "The killer used a ligature. Before you say you didn't see a rope or scarf, he most likely took it with him."

"Him?" April's heart went out to Pedro. "You think it was a man?"

Deana shrugged. "My guess. It takes a lot of strength to kill someone that way."

"Strength and will," April said, trying to

166

imagine how long it took someone to die. Someone as full of life as Xenia. With five kids, she would have fought to stay alive.

"Who did this?" April said. "I really don't believe her husband killed her. I saw his face when Mitch told him. No one can fake that kind of anguish."

April's eyes misted over as she remembered the scene. Pedro's grief was visceral. No one was that good an actor.

Deana drained her glass. "Whoever did it was very angry. It was a brutal death."

"Wouldn't she have cried out? Wouldn't we have heard her?" April asked.

Deana pushed her glass on the tap in the refrigerator, filling it again. She offered April water, which she refused. "She might not have had a chance to get a sound out. Besides, remember how noisy it was?"

April had been the closest to the entry point. She'd heard kids all day long. By the afternoon, she'd tuned them out.

"While it could have been a random act of violence, it's more likely a personal crime," Deana said.

"As in husband?" April felt her spirits drop. Did Pedro stand a chance?

Deana shrugged, shutting her laptop. "Or lover or business associate. Other family member. Crime of passion doesn't always mean husband. Just someone with sufficient reason to want to throttle her and actually do it."

April shuddered. She'd made others mad enough to want to kill her. She knew what it was to face that kind of anger.

"I've got to get back to work," Deana said, giving April a hug and a kiss.

"Me, too. After I drop off something for Trish."

Deana raised her eyebrow in question.

April said, "Don't ask. That woman is a force of nature."

Deana laughed and waved good-bye.

April drove to the Villarreals' house, following the same route Mitch had used Saturday night. She didn't know where else to look for Xenia's sister. Maybe she was staying at Pedro's with the kids. Today was a school day, but surely the kids wouldn't have gone.

The house sat at the crossroads of two county routes. A hundred years ago, these corners had been the hub of a well-traveled road. Faded signs painted on one building touted a stable and a general store. Prushka's Bar and Grill had an odor of decades-old beer emanating from it. The only thing left besides the bar was a gas station and minimart, today's version of the variety store. The place had been bypassed by the locals for prettier corners and overpassed by the highways for quicker ways to get into town.

A few houses remained, the Villarreals' rented home among them. April stepped onto the concrete porch and knocked. No answer. She went around to the back following a well-worn dirt path through the scrub grass. She opened the screen door and knocked directly on the back door.

Still no answer. She peered in the window. The kitchen was untidy, as though the family had just stepped out. Cereal bowls were in the sink. Someone had spilled sugary cereal on the floor, and a stream of ants marched in and out of the pile. A pink plastic cup lay nearby.

This was definitely life interrupted. April looked closer. A flyer about the Pumpkin Express was tacked to the family bulletin board.

If appeared that no one had been back since Saturday morning.

April walked around to the front. A package addressed to Xenia lay on the front porch. It was the same size and shape as the one in her car. She scooped it up. In for a penny, in for a pound. Buchert's delivery service.

She stashed the box in her car with the other. The dashboard clock read 10:30. She really had to get to work.

She didn't make it to Mirabella as quickly as she'd hoped. On the road, April was stopped by a uniformed cop. His car was parked crosswise in the road, blocking both lanes.

He stepped to her car, military in demeanor, with a somber facial expression. Now that he was closer, she saw he was private security, not police. "Sorry, no through traffic."

April peered through her windshield. She thought she could see the WLUC truck up ahead. With her window down, she could hear noises. She strained to listen. The sounds were regular and repeated. She could almost make out words. The protest Mitch had told her about was underway.

The security guard was closemouthed.

Taking a different tack, April said, "I'm with Retro Reproductions. I'm due at work at the Mirabella mansion."

The man sighed. "License, please?"

He took her license and said something into his shoulder mike. To her, he said, "All the other employees got here hours ago. We cleared them then."

She didn't feel like explaining to this guy her work hours or ethic. It was none of his business why she hadn't been at work early this morning.

He handed her back her license and stood at attention at her door. They waited in silence. April leaned over her steering wheel and tried to see what was going on up the road.

His radio crackled. He listened and waved her through without explanation. Evidently someone had vouched for her. Probably Ed.

April drove onto the property of Mrs. Barbara Harcourt, owner of Mirabella, and parked her car next to the detached garage. She hesitated. If security had talked to Ed, he would get antsy, worried if she didn't come right in. But she wanted to see what was going on.

She could get there without using the road security had blocked. During her first days on this job, Mitch had shown her a shortcut through the woods to the old Castle site. She'd used it just last week, visiting his work site to help him after she was done for the day.

She had to see him now. She needed to tell him what Deana had told her, that Xenia had been definitely murdered. The state police might not release that information right away. With the finding of homicide, Pedro's chance of being released was greatly reduced. The police could find what they needed to charge him with murder.

A tinny version of the *Godfather* theme grew louder. A roach coach rumbled up the Mirabella driveway, straining as the driver shifted gears on the slow grade. She'd forgotten. Mondays, the lunch truck came early. Within minutes, Ed's crew would be out here, grabbing hoagies and meatball sandwiches.

She made up her mind. She called Ed and left him a message on his voice mail that she'd be along in a few minutes and headed for the woods.

She followed the dirt path, breaking into as light jog over ground covered with fallen leaves. Her steps made a satisfying crackle, and she had a momentary sense memory of jumping into a pile of just-raked leaves as a kid. Ed had always pretended to be horrified, but he'd make a new pile and turn his back again, just long enough for her to get a running start and land in the middle. She smiled at the thought.

She was stopped short when her ankle twisted in a depression in the earth hidden by the leaves. Damn heels. She wished she'd taken the time to change into her work clothes and shoes. But if she'd gone inside, Ed would never have let her out again.

She rubbed her ankle. It was tender, but she could walk on it. The rhythmic voices got louder. She could understand the words. "Hell, no. We won't go. We want our land back."

April slowed when she came up to a line of people standing in the clearing where the stakes, yellow pegs and string marked the locations for the third and fourth houses. From the back the group looked like ordinary folks.

The rich didn't have to protest. They hired lawyers and kept their voices quiet.

Aldenville served as a bedroom community to Lynwood, the small city up on the hill. The doctors, lawyers and bankers chose not to live where they worked. They much preferred the quiet life in the valley. The country club was surrounded by elegant homes, some a half-century old, others built in the last twenty years. Here the professionals could mingle with their own kind. More business was done in the club and at the golf course than in their offices.

On the other hand, the workers they needed to ensure their lives ran smoothly — the maids, golf caddies, launderers and cooks — found the city the only place they could afford to live. Many would never be able to afford to buy even the smallest homes. Mitch had hoped to give a leg up to several families who spent most of their income on rent. His plan was to build four homes here, and if those were a success, buy land and build more. Give them a taste of how the other half lived.

The protesters had other ideas. April wondered if any of them had spray-paint cans in their cars.

There were about twenty protesters, men and women, mostly middle-aged and older. On a Monday midmorning, the only people available are the elderly or unemployed. Sort of like the juror pool. One guy had on a T-shirt that read, "You bet your dupa I'm Polish" stretched over his big belly.

Nice.

Carrying hand-lettered signs, the group moved slowly up the gravel drive to the empty lot where the second Homes for Hope house would be built eventually, and continued on to the edge of Pedro's lot.

A crew of three men squatted by the foundation, drinking coffee and talking among themselves. Not good. Guys were being paid to sit around doing nothing. A large well-drilling truck was parked on the side yard. Well drilling was a noisy business

174

— clearly, the drill was not running.

April spotted Mitch over to the left standing out of the path of the protesters. Next to him was a short man dressed in a gray business suit. Both had arms crossed and were watching the action with thoughtful faces.

She realized she was not going to be able to tell Mitch about Deana's findings in front of this crowd. She had no desire to get caught up in the protesters' venom. She'd talk to Mitch later, after work. April turned to head back to Mirabella.

She'd only gotten a few steps when she heard Mitch call her name. He caught up to her and tapped her on the shoulder. He looked surprised to see her. And something else. Annoyance with her? Did he think somehow she'd get in his way?

He said, "What are you doing here? You came through the woods?"

Without waiting for an answer, he guided her by her elbow back to where he'd been standing. His fingers lingered on her skin and April felt herself tingle. The smell of him brought back memories of the night before, and she fought the urge to lean into him for a kiss. This was not the time or place. Instead, she said, "I heard the commotion and came to see if you needed any help." She tilted her head toward the berm.

Mitch introduced April. "This is Hector Valdez. He's with the Mexican-American Coalition."

Now she understood Mitch's agitation. He was nervous.

The protesters walked in front of the camera, poking their signs up and down and mouthing the chants. The same reporter who had been at the A.maz.ing Corn Maze on Saturday was here, directing her cameraman to focus on an older woman with a cloud of wispy pinkish hair. The woman's lipstick was smeared and she sounded hoarse.

April realized with a sickening jolt that the woman was Vince's mother. She saw his father holding a sign that read, "Protect Our Heritage."

Before she could decide whether or not to greet them, Valdez caught her attention.

Valdez looked April up and down. "Are you, by chance, a lawyer?"

She looked down at her pencil skirt and tugged on the hem of her matching jacket. He must not have noticed the scratches on her legs from coming through the woods.

"No," she said.

"Too bad," he said. "We could use one right about now. My counsel is late."

He stroked his chin and seemed to make up his mind about something. He touched her on the arm.

"Come with me," Valdez said, striding away without waiting for her answer. "I want to practice a little intimidation of my own."

April looked at Mitch. Mitch gave her a reassuring smile. "Just play along," he whispered. "Hector knows what's doing. He's on my side," he added.

She would do whatever she could to help Mitch, so she followed Valdez.

"Stand next to me," Valdez said quietly. "Don't say a word or react to anything I'm going to say. Can you look tough?"

April furrowed her brow earnestly. She fought the urge to giggle. Giggling was not intimidating. She glanced back at Mitch, who gave her a thumbs-up.

She felt the eyes of the protesters on them and squared her shoulders. These people were trying to prevent a good family from a better life. What was wrong with a little deception?

Valdez got in between the camera and Jocelyn Jones, the reporter. The cameraman stopped filming the protesters and swung the lens over to him.

"Good morning," he said cheerily. "I

know you want to cover both sides of this story, so I've cleared my schedule and am available to talk to you."

"Not now," Jocelyn said. "I'm filming the protesters. Perhaps when that is over."

Valdez shrugged his slim shoulders elegantly. "I am sorry. My colleague has to get back to court by noon."

Jocelyn lowered her microphone and looked at April. April thinned her mouth as she felt the reporter's eyes take in her mode of dress. The suit might be three years old, but it was an Ann Taylor classic, well-made and expensive. She sucked in her tummy and thrust out her chest. The reporter was wearing a Boscov's special, a cheap suit that probably came with matching slacks in the same brown polyester. Fashion round one to April.

April felt a trickle of sweat crawl down her back. She pictured Jocelyn with a *Glamour* magazine "Don't" banner over her face.

That helped.

"All right," the reporter said, giving in. "What does MAC have to say about the protests?" The camera stayed on Valdez, so obviously Jocelyn would later film herself asking the questions.

Valdez was prepared. His voice was smooth, unaccented. "MAC is well aware of the efficacy of protest marches. We have a long history of civil disobedience going back to Cesar Chavez. However, these people are not residents of the valley. They've been bussed down here to put on a show. This is unlawful assembly and we will sue. Our attorney is assessing the situation."

April looked over at Mitch. His handsome face had been creased with worry. She saw a glimmer of hope as Hector talked. He seemed to think that MAC's influence could put an end to the protests. April didn't understand Mitch's fascination with this guy. He didn't seem too interested in the Homes for Hope houses.

Jocelyn poked the microphone in April's direction, but April took a step back and gave her a stern shake of the head. She tried hard to indicate silently she was far too important to bother with short, big-busted news reporters.

One by one, the protesters stopped marching and watched the interview.

Valdez continued. "My organization will not rest until we have rid this valley of the element that would destroy my people."

April touched Valdez's elbow, and channeling a high-powered lawyer at a congressional hearing she'd seen on C-SPAN, whispered in his ear. "It won't be pretty if

I'm discovered," she said.

Valdez ignored her and continued. Bluffing seemed to be his forte. His voice rose as he directed his comments toward the protesters. "MAC is not going to lay down in the face of a little shouting."

April muttered, "Wrap it up."

Next to her, Hector Valdez stiffened. She glanced in his direction, but his attention was not on her. She wasn't even sure he'd heard what she'd said. He was the kind of guy whose own words were the only ones that truly interested him. He talked, then waited for the next chance to spew his carefully constructed arguments. But now he looked rattled.

April followed his gaze. A man was approaching. He was rail thin, tall and, despite the heat, impeccably dressed in jacket, vest and tie. He was smiling, or at least his lips were curved.

He held his hand out for Hector to shake. Mitch started toward them, his face a storm of emotion. April saw Mitch's eyes stray to the half-finished house behind him. He gave a nod to his crew, and they all stood with new purpose. The tallest one picked up his pipe wrench.

"Hector," the man said with no warmth.

Hector's eyes remained hooded as he

returned the greeting. April glanced at Mitch. His mouth was set in a thin line.

The protesters applauded the new arrival.

"Mr. Ted Traczewski," Jocelyn said, her microphone at the ready.

Now April understood the activity. She knew that name. Traczewski was the head of the opposition movement, the Lynwood Border Patrol. They called themselves preservationists, but in reality they were only interested in saving their lifestyle without any thought to whom they hurt to maintain it. The influx of Mexican fruit pickers settling full time in Lynwood and the surrounding area had become a flash point.

"Why are you here?" Valdez asked.

Traczewski said, "A citizen has certain rights."

The reporter's eyes were darting from one man to the other. The cameraman moved back so he could get both men in the shot. The air was as charged as if a summer afternoon thunderstorm was approaching. The two men were taking measure of each other, like rams in a field. The silence was excruciating.

April could see how this was going to go. Hector was here representing his organization, not the Villarreals. Traczewski had his

point of view to espouse. Hector and Traczewski would go toe-to-toe, touting their
party lines. Immigrants are good. Immigrants are bad.

Nothing would be said about Pedro,
suspected of a murder he didn't commit.
Or about Xenia, dead.

April had had enough.

She turned to Jocelyn. "Xenia Villarreal,
the woman that was supposed to move into
this house next month, has died."

Mitch's head snapped up and his eyes narrowed. April knew there was a chance that
this kind of publicity would make things
worse for him. Without Hector's support,
the house might never get finished. She
looked away from him. The Villarreals
needed to be represented.

April grabbed Jocelyn's arm. The reporter
was startled but recovered quickly. She
moved closer to April, her reporter's in-
stincts telling her April had something
important to say. Mitch shot her a warning
look.

Traczewski and Valdez were annoyed at
being interrupted. April knew it wasn't too
smart to make enemies of these powerful
men, but tough. Xenia could not speak for
herself. They could go back to their pissing
contest after April had had her say.

"Xenia Villarreal was an American citizen," she began. "She was born in New York. Her husband, Pedro, was born there, too. All five of her children were born three miles from here, in Lynwood General."

April faced the camera, trying to think of what else to say, how to get everyone's full attention. She knew the camera would pick up any hesitation, so she banished her reserve to the furthest recesses of her brain.

The scene behind her faded away. The noise of the protesters, shuffling their feet, talking among themselves. Mitch and the well drillers, Valdez and Traczewski, all of it faded.

She remembered Xenia in her kitchen, so thrilled with her new house, so eager to embark on a new life. And she saw Xenia's lifeless body, lying among the broken cornstalks.

April said, "No one deserves to die alone, robbed of her last breath. Murdered."

CHAPTER 14

"Murdered?" Jocelyn echoed. "Who says? Get the state police on the phone," she barked at her producer, a young girl with pink highlights in her blonde hair. She pulled out her cell.

April couldn't look at Mitch. This wasn't the way she wanted him to find out that Xenia had been murdered. She felt Valdez's ire at being upstaged coming off him like waves of heat.

Traczewski shifted his weight, a smug expression on his face, as though the slaying of Xenia just proved his theory that immigrants were awful human beings.

Jocelyn Jones moved away from them, dialing her phone and motioning for her camera guy and the producer to follow her. They jumped into the WLUC truck and quickly drove off, skidding on a pile of leaves before straightening out and hitting the road. Murder was a bigger story.

The protesters gathered around Traczewski, no longer marching now that there was no audience. He said a few words, dismissing them. The crowd dispersed. Hector Valdez nodded curtly at Mitch and turned on his heel and left.

Mitch was steaming, his face a shade of red April had never seen on him before.

He watched Traczewski interacting with a few lingerers. "It was no accident that the TV station showed up. Traczewski had this all planned. He has those protesters and the media under his command. I wasn't expecting that," Mitch said.

April was surprised by his singlemindedness. Had he heard what she'd said?

"Mitch?"

He turned his attention to her. "Damn it, April. I had a deal. I let him have the exposure, and Valdez was going to bring me more backers."

April was dumbfounded. "Are you serious? Did you hear what I said? Xenia's been murdered."

"I heard you, and I'm sorry, but I can't do anything about that. Let the police deal with that. I can only do one thing. Save their house."

"Mitch —"

Mitch interrupted, his hands raking

185

through his hair and his face grim. "This isn't just about one house, their house. My entire project is at risk."

"I'm trying to give Xenia a voice. She's being ignored."

"Tell that to her kids when they're living in the family van," Mitch said. He stalked toward the house.

"Mitch," April called.

He didn't look back.

April could do something. She could let everyone know who Xenia was and help bring her killer to justice.

Doing her supper dishes that night, April had a giant knot in her stomach that had nothing to do with the frozen burrito she'd eaten. Mitch hadn't returned her calls.

She'd eaten her dinner with the TV news on. The protesters had looked more effective on television. The crowd of them looked larger, louder, more vociferous.

Jocelyn Jones had interviewed Traczewski. His gray hair was swept off his forehead in a dramatic wave. He was tall, and sounded perfectly reasonable. "We need to protect the American way of life," he'd said.

What he hadn't said was that he was okay with immigration as long it was Christians from western Europe. For all others, he wanted the door slammed shut.

Not that he'd mentioned his ancestors. He talked about the quality of life to be maintained, the sanctity of the English language, the overcrowding and crime that was sure to result.

April pulled off her glove roughly, catching her fingernail in it. Her actions ripped it off close to the nail bed. Damn, that hurt. She sucked on her finger.

Her phone rang. Her heart leaped, but a glance at the caller ID indicated it was not Mitch.

"April, why were you on the television?" Her mother's voice came through the answering-machine speaker loud and clear. She could hear Clive prompting her mother as she continued. "Did you go to law school while you lived in California and forget to tell us?"

April cringed. She would have some explaining to do. She made no move toward the phone. Trying to tell her mother she'd had no intention of misrepresenting herself was futile.

Clive chimed in, loud enough for her to hear. "You looked stellar, luv. Like a real barrister."

"Call us back," Bonnie said. "I've been thinking about suing my neighbor for letting his dog poop in my yard." She heard her mother cackle as she hung up.

Next, her cell rang. She saw by the readout it was Mary Lou. She let that go to voice mail, too. Mary Lou's message was brief. "Saw you on the news. Call me."

Hoping to find something to distract her, April went back to the TV and flipped through the channels. She put on MTV, but after several minutes of waiting for commercials to end, she gave up. She'd have loved some of the old MTV right now. Just music videos and a VJ to soothe her mind. Where was Nina Blackwood when you needed her?

Her cell rang again, this time with the strains of Bob Seger's "Like a Rock." Deana's ring. The one call she had to answer.

She turned off the television and picked up the phone tentatively, as though it were hot. "Hi, Dee."

April plunged ahead, not giving Deana a chance to speak. "Look, I'm sorry if I said too much."

"About what?" Deana sounded perplexed.

April knew the warmth in Deana's voice was about to go away. She felt a chill ripple down her spine. "Did you see the news?"

"I guess Mark has it on in the study. Should I go look?"

"No." Damn, she had to come clean. "Listen, I was interviewed at the protests at Mitch's after I saw you today. The reporter made me say more than I wanted to."

April heard herself making excuses. That was not acceptable. She needed to take responsibility for what she'd said. It hadn't been Jocelyn's prodding. It had been her own big mouth.

She cleared her throat and spoke clearly. "I let it slip that Xenia was murdered."

There was a long silence. April strained to hear Deana's voice. Her breathing, anything. "Deana?"

"Did you tell them I told you?" Deana asked, her voice forced, as though she'd been running and was out of breath.

"Of course not," April said.

"Still, the police are going to assume I did. My reputation . . ."

April sighed. She knew Deana's reputation was critical. Her job as deputy coroner had just begun. She wouldn't be reappointed if her superiors thought her untrustworthy.

"I'll tell Yost that I forced it out of you," April said.

Deana said, "So I just look weak and not like a breaker of confidences."

"Or I read the report on your desk. Upside down."

"Proving I'm not to be trusted with important paperwork."

"Deana," April pleaded, "Xenia was being forgotten in the wake of the protests. No one was paying her any attention."

For a moment, there was silence, then April heard Deana take in a deep breath. "I'm going to have to think about this some more, April. I'm sorry."

April felt the words "I'm sorry" pierce her heart. Deana would have to apologize for April's mistakes. She started to speak, but Deana cut her off.

"We're stamping over here Wednesday night" she said. "I'm going to get the envelopes for your mother's invites. I was thinking aqua and brown. What do you think?" Her words were clipped.

"That sounds pretty," April said, unable to shift gears. What did the colors matter anyhow? But she didn't want to hurt Deana's feelings by voicing those opinions.

"Seven o'clock. If you want to come," Deana said abruptly. She hung up before April could respond.

Of course she would be there. She glanced at her calendar.

A red circle on her calendar caught April's

eye. Xenia had been scheduled to come back tomorrow and talk about the stamping in her new house. A date she wouldn't keep now.

Her heart was heavy. Xenia's boxes were still sitting in her car, awaiting delivery. Calls to her sister had not been returned. April decided to bring the boxes in and hope that there were invoices or addresses inside.

April ripped open the tape holding the box from Trish first. It contained six smaller boxes of various sizes with the Bella Beauty distinctive blue packaging. She pulled them out, pleased to find each printed with a label with the name and address of the recipient. Furthermore, the labels contained the contents and the amount due. She'd be able to deliver the packages without any problem. She could collect the money and deliver it to Pedro.

The other box, the one she'd found on Xenia's porch, was a different can of worms. Inside were eight identical size boxes. The boxes were hot pink with scalloped edges, much like the packaging in Trish's box. The font was very close to the Bella logo, but the name of this product was Bonita. Tiny writing along the outer edge was in Spanish. She couldn't read Spanish.

April ran a fingernail under the opening and popped up the top of one of the boxes. Inside was a plastic case, fitted with five lipsticks with matching glosses, one eye shadow pad and several shades of foundation. A sample kit, very much like the one Trish had showed her the other day.

Except for the color of the boxes, and the name of the products, this line was exactly like Trish's.

The product had obviously been styled after Trish's line. Ripped off, some might say.

Xenia had been going into business on her own. Probably using her customer base that she'd built up selling Trish's products. That was pretty unethical. Xenia had hinted that her suggestions had not been heeded by Trish. April knew firsthand how bull-headed Trish could be.

If Xenia had felt Trish was not answering her clients' needs, she might have gone off and created her own cosmetics.

She stood to make her own fortune.

An invoice on top listed this box as one of six. Five more boxes like this meant forty eight starter kits. The total for all boxes was nearly five thousand dollars.

Where had she gotten the money?

April sat down heavily at the kitchen table.

When she and Xenia had been picking colors the other night, they'd talked about Xenia's jobs. She often cleaned businesses with her sister as well as selling the cosmetics. April knew she was ambitious and a self-starter. If she had income she hadn't reported, their family might not have been picked for the Homes for Hope house.

Mitch had very strict guidelines as to how much money a family could make to qualify for one of his houses. The earning limits were set according to how many kids a family had. If Xenia was working under the table, hiding income, that could be a problem. Not just for her and Pedro, but for Mitch. If word got out that the process had been compromised, his opponents would have a field day. He couldn't stand any adverse publicity.

CHAPTER 15

On her lunch hour the next day, April drove to the first address on the box of Trish's products. It stood to reason that these deliveries were meant for baronesses, who ordered these products for others. If Xenia had started her own line, then they would be the logical people to buy the starter kits for Bonita, too. She would ask them what Xenia was up to.

Could this have contributed to her death? Two things nagged at April: Where did Xenia get the money to fund these starter kits and what would Trish do when she found out that Xenia was taking her business?

April hoped some of the answers lay ahead.

The addresses she got off the Internet led her to neighborhoods she'd never been to in small patch towns, remnants of coal-mining, company-owned villages. Here, housing was still cheap. Many of the homes were row houses, leaning into each other like tired siblings.

April knocked on the first door. The woman who answered peeked out tentatively. The house was covered with asphalt shingles, many cracked and some missing, creating gaps like a jack-o'-lantern's smile. The steps leading up to the porch were crumbling concrete. The ripped screen door should have been replaced with a storm door by now to keep out the inevitable cold air.

The woman was wearing a housedress and had a bright pink duster in her hand. Her makeup, however, was fresh and perfect. Her cheeks stood out against her skin. Her lips were red, lined in a darker color.

April could see past her into the living room. The floor was covered in lush dark brown carpet. Two couches, covered in swirling cut velvet, faced each other. The white brick fireplace was flanked by gleaming brass tools. In the dining room beyond, the oak table was set with a lace tablecloth.

The well-kept interior was at odds with the house's shabby exterior. April realized these people probably didn't own their homes, but they did take pride in what was actually theirs.

April introduced herself, and the woman

answered in rapid Spanish.

"English?" April asked.

The woman shook her head. This was going to be harder than April had thought. She tentatively held out the order. The homeowner nodded, fetched her purse and counted out the money owed.

But by the time April had delivered the third package, she knew her questions would not be answered there. All of her transactions were carried out in sign language. The first two women had given her cash in the exact amount due. They'd been expecting their delivery. She didn't know if they knew about Xenia's death or not, but they took the products from April and closed the door.

Those three deliveries had already taken up most of her lunch time. The rest of the Trish order and the box of starter kits remained on the backseat of her car. She had no idea who was supposed to get them and she was no closer to figuring out why Xenia was killed.

Disheartened, she left the rest for another day and went back to work.

Around six, April headed to Deana's for the stamping meeting. She planned to arrive a little early hoping to have a face-to-face with her friend.

Deana called her just before she turned onto the road where Hudock Funeral Home was. She was brief. "Could you run up to Trish's and pick up the envelopes for your mother's invites?"

Dang, it was a forty-mile round-trip. It would take her the good part of an hour to get up there and back.

But how could she say no? She would do whatever Deana asked her; April needed to be back in her friend's good graces. She didn't like being on the outside of Deana's affections.

April agreed and drove as fast as she could, happy to see her time out to Pine's End was just eighteen minutes. At this rate, she'd get back to the stamping before the snacks were put out. Stopping in front of the closed entrance gate, she rolled down her window and looked expectantly into the guardhouse. The security guard stopped texting and gave her old car a disapproving look. Suddenly he smiled. "Hey, I saw you on TV yesterday. You're that lawyer, right?"

April hid her confusion with a wary smile.

He didn't notice. The metal barrier was already opening. "You going to see Trish again? Be my guest," he said, bowing slightly.

April waved jauntily, matching his mood.

Being mistaken for a lawyer had its advantages.

No one answered the door at Trish's. Damn. April flipped open her phone, annoyed to see the smallest of bars showing. Trish's house was hemmed in by tall evergreens. Her neighbors' houses were just as dark as hers was.

April walked back down the drive, watching the bars waver. She called Deana, pacing, trying to make sure the phone coverage remained. "No one's home."

"Okay. Don't leave. See the keypad by the garage door?"

She moved closer to the garage and spotted it on the side of the door frame.

"I do."

"I'll give you the code to get in. The box of envelopes should be right inside the door."

"Deana, really? I'm not comfortable going in."

She heard the ominous crackling sound that meant her phone was losing the connection. She raced back to the end of the driveway.

Deana was saying, "It's all right. I've used her garage code plenty of times." Deana broke up again. "Go ahead. It's 8-7-4-7-4."

April looked around. No one was likely to

call the police on her. She swallowed her discomfort and logged in the numbers. Nothing.

"Deana?" But the phone was dead.

She took a deep breath. She wanted to do this for Deana. And her mother. They needed to get the invitations in the mail.

She tried the numbers again, being more careful this time. It worked. The garage door rumbled open.

She hurried inside. The automatic overhead light came on. No cars were parked here, though two oil stains gave away their usual positions. April turned her attention to the shelves lining the garage and found the box with an invoice made out to Deana.

"One hundred Regency envelopes," she read off the paper stapled to the top.

She grabbed the box and headed back to the car, stopping only to close the garage door. She threw the box on the passenger seat and peeled out.

She slowed when she reached the guardhouse, waving to the security guard, as he stuck his head out.

"No one home?" he said.

She shook her head, covering the box with her free hand.

"I thought I saw her and her husband go out earlier," he said.

"Thanks anyhow," April said, feeling like a criminal.

Back at Deana's, April made her way downstairs to the Hudock Community Room, used for funeral dinners and stamping meetings. Mary Lou waved hello, and Rocky raised her glue stick to her in greeting. Suzi was leafing through the latest issue of *Cloth Paper Scissors* magazine. She pointed out an article to Rocky. April wondered if Rocky had ever been published. She was certainly good enough.

Deana came in from the hall, carrying a large box of Stamping Sisters ink pads. "Got 'em?" she asked when she saw April had arrived. April held up the box as proof, hoping it was enough to earn her friend's forgiveness.

Deana said, "Good. Your mother dropped off the addresses earlier. We should be able to get all the envelopes done tonight."

April stopped by Rocky, who was spreading glitter glue on the vellum overlay. The floor around her sparkled.

Mary Lou waved her over and pulled out a chair next to her. She patted the seat.

"What's this I hear about new stamps you designed?" Mary Lou asked. "I want to make a scrapbook page for my niece. She

200

just got back from a soccer tournament in California and she loved it."

"Soccer balls and sporty things? I don't have anything like that," April said.

"No, your San Francisco ones," Mary Lou said.

April caught Deana's eye. Had she told them about the debacle with Trish? April didn't like that idea. Deana shook her head quickly.

"I was just telling the girls that you're creating your own line of stamps," Deana said.

Mary Lou was still going on about her niece. "She fell in love with the city when the soccer team went there on a field trip. Fisherman's Wharf, Coit Tower. She's already looking into colleges there."

April pulled out the selection of stamps she'd shown Trish yesterday. Mary Lou fell on them, exclaiming. Suzi joined her to see what the excitement was all about.

"Ahh. Look at the sea lion," Suzi said. "Can I use this?"

"Of course," April said, pleased that the stampers liked her work.

Deana laid out the invitations they'd made at the last session. Mary Lou had printed the vellum with the information about the wedding.

April picked one up. "These look great," she said. "I love the font."

The wording was simple. "Bonnie Buchert and Clive Pierce invite you to their nuptials. Wednesday, November 18 at 7 p.m. at the Aldenville Country Club."

No mention of Homeland Security or the real reason for the wedding. April held the fragile piece of paper in her hand. Her mother was getting remarried. Wow.

April felt her eyes mist. Deana saw and came over to give her a squeeze. April knew Deana would always be there for her.

The group settled into the business at hand: addressing envelopes. Deana had the list of Bonnie's invitees. Each of the stampers claimed a few of the names and a stack of envelopes, and began.

"Suzi, did you have your Pumpkin Express meeting?" Deana asked after a few moments of silence.

"Tomorrow," Suzi said. She gnawed a cuticle. "They're meeting tonight without me. Deciding if I can come back."

"They might keep you out because of Xenia's murder?" Rocky asked.

Suzi shrugged. She could use a little Wonder Woman magic right about now.

Rocky went on. "Everyone's been affected. Mitch needs to raise more money, too. Right now my brother doesn't have a pot to pee in. He remortgaged his own house to buy the land from Aunt Barbara that he's building the houses on."

"I thought she gave it to him," April said.

Rocky answered, "No, he had to pay her. And she wouldn't let him pay it off gradually, either. She wanted all of the money up front."

The stakes were much higher than April had realized. Mitch was in danger of losing his house as well as the unfinished Hope houses.

April's thoughts were interrupted by a loud voice coming from upstairs. The group turned as one. Two voices. Mark, Deana's husband, and someone else. A female.

"Is Bonnie coming?" April said, straining to hear if it was her mother. She wanted to see her face when she saw the finished invitation.

"Not that I know of," Deana said.

The voices grew louder, the feminine one prevailing. All of the stampers had stopped working and were watching the stairs. A minute later, the clatter of heels was heard and April could see two-tone spectator pumps leading the way. Whoever it was, she moved quickly, like an aerobics instructor with no time to spare.

"Good evening," the voice said. A face appeared, bending down to be seen through the slats of the railing.

It was Trish. April shrank back in her chair. For crying out loud. If Deana had known Trish was coming, why didn't she ask *her* to bring the envelopes? April knew she was being petty, but she resented being made into a delivery service.

She glanced at Deana, who shrugged.

That thought led to another. She still hadn't found Xenia's sister to give her the rest of the orders that needed delivery. If Trish knew the box was still in April's car, she would blow her stack. April decided she'd best stay out of Trish's periphery. She got busy spreading glitter on the vellum.

Deana looked surprised, and somewhat wary, to see Trish in her home. Deana's eyes strayed to the materials on the table. Most of it was not the official Stamping Sisters brand. Was Trish in the habit of checking up on her salespeople? April wouldn't put it past Trish to have some kind of noncompetitor clause in her contract.

Trish waved a hand at the group and made a beeline for Suzi. "I've got the prizes for the Pumpkin Express in my car. I brought a full set of Bella cosmetics, the fall Sparkle stamping line and the Honk if You

Love the Holidays stamps."

"Thank you," Suzi said, backing away from Trish's aggressive approach. "I'll let the committee know about your generosity."

Suzi sounded wooden, insincere, like someone who was wondering if Trish's generosity was worth the price she seemed to demand — undying thanks.

Deana said, "Mark will unload the car. Let me tell him."

Trish fluffed her hair, pulling it off her neck and letting it fall back down. "I already charmed him into doing it. That man is easy. One flutter of my lashes was all it took."

April saw Deana swallow a comment. Mark was a polite, helpful guy — not a hapless fool swayed by a woman's manipulations.

"Can you stay?" Deana asked, just barely managing to mask what April suspected was hope for a negative answer.

"Not too long," she said. "I'm on my way home from an affair in Lynwood."

Deana put on her best hostess face. "Well, have a seat. We're addressing invitations for April's mother's wedding."

"So you said on the phone," Trish said. "I see you got the envelopes. I didn't realize you were stamping, too."

They were using stamps to add color to the envelopes. The lattice was not a Stamping Sisters product. Neither were the inks they were using.

Trish turned away, and Deana swept a pile of store-bought stamps into the trash at her feet.

Trish pretended not to care. "Suzi, how are things at your nursery? Recovering from finding a body there?"

Suzi, stricken by the comment, looked around the table for help.

Trish continued. "Of course, it's a very sad ending for Xenia. She was one of my salespeople. I'll miss her."

"We all will. I'm determined not to let her be forgotten," April said, looking at Deana, not Trish.

"I get that," Deana said. She touched April's shoulder and smiled at her. "I totally get that."

April felt as though she'd been blessed by the pope. Life was so much nicer when Deana was not mad at her.

But Trish wasn't feeling the love in the air. Her brow would have been furrowed but for the Botox. "I thought you were having a Stamping Sisters meeting?" Trish said. "Isn't this your usual time for that?"

"Well, yes, but . . ." Deana began. "Bonnie's wedding . . ."

"Stamping Sisters has a wonderful line of wedding stamps," Trish said. "With doves and bells. Even the invitation matches. I don't see those here."

April had seen those stamps, suitable for a twenty-year-old bride.

"My mother has particular tastes," April said.

Deana was still straightening the table, but each of the stampers had her own equipment and a range of supplies from different manufacturers in front of them. Deana couldn't sweep it all into the garbage.

April remembered what Trish had said on Monday about Deana underperforming. Would Trish take her Stamping Sisters away from her?

Trish glanced at the lineup of Suzi, Mary Lou and Rocky, who were all watching her intently, like birds on a telephone wire.

"Pardon me for the interruption, but this is my business," Trish said tightly.

"Well, we don't want to talk business right now," Rocky said. "We're working on a worthwhile project here. What stamps we use are nobody's business."

Trish regarded Rocky. April wondered what was going on between them. After a full moment of quiet, Trish recovered. "Of course not," she said, blinking brightly.

April knew that this was not the end of the discussion. Deana would hear about this indiscretion later.

Trish wandered the room, looking over Mary Lou's shoulder, picking up the page she'd made using April's stamps. Trish looked up at April and back down to the designs, as though she couldn't reconcile the two.

Suzi showed her the tag she'd made with the sea lions.

"Aren't these cool?" Suzi said, spreading out April's stamps. She inked up one and stamped a line of palm trees on a piece of scrap paper. "I love April's aesthetic, don't you?"

Answer that, April thought bitterly. Trish had barely looked at her designs yesterday.

"April's very talented, obviously," Trish said, handing the page back to Suzi crisply. She smiled at April ingratiatingly.

She pulled out a chair next to April and sat down. She leaned toward her and said softly, "I feel as though we got off on the wrong foot the other day. I didn't mean to insinuate that you needed to buy your way into my good graces."

April kept mum. The woman hadn't insinuated. She wasn't that subtle. She'd said outright that April would have to buy her way into designing stamps for the Stamping Sisters line. April folded her arms across her chest. She leaned against the back of the chair. Suzi and Rocky were across the table acting as though they were conferring about inks, but April knew they were listening.

"I had a call after you left," Trish said. "A client who is very interested in a travel series of stamps, based in California. Isn't that what you've created?"

April narrowed her eyes. She doubted that Trish had a new customer. April waited for her to get to the point.

Finally Trish said, "I would like to commission you to make this the line of stamps."

Commission would mean no money coming to April if Trish didn't sell any of the stamps. She looked over to Rocky. She couldn't imagine Rocky giving any of her artistic work away. April had a right to be paid for her original ideas.

She pulled herself upright and faced Trish. The other stampers looked over in anticipation, feeling a change in the air. "That offer is no longer on the table."

Trish leaned away from April, surprised to find herself in a negotiating position.

April felt the support of the other stampers and went on. "If you want to do business with me, you will pay me an advance against sales and royalties on every stamp sold."

Trish's mouth hung open unattractively. April caught a smile from Deana and a smirk from Rocky. Mary Lou slipped her hand under the table for a high five.

Trish began, "I —"

"I'm not finished," April said. "The stamps will be marketed under the name 'April Buchert,' not Stamping Sisters. I'll retain my name as a separate copyright."

Trish looked around her for support but there was none. She was surrounded by April's friends.

The clock on the wall ticked as the minute hand moved. No one said a thing.

Trish stood up in one smooth move. She smiled brilliantly, as though she'd just scored the biggest deal ever. "That will work," she said. "Come by Sunday afternoon and we'll go over the details."

She waved her fingers, one at a time. "Well, ladies, have a wonderful night with your wedding project. I'll look for my invite in the mail," Trish said.

Without a backward glance, Trish tapped her way out of the room. April laid her head on the table, then slowly sat upright again. "What have I done?" she said, wiping her brow dramatically.

"You just invited Trish to your mother's wedding," Rocky said.

"Never mind that. You've sold your first line of stamps," Mary Lou said.

"I did, didn't I?"

"You did," Deana said. "I'll be honored to add the April Buchert line of stamps to my sales kit."

"Only at Stamping Sisters– sanctioned events, of course," Rocky said with a twinkle in her eye.

"Of course," April and Deana said in unison.

CHAPTER 16

April's work at Retro Reproductions on Thursday was held up by the electricians Ed had been so worried about, so after a futile hour of waiting around, she took off. She ran some errands, then decided to swing by Bonnie's before her mother went to work and show her the invitations. She ran home to drop off her groceries and pick up a sample.

But her plans were thwarted.

A moving van was in front of the barn. April had to park to the side and walk around. The two oversize barn doors were wide open. Planks of wood had been laid on the stone steps to make a ramp. A burly kid, a few years north of being a high school linebacker, wheeled down a dolly covered with gray quilted mats.

April could hear her father's voice coming from inside. She hurried through the door, barely dodging a bureau she hadn't noticed in the shadowy interior. It had been set down just over the threshold.

"Dad?"

April moved around a stack of boxes. Her barn, the empty space she'd been trying so hard to fill, was overflowing with old-fashioned heavy furniture, dark walnut dressers and a big bed. A coverlet made of tiny circles of fabric was covering a horse hair chair.

Worst of all, there was a blue corduroy recliner in the middle of the room. From the looks of the worn, stained pillow that rested on the top of the back, it was well used. Somebody couldn't live without it.

Her father turned away from scribbling his name at the bottom of an invoice. A middle-aged man with a "Monster Movers" hat nodded at her and left. She heard the rumble of the big truck start up.

"Dad?" she repeated.

He mopped his head with a handkerchief. "I'm sorry, April. They had nowhere else to go. Vince's sister flat out refused to take them."

"Vince's parents are moving in?" She tried to take in the enormity of this turn of events. The barn was no longer hers.

"I'll have to pack some things." April's chest tightened. Where would she go? Deana had no extra space. Mitch's was out of the question. Her old room at her mother's had been turned into a craft room, and unless she wanted to take her chances stepping on a pin or a bead every time she moved, she couldn't bunk there. Besides, they were a couple in the happy throes of prewedding jitters. Not for her.

There was a motel out on the highway, but she couldn't afford a prolonged stay there.

"You don't have to move out," her father said. "You've still got the loft. We had the movers put their bed over there." He pointed to the far side of the main floor where his office had been housed until recently.

"A couple of their dressers for their clothes, and that's all they need. They're good."

"And the couch and the chair. A TV," April said, unable to stop herself. She pictured an old man in the recliner, changing the remote, tuning in ancient golf games and documentaries on the sex lives of baboons.

"Well, you can't expect them to sit on a futon, can you?" Ed said. He mopped his face again. She could see how tired and stressed he was.

April winced at his tone, but it snapped her back to reality. She was acting like a spoiled brat. Her father and Vince had been letting her live in their barn, rent free, for nearly five months. The Campbells were old and had nowhere to go. That was truly sad. She hoped in her own life, she'd have her living situation straightened out by the time she turned eighty.

She took in a deep breath. "All right, Dad. We'll make it work. I can live in the loft. We'll share the bathroom and kitchen."

The floor was littered with boxes. April picked up one. "Let me help unpack."

She pushed a box with hanging garments toward the closet. "Your walk-in is too big for one person anyhow. In fact, if things get really tight, I can move in there," April said, keeping her tone light.

She was rewarded by a smile on her father's face. "A family of four could live in the shower, for that matter," he said. "It's big enough."

"That's true." April shoved her clothes to one side of the closet and hung the polyester pantsuits and men's plaid shirts. A few hangers held khakis. There wasn't much. She was done in a few minutes.

She opened another box. This one held

folded sweaters. "Where are the Campbells?"

"Vince took them out to eat," Ed said. "He'll bring them along in an hour or so. I want to get as much done as possible before they get here. Let's put the bed together."

She watched him strap on his tool belt. Ed was a hands-on guy, and April admired that he was always the first one to pitch in whenever there was work to be done.

She sorted the screws as he laid out the rails. After a few false starts, they fell into a familiar rhythm. April had spent much of her childhood in just this position, searching through a paper bag of nuts and bolts and screws, looking for the right one, trying to hand it to him just before he knew he needed it.

She found herself humming along with her father, even breaking into the chorus of "The Weight" when her father starting singing about pulling into Nazareth about half past ten. When he started on James Taylor, she surprised both of them by knowing all the words to "Sweet Baby James." They'd spent many hours listening to his favorites: Carole King, Janis Ian, The Band.

A longing for the way things used to be washed over her. It was so strong, she had to turn away from her dad to hide the tears in her eyes. She didn't want him to think she was unhappy. Just the opposite. Moments like this, when they were working together, in sync, she felt so close to him. She loved that she knew him well enough to know that he would launch into "Sweet Home Alabama" right after "Sweet Baby James." Well enough to know he wouldn't mind if she took her time looking for the right size screw but would go nuts if she handed him a hex wrench instead of a socket. Well enough to know that he was happy to be building things with his daughter.

Her heart filled with joy and she smiled at him.

"What?" he said, looking up from the knob he was tightening.

"I just love working with you," she said. "I'm glad to be back home."

He sat back on his heels. She worried about his knees. Bending so much at his age couldn't be good for him.

"Ape, you coming back to Aldenville is the best thing to happen in years."

Within the hour, they had the place semilivable. The couch and chair had been moved under the loft. Ed hooked up the Campbells' TV close by. April had been getting by with the small TV built into the kitchen wall. She wasn't big on watching network TV, preferring to watch movies on her laptop in bed or catch up on series online.

Now she'd have two elderly people living with her. She was only glad that she hadn't planned on bringing Mitch home anytime soon. Talk about awkward.

One last problem remained.

Ed and Vince had moved their office out of the barn several weeks earlier, so the bed fit nicely on the opposite wall. The Campbells could warm their feet by the gigantic stone fireplace on the northern side. One dresser fit next to the fireplace, but the other was too large to go anywhere, unless she took down her drafting table.

It sat in the middle of the floor like an accusation.

"I'm going to have to take the drawing table apart," April said, standing back, hip cocked. She didn't like the idea but was determined to do whatever was necessary. She knew she could do without her table, sketching stamps in the loft or at the kitchen table, but it still felt like a wrench to take it down completely. A real reminder that she didn't live here. Not really.

Her father said, "We can find a place for it." He looked around the room, moving in a circle. His finger was at the ready to point out possibilities. But he couldn't come up with any. The once vast space had filled up with the large ornate furniture the Campbells favored. He pointed at the barn doors.

"If you keep them closed, you could put the table in front. Just use the kitchen door."

"Winter's coming, Dad. I doubt it would be comfortable to sit there. Look, it's no big deal."

Ed looked at his daughter, his worry lines as pronounced as a pulsing vein. He was really stuck between a rock and a hard place.

She flipped over the drafting table and worked out the first screw that held the legs on. "No worries, Dad."

The kitchen door opened just as she was stashing the pieces of her table in the closet next to the bath. She and Ed greeted the new arrivals.

Vince led his mother in gently. She was soft and pink, her hair a nest of curls. She was dressed in polyester pants and a well-worn sweatshirt with a bear dressed in a plaid shirt on the front. Her black sneakers were practical, laced tightly with neat, double-tied bows. Above the tongue were bright orange socks. A pin shaped like a ghost on her lapel blinked off and on.

She eyed the six-burner stove. "Vincent, I

don't think I could cook on this. I would be afraid to push the wrong button."

Ed kissed her cheek. "You'll be fine, Mom. I'll give you a lesson or two and you'll be good to go. You know April, my daughter."

"Call me Charlotte, dear," she said, smiling at April. She touched her cheek. "You're a pretty girl. Took after your mother," she said with a baleful glance at Ed.

Ed rolled his eyes.

Vince leaned out the door and yelled, "Dad!"

A line of profanities turned the air blue. Vince winced. His mother seemed oblivious. She put her purse down on the kitchen table and started opening the cabinet doors. She was a natural nester.

April was a little ashamed of how bare her cupboard was. There was no real food, only things that could be microwaved, usually in a cup or a bowl. Sometimes she added water.

Vince went back outside. They could hear him clearly. "Leave the damn car alone. I'll take it into the shop next week."

A strong but quavery voice came back. "You can't let it knock like that, boy. You're just asking for trouble."

"Here comes Grizz," Ed said. She and her father were lined up as though in a receiving line.

"Grizz?" she asked. "I thought his name was George."

"That's his given name. He's an old Marine. They nicknamed him Grizzly Bear in the war. Most people call him Grizz."

He might have been built like a bear at one time, but the man who came through the door, still stewing about Vince's dieseling engine, was hardly ursine. He was only about five-foot-six, the same as Clive on a good day. His barrel chest had sunk. The only thing grizzled about him was his facial hair, which looked like it needed a good shave.

"Grizz, you've met my daughter, April," Ed said.

"I don't remember," he said with a wave of his hand. "You need to have your timing checked."

"Got it," Ed said.

Vince was clenching his teeth when he gave April a hug. "I'm sorry," he whispered in her hair. "If there was any other way . . ."

She kissed his cheek. For the first time, she wondered what Vince would be like in thirty years. Did he have a choice or would he grow into this irascible, grumpy old man? April hadn't considered what a household of *two* old men might look like. She stole a glance at her dad. He was already full of complaints and worries. What would thirty more years of life do to him?

The thought gave her a stomachache. She was an only child, with two sets of aging parents. Yikes.

Living with the Campbells would be good practice.

An hour later, April was wondering if she'd make it through the first day. The TV was blaring downstairs and April couldn't concentrate up in the loft. Why did it get louder and louder when they broke for commercials? She blew out a breath, trying to calm herself, but felt herself tense up again as someone downstairs changed channels.

Then she checked her phone. Mitch hadn't called. She knew he had his hands full with the Homes for Hope houses and Valdez, but no text, no calls. She'd even checked her e-mail although she knew he hated using e-mail for personal use. Nothing. She wanted to tell him about this newest wrinkle, and let him know not to come over later.

She gave up and climbed down, using the bathroom, splashing cold water on herself and staring at herself in the mirror. No answers there. She walked into the living room. Grizz was in his corduroy recliner.

Charlotte was on the high-back sofa, crocheting.

Scott Ferguson was on TV. He was smiling at the camera, seated in a chair on a stage. Another chair was empty alongside him. He looked seriously like an actor in a SNL sketch. A crawl on the bottom of the screen told the viewer that his annual telethon raising money for the Widows and Orphans was this weekend.

"Whatcha watching," April said, sitting next to Charlotte, figuring if you can't beat 'em, join 'em.

Charlotte said, without missing a stitch, "It's a repeat of Scott's *Highland Fling* show. We never miss it. He gives such good tips on how to live life."

He sounded more like a evangelist than a TV personality. April was intrigued. Ferguson wasn't dressed in a kilt today. Maybe the prospect of crossing his legs on live TV was too daunting even for him. His suit was plaid though, and the effect was mesmerizing. The lines in the plaid seemed to shimmer on screen.

April turned her attention to Charlotte's crocheting. It seemed to be a sweater with an intricate pattern and popcorn balls. She picked up the far edge. Charlotte smiled.

"Do you want to learn to crochet, dear? I

223

could teach you. Considering we're going to be spending so much time together."

April fought the urge to flee. She could see the nights spread out in front of her. Mitchless, she'd crochet afghans and sweaters that Ed wouldn't wear. The idea was so depressing.

"Send him some money," Grizz growled. "He's got those damn kids on again."

"I will, honey, don't worry."

On cue, pictures of smiling little kids standing in front of a dilapidated building flashed on the screen.

"Don't forget the telethon this weekend, people," Scott said. "Saturday, beginning at noon. All the money will go to the AIDS Widows and Orphans. It's all hands on deck."

"We'll be there," Charlotte said earnestly to the TV. "You can count on us."

April went over to Bonnie's to give the Campbells some time to settle. She still had the box of deliveries from Trish in her car. Maybe Bonnie would know where to find Xenia's sister.

Again Bonnie and Clive were in the backyard, surrounded by kids. Vanesa sat alone at the picnic table, which looked forlorn without its summer tablecloth and umbrella.

"April," Clive managed to get out, puffing with exertion.

"April!" mimicked one of the boys. He had a dimple in his cheek and a mischievous glint in his eye. He clearly hadn't figured out his mother wasn't coming back.

"Lovely to see you," Clive said, scrambling to his feet, brushing the dead grass from his khakis. He had dirt on his knees, and his hair stood on end, as though he'd put it through a Flowbee. The little girl, Erika, helped to clean him up, slapping his knees firmly, a determined expression on her face, her cheeks reddened from the play, her bird-like chest heaving.

"Lovely to see you," the boy echoed. His British accent was pretty good.

"Knock it off, Greg," Vanesa said. "No one likes that game."

Greg pouted, his lower lip jutting out a good inch. He had huge brown eyes with long eyelashes, and April suspected he was used to getting his way with that pout. She hid a smile. She doubted that Xenia had been immune to his charms.

Greg and his two brothers, one taller and skinnier, and the other shorter, looked like three stair-stepped versions of the same child. Erika, the youngest, circled the boys, tapping a shoulder, a knee, trying to get a rise out of one of them.

"What are you guys doing?"

Clive peeled Greg off his arm. "We're just going in to play some music."

"Nooo," Jonathan, the youngest boy, wailed. "Hide-and-go-seek," he cried.

"Shut up, Jonathan," Greg said.

Jonathan punched Greg and wrestled him to the ground. They rolled around like puppies. Tomas, the oldest, watched them. He looked like a referee, ready to step in if he was needed.

Erika toddled over to Vanesa, and hanging on to her leg, began to suck her thumb. She rubbed the hem of Vanesa's knit shirt rhythmically. Vanesa ignored her but didn't push her away. April felt tears push to her eyes as she thought of these kids growing up without a mother. This teen was bound to bear the brunt of it.

"Let's show Aunt April what we sing," Clive said. "She looks like she could use some cheering up."

April raised an eyebrow at her mother. "Aunt April?" she mouthed. "No way."

"They are the closest I have to grand-children."

Bonnie laughed and linked her arm in hers.

"Mom," April said as they walked behind

Clive and the kids toward the house, "have you seen Xenia's sister?"

"She has to keep on working. She drops the kids off, but that's all. We don't really talk. She's trying to cope, but she's pretty out of it, poor thing."

Vanesa hung back, letting the kids run ahead. She was eavesdropping. April lowered her voice a bit more.

"The thing is, I have this box of stuff for Xenia's clients. I was hoping her sister could help me figure out what to do with them."

"You don't have much choice, do you? You're going to have to deliver them."

Vanesa stopped and let them catch up to her. "I can help you," she said. "I helped my mother all the time."

"Would you?" April said.

Vanesa nodded.

"Great."

Wanting to lead the way into the house, Greg pushed Jonathan aside as the two reached the back door. Jonathan began to wail.

Clive patted his shoulder. "No worries, mate. Being first don't mean nothing. Being last is the best."

Erika, who was being carried by Vanesa, climbed down. She stood by the door, giving each of her brothers a gentle push through the door. Then she piped up, "I'm last. I'm best."

Clive scooped her up and she giggled. "You get to pick first, Erika. Tambourine or bells?"

"Bells, bells," she shouted, dropping out of his grasp and heading for a wooden trunk that April had never seen before. It was standing in the middle of the living room. The kids must have been spending a lot of time here.

Erika opened the trunk with help from Tomas. He hadn't said a word, but he'd been observing. April wondered if he'd always been so solemn. He held the lid open so his sister and then his brothers could pick out their instruments. Jonathan pulled out a washboard and a stick, Greg a pair of maracas. Erika rang her bells, racing around the room.

Tomas handed the tambourine to Vanesa, who took it gingerly. She stopped the noise it was making with the palm of her hand. April recalled watching Clive on his old TV shows, spinning the tambourine, twisting his body as he tossed the disc in the air and caught it behind his back.

He had the same sparkle in his eye now.

"Tomas," Clive said, bending with a flourish. "Maestro."

Tomas sat at the piano, with his fingers poised to strike. Clive sat next to him. Bonnie settled into her favorite chair and picked up her knitting.

"He's a natural," Clive said to April.

Jonathan, Erika and Greg were getting maximum noise from their instruments. April began to wonder if Clive had any earplugs around. He was already half deaf himself.

"Okay, kids," he said quietly.

The cacophony, miraculously, ceased. Vanesa raised her eyes up from the floor for a moment.

Clive raised his hand like a concertmaster. All ten eyes were on his fingers. He pointed to Erika, who jingled her bells. Next was Jonathan on the washboard. Each of the kids took turns, making their instrument sing until Clive stopped them with a crisp snap of his hand.

April clapped.

"That's just our warm-up," Clive said with a grin. "Wait until you hear this."

He sat next to Tomas on the piano bench. "One, two, three . . ."

He began playing. Tomas played along. Clive sang, his voice still strong and easy on the ears. The kids joined in, blending their voices with his, hitting the high notes Clive could no longer manage.

It was a song April hadn't heard before, reminiscent of his old stuff but with a modern twist. She found herself moving her hips along with the beat.

Vanesa closed her eyes and sang, her general sullenness forgotten as she caught harmonies with Clive. She had a lovely voice. Her face was transformed from sad to beatific. Erika tucked her hand into her sister's and watched her as she sang along in an earnest, piping tone.

"Wow," April said, clapping. Her hands seemed inadequate to make enough noise to truly appreciate what she'd just heard. "You guys are amazing."

"I wanted to sing 'Banana Pancakes,' " Greg said solemnly. "But Clive made us sing his song."

"I've never heard that song before. New?" April asked.

"I'm working out some stuff," Clive said. He looked away, suddenly shy. He turned his attention to Jonathan, who had come over to the piano and was pounding the keyboard.

Greg, on the floor, had untied Clive's shoelaces and was retying them to each other, sneaking glances up at Clive, who remained oblivious. Tomas stopped his brother and fixed Clive's shoes.

Greg looked up. "Clive says we're his music," Greg said.

April turned to Clive with a question on her face.

"My muse," he said.

April laughed. Greg shrugged comically, his skinny shoulders rising up to meet his ears.

The doorbell rang. Bonnie started out of her chair, but April gestured to her to stay put.

"I'll get it."

She'd barely gotten across the living room when two men entered from the little-used front door.

Her heart leaped when she recognized Mitch. She couldn't see who was behind him. She felt a rush as the kids ran past, Greg shoving Jonathan, Tomas right behind them and little Erika trying to catch up.

"Daddy," Erika screamed.

Vanesa stayed where she was, but April was glad to see a smile grow on her face.

Pedro Villarreal was nearly knocked over by his children's joy at seeing him. He took it in stride, grabbing Jonathan by the arm and lifting him and Erika up without a struggle. Tomas and Greg stood at his feet, jockeying for position, but not fighting.

"I got him a lawyer," Mitch whispered to April as Pedro's kids jumped on him.

April felt her own frown lines deepen. "How? With what?"

Clive tinkled on the piano, joyous music underscoring the sweetness of the reunion.

April led Mitch to the kitchen where they could talk in relative peace and quiet.

Mitch crossed his arms over his chest and leaned against the wall. Bags had formed under his eyes and his skin looked sallow. April didn't like how tired he looked.

"What did you use to retain the lawyer?"

"The Foundation money."

"Is that smart?" April cried. "How are you going to finish digging the well? They can't move in without water."

He put out his hand and she took it. He squeezed it, giving her a wan smile. "Don't worry about it. I'll figure it out. I've got options."

Whatever money sources he'd been relying on had to have dried up. People had to be scared off by Xenia's death, the graffiti and the protests. April knew that the supply house needed to be paid. The well drilling wasn't going as planned. Every extra foot costs another couple of hundred dollars.

April couldn't keep the worry out her voice. "Is Hector Valdez helping you?"

Mitch shrugged. "Look at that," he said, smiling as Erika screeched happily. Her little cheeks had bloomed with color. Greg had Jonathan in a gentle headlock and was rubbing his head gleefully. Vanesa had moved to her father's side, nestling under his arm, her face in his neck. He kissed her hair. Tomas was talking to his father, the words lost across the room. His eyes wouldn't leave his father's face.

Mitch said, "I couldn't let him be stuck in jail while they look for Xenia's killer. He needs to be out and working and taking care of his kids."

April was proud of Mitch. He did have his priorities straight. Earlier in the week, she'd worried that he'd forgotten about Xenia and Pedro. Now she could see he was trying to keep all the balls in the air.

A germ of an idea snaked into April's mind. Mitch needed to raise money fast. Scott Ferguson was having a telethon this week. What if she could persuade him to donate even more than he originally promised to the Homes for Hope? Mitch could raise some capital without risking his principles.

Mitch straightened and gave April a peck on the cheek. "Pedro wants to take the kids to the house and do some painting. I'm going to go with him," he said.

April hugged him. She felt him relax, but only for a moment. There was work to be done. She couldn't wait for the day when they could spend some time in each other's arms.

Maybe she could hurry that scenario along. Raising money would help.

"Vanesa, let's go make those deliveries," April said. "We've got one stop to make first."

CHAPTER 17

April and Vanesa drove silently up the mountain to Lynwood. She passed the small mall that served the area. Boscov's, the local department store, was the anchor. The other twenty stores changed with the vagaries of the local economy. Right now a Halloween Superstore occupied the space left vacant by a drugstore chain.

For a more extensive shopping experience, most of the residents drove thirty miles to Wilkes-Barre or sixty miles south to Allentown. At Christmas, many drove a hundred miles to King of Prussia. Of course, the country club set went to Philadelphia or New York. Or Paris.

The regular folk had to make do with the local shops, which made services like Trish's even more valuable. Ordering products from your home had special appeal.

April explained to Vanesa what she needed her to do. She told Vanesa about the box she'd found on the porch and the starter kits that were inside. Vanesa said nothing. They would deliver the remaining Bella orders, and Vanesa would determine which of these baronesses were going to be part of Xenia's new business venture.

At the first stop, Vanesa spoke to the woman of the house. She handed over the box of Bella Beauty, but nothing else.

"What did she say?" April asked.

Vanesa shook her head. "She didn't know anything about the new line."

April worried that Vanesa wasn't asking the right questions, but she had no choice but to trust her.

At the second stop, they had better luck. Vanesa and a young mother talked in rapid Spanish. She not only accepted her starter kit, but wanted three more. April asked Vanesa to ask her what she knew about Bonita, but after a torrent of words from the other woman, Vanesa's answer was short and curt.

"Not much. My mother only told her something new was on the way."

It was the same with each of the deliveries. Many of the women were enthusiastic about the new line of cosmetics aimed at the Hispanic market, but no one knew anything.

Disheartened, April started back to Bonnie's. Vanesa was silent. April reminded herself that Vanesa's mother had just died, and the kid was bound to have moments of disquiet.

Passing a billboard advertising Ferguson Enterprises, April remembered the second part of her errands. Talk to Scott Ferguson.

Ferguson had a store on Route 309 outside of town where he sold Scottish imports, woolens and jewelry. She found it easily thanks to the large rolling sign with removable letters out front that read, "Ferguson Enterprises. Day trip to Atlantic City every Tuesday. Sign up inside." It looked like the signs churches used for the homily of the week. This was a different kind of devotion.

April pulled into the large parking lot. Bright black and shiny, the asphalt appeared freshly sealed for the winter. Several buses emblazoned with "Ferguson Enterprises" spelled out in plaid letters were parked next to a concrete block building at the back of the property.

She peered out of her windshield, looking for an indication that his office was here, too. Two storefront windows took up about two-thirds of the building, with two glass-fronted doors located midway between them. One window displayed a plaid-dressed mannequin family, two parents and three kids of varying sizes. A motorcycle with plaid saddlebags was in the other window.

The other third of the building had no windows in the front, but several small windows around the side. Ferguson's office could be housed there.

"Stay in the car, Vanesa, okay? I'll leave you the keys. You can listen to my radio."

Vanesa shrugged and set to work changing the stations. April winced when the girl switched one of her preset buttons to the hip-hop station.

"I won't be long," she said.

She approached the building. A chime sounded as April stepped on the black mat going inside. A cheery woman greeted her from behind a counter that ran across the back of the room. She laid a paperback best seller on the counter, facedown.

"Welcome. Need some help?" she trilled. Her middle-aged face was layered with wrinkles, but she didn't seem to mind. She smiled with the enthusiasm of someone who knew she had a place in heaven.

"I'm looking for Mr. Ferguson."

Her eyes narrowed, and her lips pursed. The clerk's eyes trailed to a door at the far

238

end of the counter. April looked that way. The door was unmarked.

"He's not in," the receptionist said. She looked April up and down.

April looked closer at the woman's name tag. Olivia Ferguson. Must be his wife. Why was she so protective? He hadn't struck April as a guy who needed his wife to run interference for him.

Unless it was just women she had a problem with.

"I have something to deliver to him. From my father, Ed Buchert of Retro Reproductions?" April asked, letting her voice rise up at the end.

Mrs. Ferguson's eyes strayed back to the closed door. Her shoulders twitched as though she heard a sudden noise. April heard it, too. A door had opened and closed in the back. April walked quickly to the front. She saw a figure hurrying to a Porsche parked on the side. His remote key lock beeped twice. She looked back at Mrs. Ferguson, who sank back down onto the stool behind her, pulling her paperback out again. He'd made a clean getaway as far as she was concerned.

By the time April got to his car, he was seated in it, looking at something in his lap. She grabbed the door handle as he was about to turn the ignition key.

He turned toward her, startled. She looked in the window and was surprised by a view of hairy knees. Scott Ferguson was in another kilt, this one a solid red wool. The leather sporran laid in his lap like a fancy fanny pack. The screen on his phone glowed from the passenger seat.

April tore her eyes off his bare knees and met his gaze. "Mr. Ferguson, a word, please," April said.

"Look," he said. "I know who you are. A lawyer with that MAC outfit, right? I told the Campbells not to worry. They will be paid back, I assure you."

April was confused before she realized he must have seen her on TV with Valdez. "I'm not a lawyer," she said. "I'm an interior designer. I have a business proposal."

He got out of his car, suddenly much more cordial. "Why didn't you say so? Come into my office," he said.

His ever-present snakish smile deepened into something more human. He moved in to shake her hand. Up close, she could see his appeal. He put her hand in his and rubbed the top familiarly. His eyes never left her face. He made her feel special. She looked down, breaking the contact first.

"I was just about to go out, but it can wait.

I always have a few minutes for a lovely lady. Follow me," he said. He acted as though he hadn't been trying to run from her a few minutes earlier. This was a man who liked to be in control. And who was comfortable creating his own reality.

They walked back, passing a large concrete block building. It was painted dark green and had no identifying signage.

He led her to a door on the side of the store. It was nearly invisible, painted the same mustardy gold color as the brick side of the building. The door led directly into his office. "After you," he said, touching April gently on the elbow. "Have a seat."

"I have a proposition," she said.

"So you said," he said. "I'm always up for a new idea."

He closed the door firmly behind her. She stopped, several feet inside the door, confused. She couldn't find the couch. The entire room was decorated in tartan. The same red plaid was in the rug, the wallpaper, the curtains. It was like being inside of an antique lunch box.

April's eyes shimmered, trying to take it all in. She closed her eyes against the assault. When she opened them again, she headed to the long wall opposite his large mahogany desk. She led with her foot like a blind person and bumped into an umbrella stand that held a collection of walking sticks. The rattling was loud, and as she grabbed them in an effort to stop the whole collection from falling on the floor, she wondered if Ferguson's wife would come back here to see what was going on.

She perched on the edge of the couch, unwilling to sink into the cushion and risk being obliterated by the plaid. She was glad she was wearing black. Maybe he could see her.

April blew out a breath. "I'll get straight to the point. Winchester Homes for Hope needs a cash influx. Your offer the other day when you cut the ribbon at Suzi's A.maz-.ing Maze to donate one percent of the telethon profits was quite generous."

Ferguson leaned forward, arms on his desk. His desk was completely clear, the glass top protecting the antique finish from fingerprints. He must do his work elsewhere. There wasn't even a laptop in sight. On the credenza were pictures of him with the pope, Bill and Hillary Clinton and Mike Murphy.

Now that her eyes were starting to adjust, April saw the walls were covered with photos. Bus trips to Atlantic City with smiling seniors. There were pictures of groups standing with piles of luggage in front of Vatican City, the Eiffel Tower and the London Bridge. The buses behind them were emblazoned with the Ferguson Enterprises logo, the same plaid lettering and bagpipe.

She focused her attention on him. "I was hoping I could convince you to increase your end just a bit."

Ferguson blew out a breath and sat back in his chair, obviously reluctant to continue the conversation. But April had had many clients balk at the price of her work or at the length of time it would take her to implement their visions. She knew she was good at bringing people around.

"That money is meant for the AIDS widows and orphans of Scotland," he began.

April hadn't known AIDS was a problem in Scotland. She leaned forward. "Hear me out. What if I can raise the total amount of the donations? Bigger totals means more money all around, right?"

She saw the idea of raising more cash spark his interest.

She leaned in farther, smiling at him. He'd used his charm on her. Now it was her chance to turn hers on. She reminded herself of Xenia's children, how happy they'd be when they moved into their new bedrooms. She thought of Vanesa, outside in her car, with a place to do her homework. Mitch, his money woes behind him, visiting her again at night.

She said, "That way you could give away a bigger piece of the pie without hurting your bottom line."

Ferguson stroked his chin as though impressed with the size of his mandible. "And how do you propose to increase donations?"

"I can get Clive Pierce, lead singer of the Kickapoos, on stage. Singing."

Ferguson hesitated. April was afraid maybe she'd overplayed her hand. Maybe Clive wasn't enough.

Ferguson tapped his veneers. "He doesn't perform anymore. I heard he suffers from stage fright."

"Exactly. He hasn't performed anywhere in years." In fact, the last time might have been when she'd gone to his concert in the early eighties. "But I will deliver him. To you. On your stage," she said, hoping that was true. She knew she'd have to convince Clive, too.

Ferguson was shaking his head. "The telethon is only two days away."

He pushed back, making a show of pulling on his knee socks and rearranging his sporran. April knew he had taken the bait. She just had to reel him in.

The former lead of the Kickapoos was a moneymaker, and Ferguson knew it.

He straightened. "I'll need more volunteers to handle the phones."

Yes! She had him now. She'd prevail on the stamping group to do this.

"Got it covered. Deal?" she asked.

Ferguson stood. April got up from the couch, hand extended.

The door to the parking lot opened suddenly. "April?"

Ferguson turned quickly, surprised to see another visitor. His sporran bounced.

Vanesa stood in the doorway. "I got worried." Her eyes were hooded, her expression unreadable. April figured she was more likely bored.

"Who's this lovely lady?" he said, the words purring out of him.

Vanesa smiled and tossed her hair once. Now she didn't look distressed at all.

April said. "Wait for me in the car, Vanesa. I'm just about done here."

Vanesa was not deterred. Ferguson's charm was drawing her in. She reached her skinny arm out to shake his hand. "Vanesa Villarreal," she said.

Ferguson's eyes grew wide. "I'm sorry for

your loss," he said softly. Behind his gentleness, though, April could see wheels turning.

"Vanesa," April said again, nodding her head toward the parking lot.

"Wait. I have a question for you. I don't know what music the kids today like to listen to," Ferguson said, without taking his eyes off her face. "Do you think Clive Pierce is a good addition to my telethon?"

Vanesa had started toward the door. She stopped and looked at April. "Is Clive going to sing on TV?"

Ferguson continued. "Do kids your age know who he is?"

Vanesa nodded. "I sing with him," she said.

Ferguson's gaze shifted from Vanesa to April. She saw a spark of triumph there. Vanesa was backlit in the doorway. From where April stood, Vanesa looked like a beautiful woman, not a young girl. She glanced at Ferguson, knowing what he saw.

April cringed. "Vanesa, I'm finished here. Let's go."

Ferguson steepled his fingers under his chin. "Sing? Do you now?"

Vanesa nodded.

April moved to the door, shielding Vanesa with her body.

Ferguson said smoothly, "How would you like to sing on my telethon?"

April's heart sank. There was no way she'd let Ferguson exploit this kid on television. "No, no, no," she said. She opened the door, trying to push Vanesa through it and out into the parking lot, into the car where she belonged. Where April could get her back to her father.

"Not going to happen," April said.

"I want to do it," Vanesa said. "I want to be on TV."

"Vanesa, hold on," April said. "You don't know what you're saying."

Ferguson ignored her. "How many songs would you like to do?" he said.

"Two," she said with the aplomb of a kid who'd been booking her own act for years.

"Done," Ferguson said. He stood, shook her hand, patting her on the upper arm as he did.

"We'll see about that," April said.

Vanesa turned to her, her eyes flashing with anger. "You can't tell me what to do. You're not my mother."

CHAPTER 18

"Vanesa, you really shouldn't talk to strangers," April said, at a loss for what to say to this teenager. It was bad enough that she had to go back and tell Clive that he was singing on the telethon. Now she had to deal with Vanesa as well.

Vanessa was only fourteen, for crying out loud. Ferguson would need parental permission. Pedro wouldn't let her appear on the show . . . would he?

April relaxed a little, enough to stop squeezing the steering wheel. She sat back in the seat.

"He's not a stranger," Vanesa said. "I've been there before, with my mother. He just didn't remember me."

"Vanesa, what am I going to tell your father?"

"My father will let me do whatever I want. And I want to sing."

April took her hands off the wheel at the

light and pushed on her temples. She felt her blood pulsing and her brain hurt. How had Bonnie gotten through her teenage years? April knew she'd been just as intractable and stubborn as Vanesa.

At Bonnie's, Pedro and she were cooking in the kitchen. The heat of peppers pricked April's nose and made her eyes water. The kitchen smelled heavenly.

"Hey," Bonnie said, putting out her cheek for a kiss as she cut up baked tortillas into chips. "Pedro's making chili."

Pedro shrugged shyly. "The kids like it," he said.

April said to Bonnie, "I thought you were going to work."

Bonnie shook her head. "I called in sick. Now that Pedro's out, we needed a celebration."

Not that Bonnie needed an excuse to cook. April knew what she wanted. To keep everyone together for a while.

Vanesa went to her dad. He offered her a spoonful and she tasted the chili. She lifted his other arm so she could snuggle in. He kissed the top of her head and smiled. April could see the sadness in his eyes. His shoulders looked as though they were being pressed down by an invisible weight. A weight April knew wouldn't be lifted soon.

Vanesa could ask for the moon and the stars right now and he would deliver them on a platter.

"Where's Clive?" April asked. If Vanesa was going to sing, it had to be with Clive alongside her.

"In the basement with the boys playing Xbox," Bonnie said. "Erika's in the living room watching television."

April heard the opening strains of *Sponge-Bob SquarePants.* She opened the door to the basement in the kitchen and hurried down.

Clive was cheering Tomas on as he veered his car around a roadway on the big screen. April sat next to him on the couch.

"They're brilliant," he said. "Much better than me."

April knew Clive was doing a good job of keeping them distracted.

"You suck," Greg said matter of factly.

"I do," Clive laughed. "I really do."

April needed an answer. "Clive, can I talk to you for a moment?"

He turned to her, his face open and happy. He was enjoying his time with the kids. Too bad he wasn't a grandfather by now. He'd be a good one.

April said, "You know how Mitch needs

money to keep his houses going?"

"Of course. I'd love to give you something . . ." Clive began, reaching for his wallet.

April held up a hand to stop him. "I'm not asking for money. I just need you to sing."

Clive looked puzzled. "Me? I'm flattered, darling, but I don't see how that's going to pick people's pockets for cash."

"Ferguson's having a telethon later in the week. He wants you on it."

"Me?" His small face twisted more as he sussed out her meaning. "On the telly? Are you having me on?"

"No. Ferguson thinks you'd be a big draw. So do I," she hurried to add.

Clive's face clouded. "I don't perform anymore. You know that."

"It's for a good cause," April said significantly, nodding her head at the boys, who'd let the game go and were tussling on the floor. The cars on screen veered off the road and blew up. She whispered, "Their future. So that they can move into that house."

Clive rubbed his hands together. His big smile was gone, replaced by a down turned mouth that April had never seen before. His forehead was creased as deeply as Ed's.

"I have to think about that one, luv."

251

April hated what she had to do next. But now it wasn't just Mitch. She couldn't leave Vanesa on stage by herself.

"I'm afraid you're going to have to. Otherwise Vanesa will be singing on TV alone."

Clive jumped up. April put a restraining hand on his arm and told him quickly what had happened at Ferguson's.

"Just say you'll do it," she said.

Their quiet talking had gone on too long. The boys ganged up on Clive and pulled him to the floor. April saw the look on his face before he disappeared under a sea of little legs and arms.

She went back upstairs before he could answer, feeling his disappointment in her like a dagger in the back. She hadn't thought it would hurt so much, but it stung.

April went past Pedro and Bonnie tasting the bubbling stew and into the living room. Erika was sitting on the floor, two feet from the TV, her mouth open, her eyes fixed on the creatures on the screen. She was oblivious to April's entrance.

Vanesa said, "Move back, Erika. Mom says it's not good for your eyes."

Erika scooted backward without breaking her gaze. She went about two inches and stopped.

April picked her up and plopped her in

Clive's recliner. Erika adjusted herself and was rapt again within seconds.

"Thanks," Vanesa said. "She's not supposed to sit that close."

"Smells good in the kitchen," April said. "Isn't it great to have your dad home?"

Vanesa didn't answer for a moment. When she did, her voice was defiant. "He said I could do the telethon."

April had seen it coming. She was at a loss for an answer.

Vanesa's eyes were fixed on the television. She said quietly, "My mother and father fought, you know."

April's head snapped to Vanesa, but the girl wouldn't look at her.

"All parents do," April said slowly. "It doesn't mean that they didn't love each other. My dad and mom fought all the time."

"Your dad isn't accused of murdering your mom," Vanesa whispered. She tried to keep up the defiance, but it wasn't working. April's heart broke for her.

She snuck a glance toward the arch that led to the kitchen. The smell of the chili had permeated the house. From the sound of water running and pans clinking, April figured Bonnie and Pedro were cleaning up as they cooked. Pedro sounded happy to be free.

April suddenly understood why Vanesa was so troubled. "Did you tell the police that your parents were fighting?"

Vanesa's lush eyelashes were suddenly thick with tears. "He made me, that tall one. I didn't want to."

Yost. Damn Yost.

Poor Vanesa. She wanted to appear so independent, so tough, but she was fragile. As the oldest, she alone was saddled with the knowledge that her mother was gone in a way her younger brothers and sister could not comprehend. She had no one to talk to.

"Dinner," Bonnie yelled.

The noise of the boys clattering up the stairs seemed to come through the floor.

Bonnie called again. Mitch hollered hello as he came in the back door.

"We'll be in in a minute," April said.

Vanesa covered her ears, hanging her head as the tears dripped in her lap. Her shoulders shook with the effort of holding herself together. April's heart broke again as the waves of grief racked the young girl.

"Parents fight," April said. "It doesn't mean anything. I'm sure the police understand that."

The kitchen grew noisy as the boys clambered for attention. Erika got up as the show came to an end and joined them. April heard Pedro kissing her as she squealed.

She took Vanesa into her arms and let her cry it out.

"Vanesa, your father didn't kill your mother. I'll make sure the cops know that."

Vanesa sniffled. "My dad didn't want Mom to work so hard. Said he was the male. He was the breadwinner. She should stay home more."

"Is that what they fought about? Your mother's selling the Bella cosmetics line?"

"He was okay with that. But the Bonita stuff we delivered today."

The truth dawned on April. "You knew your mother was starting a competing line." April cocked an eyebrow at Vanesa. She'd been her mother's confidante. "Tell me."

"Mom said I could take over her cosmetic business someday. Start with a line for teenagers. She was building a legacy for me. That's what she called it."

Xenia had realized that she could make a lot more money being her own "queen." She could expand rapidly through the social network of the Latinas and outstrip Trish's success, probably in a manner of months. A very smart business move.

Did this maneuver get her killed? April

shut down that thought before Vanesa picked up on what she was thinking. She didn't need to add to the girl's troubles.

But it was possible. If Trish had gotten wind of Xenia's scheme. Xenia jumping ship and taking a dozen baronesses with her would cost Trish plenty.

Trish had to be livid. If she knew.

But one more question popped into her mind. "Where did Xenia get the money for startup costs?" April said.

"That guy. That Ferguson guy. He lent her the money."

Dinner went by in a blur. The little kids climbed onto the banquette and ate with gusto. The adults crowded in. April couldn't remember her mother's kitchen so full in a long time.

Vanesa stuck close to her father's side. Clive was unnaturally quiet.

Mitch volunteered for cleanup duty. Bonnie and Pedro and the kids went into the basement for another round of Mario Kart.

Clive and April cleared while Mitch washed. They were just about finished when Clive said to Mitch, "Mind if I borrow your girl for a few moments?"

Mitch looked at April. She nodded. "Go ahead."

Clive opened the door and led April outside to the garage. "I want to show you something."

He opened the small side door, and they walked in. Most of the garage was empty, but April could see that the concrete floor, painted barn red, was swept clean and the walls were newly painted a soft gray. As her eyes adjusted to the dim light and she walked farther in, April saw there'd been a transformation in the back half of the garage.

It looked like a rock club. The walls back here were painted midnight blue with stars on the ceiling. A shiny drum kit with the Kickapoos logo across the bass was set up on a raised stage that had been built along the far wall. Amps and microphones were plugged in, ready to go. A keyboard sat to her left.

Clive's life as a Kickapoo was honored out here. The walls were hung with memorabilia — Kickapoos tour posters, handwritten playlists. Toys with the logo, a lunch box, a notebook and other school supplies were in a glass-fronted cabinet.

Pictures were everywhere. Pictures of Clive with Mick Jagger and Roger Daltrey hung on the walls. Paul McCartney as an obviously young Beatle, then again as a disturbingly young-looking old man. April had never been to the Rock 'n' Roll Hall of Fame in Cleveland, but she imagined much of this stuff belonged in it.

Guitars were everywhere. In floor stands, hanging on the walls. There had to be at least twenty of them. She got closer and gasped when she saw one signed by Eric Clapton. She touched it tentatively, rubbing her hand over the smooth, sparkly blue surface. It felt warm. Slow Hand.

She paused by an upright piano with the lid open, exposing yellowed keys. She glanced at the sheet music in the holder. The music was handwritten, in a scratch she didn't understand.

"It's not that I don't want to sing," Clive said. "I still have the need. That's what I come out here to do."

"Does my mother know?"

He screwed up his face. "Of course. She knows everything about me."

"Well, I'm sorry. I messed up. Mitch needs money —"

"Stop," Clive said. "It's done. You're right. I can't let Vanesa go on alone. And she wants to sing so badly. She's a wonderful talent. She should have a shot. And it'll do her heart good to help out in some fashion."

■ ■ ■ ■

"Vanesa did what?" Mitch said.

Mitch had followed April home in his car. It was eight o'clock, earlier than their usual rendezvous, but because of the Campbells inside, they were sitting in his Jeep.

"She told Ferguson she'd appear on his telethon this weekend, trying to raise money for the Homes for Hope houses."

Mitch frowned. "I didn't ask you to go to Ferguson to raise money."

April'd hoped that tonight's dinner had helped to normalize them. But he was still mad.

"Mitch, you need money. He's been wanting to help. He said that the day we worked at the A.maz.ing Maze. Putting the two of you together made sense."

"I don't need his help," Mitch said. "You should have talked to me first."

"Look at it this way. If we raise enough money, you'll be able to build that second house even faster."

Mitch was quiet for a few moments. April's stomach churned as she watched his reaction.

"I'm going to let Hector know. He and

MAC have a family in mind for the second house."

"You're going to let Hector Valdez pick the second family?"

Mitch nodded. "Goodwill. Hector has a lot of connections into the immigrant community that I can never have."

April didn't want to fight with Mitch. She wasn't sure Hector Valdez had his best interests at heart. The other day it seemed as though he was just out to promote himself. But these were Mitch's decisions. She'd done enough asking Ferguson to chip in.

"Want to come in and meet my roommates?" April said. She looked at the barn. Light leaked out the clerestory windows above the door. "They might be still up."

"I need to get home," Mitch said. "I'm really bushed."

April sighed. He had every reason to be tired, but that wasn't why he was hurrying home.

April sat in her car in her driveway, unable to get out. The barn, so empty just a few days ago, had lights blazing from all the windows. One of the huge dual doors was pulled back on its track. Grizz liked fresh air. April preferred her air indoor and recycled. Plus she knew the local raccoons that raided the garbage cans would have no reservations about sauntering inside in search of snacks.

She'd stopped just short of the first motion-sensitive light. She didn't want the Campbells to know she was home just yet. She didn't want to have to fake polite conversation. Maybe they'd go to bed soon.

April was barely aware that a car had pulled up behind her. The headlights had flashed for only a moment in the mirror.

She sat up quickly, hearing tires on gravel as the car drove the last hundred yards with no lights on. Someone was trying to sneak up on her. She grabbed for her phone, only succeeding in knocking it out of reach.

A figure got out of the car, features momentarily illuminated by the indoor light. She could see it was a man.

She knew remaining in her car was safer than getting out. She locked her doors, the sound of which was so loud in the quiet night that her heart pounded in response.

The man moved quickly, rapping on the back passenger window. She turned. All she could see was a belt buckle. She heard the scuffing of the gravel as he came around to the driver's side door. He dropped down so his face filled her window.

Ken.

She screamed anyway, not recognizing her husband before the sound was out, her pent-up emotion busting out of her.

She turned the scream into a stream of obscenities, surprising herself with the variety and scope of blue words she knew.

April tried to open the ungiving door, forgetting she'd locked it. Ken was grinning at her, making an unlock motion with thumb and forefinger. She cursed him again.

When the door opened, she was pushing so hard, she nearly fell out. She recovered, struggling to plant her feet. Her legs had gone to sleep while she'd been out here contemplating.

"Damn it, Ken. I told you not to come."

"How could I resist?" he said. He put his hand under her elbow, steadying her. She pulled away, threatening to topple over again. Ken was very bad for her equilibrium.

She steadied her stance, feeling her knees lock as though she were trying to stay afoot on a sea-tossed ship. She glanced toward the barn door, hoping the Campbells' waning hearing had prevented them from catching any of this. She didn't need any witnesses.

"How did you find me?" she said. She hadn't told Ken where she was staying, and she was sure she'd never brought him to the barn when Ed and Vince lived in it. He'd only been to their place before this one, a seventies ranch.

Ken brushed back the hair from his face. That was a move that used to make her heart beat faster. Not anymore.

"Are you kidding? Small-town America, girl. Every gas station attendant, every crossing guard, every bartender I asked knew about the California girl living in the barn. It took me a while to find the right barn. You almost fooled me with the octogenarian roommates."

"It's a long story," April said. "Sorry you can't stick around to hear it. Have you got my papers signed?"

She held out her hand.

He tried to look disappointed, but April could see he was only playing the game. As soon as he'd seen the Campbells, he'd known he wasn't staying.

She wasn't taking any more. "I don't find your helplessness cute or fixable. I've had enough of you to last me a lifetime."

"Baby . . ." Ken said.

The "baby" did it. She was nobody's baby. She moved away from the car door, no longer needing to hide behind the metal. He wouldn't — couldn't — hurt her.

"I'm a different person than you knew, Ken. I don't back down anymore. I've seen people die too young, leaving nothing but pain in their wake. I'm sick of not being true to myself. I'm ready to live my life now, on my terms. And that does not include you."

Ken looked her over, starting at her feet and ending several seconds later at her hair, as though no longer sure this was his wife. April straightened her spine, thrusting her chest forth and lifting her chin defiantly.

"All I need from you is the legal paperwork," she said. "Hand it over."

Without a word, he went to his car and reached into the backseat. He pulled out a brown envelope. April could see the long logo of a famous San Francisco law firm.

Her heart in her throat, the prospect of real change on her horizon for the first time in years, she felt her resolve strengthen, as she felt the freedom that was at hand.

April made a quick trip into the house to grab the champagne she'd been keeping in the fridge and two glasses. The Campbells roused themselves from the TV, but she waved off their questions. Mitch would be where he always was. At the Villarreals' house. April backed her car out fast. She waved to Ken, who was parked in the turnoff at the top of the driveway.

"Have a great trip back to Cali," she yelled out her window. "Watch out for skunks on your way out of town."

She didn't take in any of the scenery on the five minute trip to the site.

The job site was quiet. All of the workers had gone home. The surrounding trees were filled with soft sounds. The bare trees and warm weather seemed out of synch, but April was grateful for the warm air. It seemed to be a harbinger of things easing up, one last respite before the winter.

Her life with Mitch could begin now, really begin. The weight of Ken had been lifted and she felt nearly giddy. All the disagreements she and Mitch had had this week faded. She set out the bottle and glasses in the kitchen and dropped her paperwork on the countertop, still dusty from installation.

"Where are you?" she called.

"Kid's bath," was the answer.

April went down the hall. The walls had been painted the color that Xenia had picked out. She pushed down the sadness she felt. Now she had something to celebrate.

Mitch was in the bathroom hanging the medicine cabinet. "Hey, you're just in time.

I could use an extra hand," he said. "Push up while I attach this side."

April obliged. She had to use two hands to hold up her end.

"Good news," she said.

"Really? I could use some." The sound of the electric screwdriver drowned his voice out.

She wanted his undivided attention. "Finish up first."

Together they installed the mirrored cabinet. April could see her grinning reflection. She couldn't stop smiling.

"That your last job of the day?" she said. "Please?"

"Well, I was going to caulk the shower again."

April put on a pout. She didn't often resort to feminine wiles but she'd make an exception. "I've got something to show you."

She pulled him toward the kitchen. She pulled the cork on the bottle and poured.

"Champagne?" he said. "What's the occasion?"

She waved the papers in front of him. "Ken was here . . ."

"Ken?" Mitch looked around. "Here?" He was on high alert.

"At the barn. It's not a problem, though.

He dropped off his divorce papers. Signed."

"You're divorced?" Mitch said, accepting the glass April gave him.

"Good as," April said.

The declaration had the desired effect. The worry lines around Mitch's eyes smoothed out.

He caught her around the waist and lifted her off the floor. He kissed her heartily. She giggled at the feeling of being airborne. The feeling of freedom.

He put her back on her feet and raised his glass. She grabbed hers.

"To us?" she said. She couldn't keep the question out of her voice. He'd been saying all along he wanted her to be free to date him, really date him, but what if he didn't mean it.

Mitch tilted his head back to drink. His throat exposed. All April wanted to do was kiss it.

"To us," he said, banging his glass on the table.

She felt her heart soar as his smile grew larger. This was a real beginning for them. She was glad to see he was as excited as she was.

April grabbed Mitch by his shirt front and pulled him closer. He was wearing a golf-style shirt and her legs weakened at the sight of the hair on his chest peeking out. She kissed him.

"You know what this means, don't you?" She had to stop kissing him long enough to breathe. His response was lost as he moved down her neck, his lips hot. Her feet felt disconnected from her body.

"All those nights you went home . . ."

He stopped nibbling on her collarbone, and straightened.

"Yes?"

She laughed at his eagerness. Instead of answering, she leaned in for another kiss. She couldn't get enough of his lips. Her insides were molten, each contact with him melting her a little more.

"We won't have to stop anymore," she said breathlessly.

"That's the best news I've heard in a long while," he said. "Let's go back to my place and get started."

Their bodies refused to untwine, and they kissed their way through the kitchen to the front door. Mitch turned off lights as they went. She held his hand as he ran back to turn off the bathroom light, and followed as he turned the deadbolt on the kitchen door.

"Beat you home," Mitch said, as they exchanged a kiss just inside the living room.

"It's a bet," April said, digging her keys

out of her pocket. She reached in his pocket and grabbed his car keys. She tossed them into the darkened dining room.

"Hey," Mitch said. "Unfair practices."

April laughed, and ran out the door. She'd just gotten to her car when she heard a crash. It sounded like glass breaking. April's skin went clammy.

"Mitch!" she yelled.

"I'm fine," he said from inside the house. "Someone threw a rock through the window. I'm going out back to see if I can see who did it."

April caught sight of something — someone — moving around the house. A car door opened and closed. April moved in the direction of the noise. A car was parked a hundred yards away. She heard the engine sputter, and ran.

The driver tried to make the ignition catch, but it was not turning over. She moved quickly. The whitewall of the tire shone in the darkness. April knelt down and felt her way to the valve. She pulled it open and heard the tire let out its air. The car settled, listing to one side.

"Over here, Mitch," she said.

April pulled open the driver's side door. The man at the wheel cowered as though she was going to hit him.

"Hector? What are you doing here?"

Hector turned the ignition key. The engine started with a roar. He put the car in gear and stepped on the gas. April jumped back to avoid being hit by the door. The flat tire dragged and the car lurched to a stop.

April heard a metallic rattling and looked into the back seat. A can of black spray paint lay on the floor of the backseat. Hector was their vandal.

April knelt by the open window. "Why did you do this?"

No answer. She looked in his car and saw an envelope addressed to Mitch. "Are you behind everything — the letters, too? Why?"

Hector reached for the door handle. April backed up to allow him to get out. Her heart beat faster and she called for Mitch again. She could hear him in the woods over to the right.

Hector Valdez pulled himself up to his full height and regal bearing. He kept his arms limp at his side. April relaxed.

He said softly, "Everything I do, I do for the cause. Our fight is never over. I needed to keep it alive in the hearts and minds of the people."

"So you sent threatening letters?"

He nodded. "But your boyfriend never told anyone. I had to escalate things. I can't let the plight of my people be ignored."

"All for TV coverage?"

April opened the back door and picked up the can of paint. Mitch raced up, breathing hard. April handed him the can of paint.

"What's going on?"

"Hector Valdez has been sabotaging your houses. He's the one that sent the nasty notes, the letters to the editor, the spray paint. All to further his own agenda."

"Is this true?" Mitch said, his eyes narrowing at the older man.

"This problem is bigger than your four little houses, sir. Bigger than your little project. Much more is at stake. I saw an opportunity to bring more attention to the plight of my people, and I took it."

"I could have you prosecuted," Mitch said.

Hector stuck his chin out. "Do what you will."

That would give him more publicity, April thought cynically.

"Let's bargain," April said. "Let him give you more money for the Foundation."

"I don't have any money," Hector said. "MAC is broke, too. I could give you some men to help you paint. And some landscapers."

"I don't know," Mitch said.

"No, it's a good idea," April said. "You

could get done much faster that way. The family could move in earlier."

April searched the man's face. He was trying to do the right thing.

"I'd watch out who your Foundation gets in bed with," Hector said.

Mitch started. "What do you mean?"

"I mean, Ferguson."

CHAPTER 19

The next morning April was up much earlier than she'd planned. She'd been so quiet, tiptoeing up to the loft just past two when she'd come home from Mitch's, but this dawn, her roommates weren't as considerate.

"Maybe she doesn't want holes in the wall, Grizz." The whispery voice traveled up the barn walls, more disturbing than a shout. April came awake and sat up in the loft.

The Campbells were early risers. Like predawn. In the pitch dark. They couldn't see well, so had turned on every light downstairs. The brightness struck April like a dentist's drill on a cavity.

She lay in her bed, turning her face to the wall, pulling the covers over her head. This was only the second morning with her new roommates and already she was running a sleep deficit.

A hammer hit the wall beneath her, sending her down the ladder before she could consider whether she was fully awake or what she was wearing. As she descended, she noticed Charlotte frowning. She realized she was dressed only in a threadbare T-shirt that barely covered her tush. She went back up for her robe.

A moment later, now properly covered, April approached Grizz, who had used a twenty-pound hammer to put up a picture. She wanted to protest, but words wouldn't come. Her throat was raw and her brain slow from lack of sleep.

"Told you she wouldn't mind," Grizz said to his wife. "Besides, my son owns the place."

"Half," Charlotte said. "Ed and Vince are co-owners."

April moved closer to what he'd hung up. What was the urgency? Not a picture. A certificate of some kind, with fancy writing. She deciphered the calligraphy across the top: Ferguson Enterprises. The certificate was for one thousand shares.

Another hammer blow. April spun around. Grizz was hanging another picture, this time on the post just below her California art. She grabbed her frame before it fell. The Campbells' photo was one of a multistory building on a beach. The pink stucco walls undulated. Looked like Florida.

"Will you be needing more wall space?" April asked.

"That's all, young lady," Grizz said. He missed her ironic tone completely.

April decided she had to choose her battles. The smell of coffee tickled her nose. The Campbells had used her French press. April poured herself a cup. Charlotte was manning the stove like a short-order cook, flipping eggs.

Grizz seated himself at the table, unfolding the daily paper. He must have already walked the mile into town to buy it, unless he stole the copy from one of the neighbors. April wasn't sure she wanted to know.

She sat at the table, sipping coffee, waiting for the caffeine to break through the brain fog that four hours of sleep engendered. She ate what Charlotte put in front of her. She already knew it was useless to protest. Besides, Charlotte was a good cook and April had enjoyed yesterday's hot breakfast. She'd forgotten what homemade pancakes tasted like.

Charlotte settled into a chair when everyone was served. Her husband was done eating already. He grunted at his plate. She got up and cleared it, then sat down to eat. April worried that Charlotte's eggs would be cold. Nothing worse than cold eggs. She'd already finished hers and was starting in on the grits.

"Sit," April said.

Charlotte looked worried. "Sorry about waking you," Charlotte said. "When Grizz gets a notion to do something, he just does it. We're not used to living with other people."

"Is that your place?" April said, pointing her fork at the photo. "Is it in Miami?"

"Is it, Grizz? I always forget," Charlotte said. She ate with tiny, quick bites as though she didn't deserve to take time out to eat.

Grizz looked up from his paper, his lips moist from his fried egg. His whiskers never seemed to grow; they were always at the same level of straggle. If he were fifty years younger, the scruff might look sexy. As he wasn't it merely presented a place where food could get caught. April tried not to look too closely for fear she'd see last night's scalloped potato caught on the wiry ends.

"It's Miami Beach," he said. "We have a share."

"What time of year do you usually go?" she asked. *How about now?* She chastised herself for being unkind.

"Oh no, we've never been," Charlotte said.

April was confused. "Why not?"

Grizz ignored them and went back to the paper. He seemed to be reading the minutes of Lynwood's city council meeting.

"Scott and Ferguson Enterprises use it as a sanctuary. Young people, mostly Cubans, who need refuge."

"And so you've never been there?" April said. A share to her meant you got a week or more at the place. She'd had a share in a house in Capitola one summer. She'd had seven blissful days at the beach, only slightly marred by her roommate's tendency to not flush. "Let yellow mellow" was her mantra.

Charlotte smiled. "Someday."

Grizz rustled his paper as though he didn't like where the conversation was headed. "You got firewood that needs splitting?" he said.

April had her doubts. She looked at Charlotte, who nodded her head sagely.

"There's a shed out back," April said. The sun had come up enough that he'd be able to see what he was doing.

Grizz stood, pulling up black suspenders that were drooping around his waist, and went outside without another word.

Charlotte, watching him go, said, "He likes to stay busy."

April said, "He doesn't like to talk about

money."

Charlotte sipped her coffee. She started to get up to clear the table, but April stopped her, reminding her of the deal they'd made yesterday. It was her job to clean up. April knew Charlotte only acquiesced because she was afraid of the high-tech dishwasher.

"Tell me about Ferguson." Now that she was in cahoots with him, April wanted reassurance that she'd hooked up with the right guy. "He seems to have a knack for making money. You own stock in his company?" April pointed to the certificate.

They could hear Grizz splitting wood, the thwack of the axe like the sound of someone slapping the side of the barn.

Charlotte pulled out a bag of crocheting. She was making hats for newborns to send to a hospital in Costa Rica. The yarn was striped with pink and yellow.

"A thousand shares, at ten thousand per," Charlotte said proudly.

April did the math quickly. A hundred thousand dollars, no wonder they lost their house. That had to be their life savings and then some.

Charlotte continued, "Indeed. He was paying us interest well over the bank rate, and we were getting great dividends."

"Were?"

Charlotte's hands stopped moving. The noise outside had stopped. April held her breath waiting for Grizz to come through the door missing a limb.

The wood chopping started again.

The crochet hook swerved in and out of the yarn. New stitches appeared. "Scott's hit a rough patch," Charlotte said. "His investments have been impacted by the global economy."

That sounded so rote, April wondered who'd fed her that line. Charlotte didn't sound like she knew anything about the economy, global or otherwise.

"As soon as he gets back on his feet, we'll start getting money and we'll be able to live in our house again."

April couldn't tell if Charlotte was naïve or just overly optimistic. The way she understood it, the house was gone. Fore-closed on by the bank. On the market prob-ably being sold to a young couple, ecstatic to get into a house at such a great price.

"All of our friends have their money with Scott," Charlotte said, turning the tiny cap around and around as it grew from the top out. "He's just devastated."

Ferguson spread his money around. In-vesting in Xenia's new company must have been part of his strategy. Judging by his reaction, the other day had been one of the few times he'd met Vanesa. Xenia had been smart to keep them apart. April vowed to keep an eye on the teen this afternoon and make sure Vanesa didn't get herself in over her head, flirting with a guy old enough to be her father.

April tried to get ahold of Trish, but her call went straight to voice mail. She left a message and asked Trish to call her back. She intended to ask her what she knew about Xenia's new company.

April spent the day at work. She rounded up all the stampers who agreed to work at the telethon the next day. She got home after dark, worn out from the week, looking forward to an early night. She was hoping Charlotte had cooked something comforting for dinner. She was in the mood for mashed potatoes and meatloaf.

The telethon was to start at noon. Ferguson would film the first three hours live and then replay it several times over the next twelve hours. The stampers had volunteered to man the phones for the afternoon.

Ferguson filmed his show out of the plain cinder block one-story structure set up behind his retail store that April had seen the other day. Inside, it was state-of-the-art, with the latest digital technology.

April was impressed. She'd volunteered at the local public television studio in San Francisco several times and hadn't seen such good equipment. The hosts at KQED would be envious of this setup.

Ferguson had spent a lot of money in here.

The first hour featured a lineup of local talent. The Lynwood High School choir; a local grunge band; Dance, Dance Academy. Between acts, Ferguson talked about the importance of his cause. He talked about the problem of fatherless children in Scotland. April hadn't realized AIDS had devastated families there.

He was dressed in full regalia today — a black watch plaid kilt, topped by a short black velvet formal jacket. His sporran was heavily fringed as was the trim on his socks.

The phone rang sporadically. April and the other stampers had plenty of time to chat between calls.

"Did your mother like the finished invitation?" Mary Lou asked.

April smiled. "She did. She teared up."

"I bet Clive bawled," Rocky said.

"You guessed right. Like a baby," April said.

The phone rang. April grabbed it, laughing as Mary Lou shook a fist at her, pretending to be angry. They'd all rather be busy answering phones.

"Hello?"

She heard nothing but heavy breathing. Great, another geriatric. Probably with a check for five dollars. She prayed for patience. "Can I help you?"

"I like your hair color," a soft voice said.

April strained to figure out what he was saying. "Okay?"

"Your lips are so plump and pretty."

April gasped, unable to contain her surprise. Rocky looked questioningly at her. April realized she was staring wide-eyed at the phone. She couldn't believe what she was hearing.

"And your boobies look good in that sweater."

April jumped out of her seat, her hand covering the front of her. Some twisted sense of duty made her ask, "Would you like to pledge something?"

Deana took the phone from her hand and hung it up quickly.

"Did you get a pervert?" she asked. "Every time I volunteer at the public radio station, I get one."

April had never had that happen before.

"It's amazing how violated I feel right now," April said. "I mean, he barely got started."

"That's how he gets his jollies," Suzi said. "Don't let him get to you."

Across the room, another phone rang. Mary Lou answered and hung up after listening for several seconds. She exchanged a look with April. She raised her finger to her temple and twirled it, a time-honored sign of a nut job.

On stage, Ferguson was introducing a local comedian who wore a porkpie hat and skinny tie. His untucked shirt was covered with a vest. He started out by mentioning that his girlfriend was homeless. She lived with him, but he was getting ready to toss her out. Funny.

The phone rang again. April felt the jangling noise in her spine. Her hair crawled with anticipation. Rocky picked it up. She listened for a moment then said, "Really? You like them, huh?" She motioned for the cameraman to turn her way. He obliged.

"I've got something special, just for you," Rocky said, looking directly into the camera and standing. She turned her back on the camera. She unbuckled her belt and bent at the waist. Deana, who was closest to her, put a restraining hand on her waistband. Suzi gestured for the cameraman to change his focus and hung up the phone. The comedian appeared on the monitor.

The stampers fell back in their chairs, laughing.

"You really wouldn't have mooned that guy, would you?" April said.

"I would, too. He deserved it."

"Oh lord, it's a good thing Mitch had to work today."

"He's perfectly aware of what his sister is capable of," Rocky sniffed.

"Sad thing is," Mary Lou said with heavy irony, "it wouldn't be the first time."

Rocky said, "Hey, I haven't mooned anyone since the Red Barons got the Yankee franchise. The other team loved it."

"As I recall, they joined in," Mary Lou said.

The Campbells were manning a phone in the row behind April. She went over to say hello.

"Nice of you to come," April said. "I appreciate it. I didn't realize Vince told you about Mitch's cause."

Grizz Campbell looked blankly at her.

Charlotte said, "We always work Scott's telethons. We didn't know you'd be here."

April backed away as fast as she could without appearing rude.

Finally, it was Clive's turn on stage. April

felt a thrill of anticipation.

"Here we go, girls," she said. "Now the phones will ring."

She saw Bonnie enter the studio and waved her over. She shifted in her seat so Bonnie could share her chair. Bonnie sat, keeping her eyes on the stage. April could feel her knees shaking.

"He'll be great," April said.

Bonnie squeezed her hand. "He's nervous."

April watched on the monitor as Clive took his position at the keyboard. Clive, so diminutive in person, was just the right size on the television. His toothy smile sparkled and his over-the-top gyrations worked on the small screen. He oozed personality. Anyone would want to be at a party where he was.

He sang his old Kickapoos anthem. His voice wasn't as pure as it once had been, but the gravelly quality that age had added gave the song additional verve. He slowed down the verse, but as soon as the familiar chorus began, the energy in the studio was electric. The stampers clapped and sang along. Mary Lou and Suzi reprised their Kickapoos kick like schoolgirls.

It was a rousing first number. But no phones were ringing. Was Clive too far past his prime?

April stared at the black phone, willing it to ring. Rocky waved her hand over hers as if she could magically make people call. Suzi and Mary Lou were still standing with their arms slung around each other. Deana shot April a concerned look.

The first phone rang. Bonnie grabbed it before April could. Another phone rang.

Soon all the stampers were busy. Bonnie had taken over April's position and was cheerfully convincing the caller to double his pledge.

Onstage, Clive took a seat next to Ferguson. "I was just a boy," Ferguson began his interview, "when I first heard you sing."

April left her station to her mother and went back to where Vanesa was waiting. A boy with a French horn was chatting her up.

"Scared?" April asked.

"Not really," the girl said. She kept her eyes front.

April was scared enough for both of them. This could be a spectacular bad idea. At best, she had exposed Vanesa to ridicule and humiliation. At worst, she'd exploited the teen for her own purposes.

Vanesa looked beautiful, dressed in a party dress that had clearly belonged to her mother. Sleeveless, it was a pretty shade of pink, with a full skirt and v-neck that left her arms and neck exposed. Her skin was unblemished, and she looked vulnerable and dangerous at the same time.

She was standing taller than usual, and April glanced down to see she was in borrowed heels, too. The sight of the gap in the back of the shoe saddened April. Vanesa looked too much like a little girl playing dress up. Xenia was not around to tell her she'd break her neck wearing heels that were the wrong size.

They heard Ferguson tell Clive how thrilled he was to have him on the telethon. Vanesa stood, readying herself to go on. She took a deep breath and moved toward the stage. The camera swung over to her, and she smiled radiantly. On the monitor, she looked possessed and in control.

April felt a thrill of pride, misplaced though it may be. *She's trying so hard to be grown-up.* Just as April finished the thought, Vanesa's foot caught on the indoor-outdoor carpet covering the floor, and she tripped. April's hand flew to her mouth. She felt as though she'd done it to her, thought a bad thought and had it come true. She was too far away to save her. Vanesa jumped up and smoothed her hair. She stumbled again.

Onstage, Clive clowned at the keyboard, standing, brushing out imaginary tux tails and bowing. The cameraman swung over to him, leaving a red-faced Vanesa struggling to regain her composure in peace.

Pedro came out of the hall that served as the wings and righted her. He kissed her forehead and gave her a gentle push. Vanesa gave him a weak smile. He whispered in her ear and she grinned. Mitch was at Pedro's side.

The phones stilled. April looked frantically at the volunteers, but not one person had a phone in hand. She felt her stomach try to crawl up into her throat and lodge there.

What a stupid idea this had been. There was no way she could raise enough money to make a difference this way. April looked at Vanesa, so adultlike in her mother's heels and makeup, but she was a child. April's heart sank. What if she exposed the kids to real danger? She thought about the perv that'd called earlier.

She rushed to the girl's side. "Are you sure?"

Vanesa looked at her dad and dismissed April with her eyes. "I'm going to Hollywood, remember?"

Ferguson began, "I have a special treat for

you tonight. Vanesa Villarreal, the oldest daughter of slain local resident, Xenia Villarreal . . ."

April cringed and watched Vanesa take the blow like a boxer might take a body shot. She straightened and faced the audience with her eyes glittering. April looked for Pedro. He was holding himself stiffly. April took her seat back at the phones. Her mother had found an empty spot vacated by one of the other volunteers.

Clive played over Ferguson's voice. April didn't recognize the ballad, but Vanesa knew it. She closed her eyes and poured her soul into the phrasing. The melody soared. Her voice was pure, untrained. She was thin in the high notes, but her technical deficiencies were offset by her passion. Her body swayed, her fingers clutched, her knees bent as though she couldn't bear the weight of the words.

April felt her eyes fill with tears. She had to close them against the onset of the emotions that Vanesa was pulling out of her. She opened them when she realized that it didn't help. Vanesa's voice was penetrating every pore of her skin.

"Don't cry," a soft voice said in her ear.

Mitch. He scooted a chair over next to her and sat down. He put an arm around her, and she rested on his shoulder. Mitch's foot tapped to the beat.

"Where's Pedro?" she asked, looking around for the father.

"He went out to the parking lot. He couldn't stand to listen."

"She sounds beautiful," April said.

"Yes she does, and she seems to love being on stage," he said. "You can stop worrying about her."

The phone ringing in her ear brought her up short. Her pulse pounded. What if she got the weirdo again? She took a breath and picked up the receiver.

The man's voice on the other end was loud, nothing like the whispering pervert.

"I'm pledging two hundred dollars," he said. "Here's my credit card information."

April took down the numbers and hung up. Her phone rang again. As she picked it up, she looked around. Everyone was on the phone. Rocky was scribbling fast, and Suzi had asked her pledger to slow down. As soon as a phone was set in its cradle, it rang again.

"That girl sings like an angel," the next caller told April. "She has the purest voice I've ever heard."

April took her information and hung up. Another caller was worried about the house.

"I want to be sure she has a roof over her head. She and her sister and brothers deserve their own place."

Mitch pitched in, gathering up pledge sheets as the volunteers finished them and replenishing the supply. He took out a calculator and began to add up what they'd taken in.

Onstage, Vanesa soared to a big finish and bowed. When she lifted her head, April gave her a thumbs-up.

Ferguson circled his hand around, signaling the duo to sing again.

Clive segued into a finger-snapping jive tune. Vanesa moved into it as though she'd been performing her whole life. Probably she had, in her bathroom mirror with a hairbrush.

Ferguson was clapping now, his bony knee bopping up and down. The phones kept ringing.

Vanesa and Clive did an encore, then left the stage. Ferguson closed the live portion of his show. The phones continued to ring nonstop for another half hour. April, Mitch and the stampers stuck around until the phones slowed. They found Clive, Vanesa and Pedro in the reception area, drinking hot tea and chatting with Mrs. Ferguson.

Vanesa had changed into jeans and a

hoodie, a teen again.

"So how'd we do?" Clive said.

Mitch said, "Fourteen thousand in credit card pledges that I saw."

"Add this to your totals," Clive said, throwing down five one-hundred-dollar bills.

"Clive!" April said. "You don't have to . . ."

"I know I don't, but I want to."

Pedro said, "And Mr. Ferguson is going to donate the money to you, Mitch?"

Ferguson entered from the studio. He pounded Pedro on the back. "That I am, sir. That I am. I expect we raised a quarter of a million dollars today."

"Really?" April had no idea that the local people had that kind of money to spare.

He slung an arm around her neck. "You had a brilliant idea. Did you ever think about a career in talent management? You have two wonderful clients right here," he said, pointing to Vanesa and Clive.

"Not bloody likely," Clive said. "I'm going back into retirement."

"Not to mention you were right. Bigger talent did translate into bigger donations. We did so well, I've decided to donate twenty percent to Mitch's houses," Ferguson said, obviously pleased with himself.

He took his wife by the arm. "We'll go do the paperwork. The missus here does all the credit card processing. You'll see the money in your account tomorrow or the day after at the latest."

He and his wife said their good-byes and left.

"He's just going to put money in your account?" Rocky asked.

"Well, the foundation's account. Not mine. I gave him all the banking information. He's going to do an online transfer."

"Nice," she said.

Mitch clasped Clive's hand. "I can't thank you enough. The Villarreals will be able to move in right away now. I can hire painters and upgrade the kitchen appliances. And I can get started on your neighbor's house much sooner."

Pedro took Vanesa home, and Bonnie and Clive followed them out. The stampers and Mitch were still milling around, excited, unwilling to go home just yet.

"Let's go get a drink and celebrate," Suzi said. April was glad to see Suzi felt like going out. She was beginning to shake off what had happened at the Pumpkin Express.

"I'd love to have you over to the barn," April said. "But I have roommates now."

"We heard," Mary Lou said. "Vince's parents?"

"How's that?" Suzi said. "Living with old folks?"

"Must put a damper on your love life," Rocky said with a dangerous grin.

April felt herself blush. Mitch frowned at his sister.

Rocky tried an innocent gaze, but it didn't work. She laughed. "Come on," she said. "Did you think no one would notice your Jeep heading over there every night?"

"I'm still a married woman," April said.

"Not by choice," she said.

"Rocky, knock it off," Mitch said. "What April and I have going on is none of your business."

Mitch ticked off on his fingers. "I can pay the supply house, and the well diggers. I'm thinking the second house should be a two-story. I can make that fifty grand go a long way to making the next family even more comfortable. I can move up the timetable, too. Get started right away instead of having to take a break."

April frowned and moved closer to him. "I was kind of looking forward to your taking a break. You've been working so hard, we barely see each other."

"I'm over every night," he protested.

"It's not enough to suit me," April said.

"Really? Really?" Mitch caught her hair and swung her face around to meet his. His eyes were dancing, and a smile played around his lips. She was trapped, but she didn't mind in the least.

"Maybe we're just not using our time wisely," he said, his voice smooth and seductive. She felt his breath on her ear and it made her gasp. He unbuttoned the top button of her blouse. "All this idle chit chat."

"Idle," April repeated, her mind going muddy. Mitch planted kisses on the bare skin of her neck. His eyelashes brushed the spots he'd just kissed, keeping the nerve endings at attention.

She slumped against the back of Mitch's couch.

He leaned back, slightly breathless, his lips red and wet. She brushed a finger against them, and he tightened his teeth on it.

"If we had more time," she began.

"It's all about efficiency," he said. "We just need to learn to use our time more wisely."

"Okay," she said, her breath returning to normal.

"I warn you, there's a bit of a learning

curve," he said, his hand entwining in hers.

"I'm a quick study," she said.

Chapter 20

April drove carefully up the winding road to Trish's place, taking the corners slowly so she wouldn't slip. The road was covered with piles of slick, decomposing leaves.

Trish had left a message while April was at the telethon, asking to meet with her Sunday afternoon. April had agreed by voice mail and so once again found herself navigating the twists and turns of Pine's End.

As she drove, April tried to decide how to play it with Trish. More forceful? Less? Give her everything she wants? Hold back?

She had to know how much Trish knew about Xenia's business activities.

Suddenly her windshield filled with the sight of a red SUV sliding toward her. April felt a jolt of adrenalin hit her system and she sat up straight. Someone had taken the curve too quickly and was on her side of the road. A crack of thunder split the clouds, and April shut her eyes, waiting for the impact.

She felt the cars hit, sending hers into a spin. Her foot stomped on the brake. Her father had spent hours teaching her how to drive, but after years of driving the hills of San Francisco, she couldn't remember if she was supposed to steer into the spin or away. It didn't matter. The wheel was moving without her.

She felt her neck snap and had the sensation that her brain was moving inside her skull like a pinball. She could only hope that her innards would end up where they were supposed to be.

She came to a stop under a bare tree. Alone. The other car was out of sight in her rear view, gone already. Either he hadn't noticed the danger he'd put her in, or he simply didn't care.

April let her heart rate return to normal. She drew in several long breaths, letting her lungs fill with air and blowing it out forcefully. She shook out her shoulders and hands. She lifted her feet. Everything seemed to be working. She might be sore in the morning, but she seemed to be okay.

She was close to Trish's house. She started her car and continued on her way.

April killed her headlights as she pulled

into the driveway. A few of the outer house lights came on, triggered by a motion detector. Inside, the house was dark, however. Trish did not appear to be home. April knocked on the front door to be sure. No answer. She glanced over at the neighbors. No one seemed home there, either. The only light was coming from the street lamps.

April moved back to look up at the window over the garage. Trish's desk was right up there. She caught a soft glow that might be the computer monitor, but April wanted to be sure. She pulled out her cell. Lo and behold, it had bars on it. She called Trish. She could hear the phone ringing in the house, but no one answered. She closed her phone just as Trish's answering machine kicked in and dropped it back in her car.

Trish was not home. April took a deep breath. This might be better. She might be able to find out what Trish knew about Xenia's new business without having to confront Trish at all. And if she found that Trish knew that Xenia was going off on her own, April would let the police know and keep herself out of it.

The other night Deana had given April the security code to her garage door. 8-7-4-7-4. Trish should have used something less obvious than her name if she wanted to be secure, April thought.

April pushed the numbers on the pad. The door began to open slowly, noisily. She ducked under it as soon as it was over her head. What she saw stopped her in her tracks. Trish's car was right in front of her.

April considered what this meant. Trish *was* at home. Her heart hammered in her chest, and her knee joints loosened dangerously. She leaned against a shelving unit, trying to gain her stability. She was sure the interior door would open, a questioning Trish behind it.

"Close the damn door," she heard, a voice hissing next to her.

April twisted, her answer dying in her throat. Her heart seemed to have stopped. She could see a shadow coming in the open garage door.

"The close switch is probably by the door leading to the house."

April recognized the speaker. "Rocky! What are you doing here?"

Rocky moved past her, a flashlight illuminating her path. She moved past the car to a door in the side wall and pressed a button there. The garage door started to slide down and an overhead light came on.

Rocky was smiling. She looked happy to catch April in a compromising position.

April wondered if she was going to tell Mitch. "I might ask you that. You're the one breaking and entering. I just followed you in."

"I was just making sure Trish wasn't home. Now I'm leaving." April turned as though she was making an exit. Once she got rid of Rocky, she would be free to find the evidence that she needed.

"Shall we?" Rocky put her hand on the doorknob. "You said yourself no one's here. I'm going in for what I came for."

April stopped moving toward the now closed garage door and turned back. "Which is?"

"Trish borrowed my favorite Louboutins," Rocky said. "I want them back. I need to wear them tomorrow."

Rocky disappeared through the open door. A pair of shoes? The door closed on April, and the overhead light clicked off. She felt the empty space cling to her like a cobweb she'd walked through.

April sought the light like a moth, finding herself in the kitchen. Rocky was walking away from her, down the hall, flipping on lights as she went.

April calmed herself and remembered her mission. Clive had pushed himself, going on TV, ignoring his need for privacy. She could put herself on the line, too.

She called to Rocky, "I'm just going into her office. Five minutes and I'm out of here."

April bounded up the stairs to the office. The quicker she found what she was looking for, the quicker they'd get out.

Trish's computer was on. The background was a picture of Trish receiving an award, her hand outstretched for the glass triangle, her smile wide. April's hand brushed against the mouse. A document came up and obscured the photo.

Hold on. She knew someone in that picture.

She minimized the document, revealing the picture again. The man beaming up at Trish was Traczewski, the head of the Lynwood Border Patrol, the anti-immigration group. April tilted her head so she could read the writing inscribed on the award. "Preserver of the Year." He looked so proud.

April felt sick to her stomach. Trish was one of *them*. She was perfectly willing to let Xenia Villareal work for her and collect the profits she made, but she was more than happy to try to run anyone with a Mexican-sounding surname out of town. What a sham.

The anti-immigration group's main strategy was to reduce the recent immigrants to something subhuman. They degraded people. Wouldn't it be easier to kill someone you didn't consider a human being?

April felt her nausea turn to fury and determination to find out what Trish knew of Xenia's business plans. She opened Trish's financial programs. The woman kept meticulous records. April could easily follow the flow of money into Trish's coffers, checks from Deana and others for inventory received.

April clicked on a file with Xenia's name. She had thirteen women working under her. All of them were selling Trish's Bella cosmetics line, no Stamping Sisters supplies. Just as Xenia had told her. Many had Latino-sounding names. The addresses were scattered over the surrounding two counties. April recognized some of the street names. She'd been there with Vanesa.

April found a chart Trish had created showing Xenia's sales over the last fiscal year that had ended in September. Xenia's income had been building, doing better each month. Until June. Sales fell off precipitously. July was even worse. Last month, her total sales had been a mere five hundred dollars, down from a high of six thousand dollars.

It must have been obvious to Trish that Xenia was up to something. An economic downturn, the summer months, none of it explained such a large drop-off. Trish would have been furious. Had she called Xenia to the maze to confront her?

If Xenia had convinced her customers — and the salespeople under her — to abandon Trish's Bella cosmetics in favor of her own Bonita products, she would have made a fortune. And Trish would have lost one.

April's stomach churned. She felt like she was in a house of pure evil. She needed to get out. She'd stop at the barracks and tell the state police what she knew.

A bang from another room startled April. Rocky. She'd forgotten about her.

She closed the program and found herself staring at the document she'd seen earlier, when she'd first touched the mouse. A familiar name caught her eye.

April glanced behind her. She could hear Rocky moving about in the other end of the house. She let her eyes travel over the contents.

It was a lot of legalese, double-talk, but April soon got the gist. On the screen was a contract between Rocky and Trish, selling Rocky the Stamping Sisters business.

Really? Rocky was going to become the

new Trish? Was that why she was here? Why hadn't she said anything?

April made her way out of the office. "Rocky," she whispered loudly. No answer. She called louder, walking through the kitchen.

Rocky appeared in the hall on the opposite side of the room. "You've got to see this," Rocky said. "You need to see the size of this walk-in." She beckoned to April to follow her and was gone again. April went through the open double doors at the end of the hall. They were dark wood carved and arched to look like those of a Spanish church.

The walk-in closet was straight ahead. Several overhead can lights made the space as bright as day. The floor was a mess. Rocky was bent over a vanity counter installed in the middle of the closet.

"Rocky, did you do this?" April stepped around a pile of dirty clothes.

Rocky looked up from the drawer she had opened. Earrings glittered from the velvet lining. "Of course not. I found my shoes in that pile, though. I'm never lending her anything again. She obviously doesn't take care of anything."

"Let's go," April said. "I want to talk to you."

"Look at this," Rocky said. She held up a

305

leather bag. It was about the size of a fanny pack.

"I'm not into handbags," April said.

"It's not a purse. It's a sporran. Her husband must be into the unbifurcated lifestyle, too."

April took a step back. "Eww. I don't want to know about their sex life," she whispered.

Rocky laughed. "Pants are bifurcated, split in two. Skirts and kilts aren't. This is to be worn over a kilt."

April had had enough of Rocky's sense of humor. "Let's get out of here."

"Hold on. I'm looking for a pair of diamond studs that she took off me in the club locker room. Go check out the room décor. It's very girly. I think they must sleep in separate bedrooms."

"I don't care what Trish does with her husband. We have something to discuss," April said. What would it mean to her stamping line if Rocky owned the company?

Rocky was studying a necklace, trying it on in the mirror built into the jewelry hutch.

She was still talking about Trish and her husband. "They're always so lovey-dovey in public. He's the big cheese, and she's his hot corporate high-powered wife. The couple that has it all. She pretends they have all this great sex. She's always bragging about his schlong . . ."

Enough. "Rocky, shut up."

"Well, she is. You'd be surprised what you overhear in the bathroom of the club."

April glanced out into the bedroom. From here, she could see only the end of the bed and the settee beyond. The room looked like the closet. Messy. The bed was unmade, some of the covers puddling over the footboard and onto the floor. April saw a picture frame lying on its side near the entrance to the closet.

She picked it up. The picture was in a heart-shaped mat. "Trish and Ted forever," it read. The glass was cracked.

"Rocky, Trish is married to Traczewski?"

Rocky poked her head out. "Didn't you know that?"

April noticed another picture on the bedside table. She could see a white dress and veil from here. She couldn't believe that Trish was married to this guy.

"But she goes by Taylor."

"So did he. I think his parents shortened it years ago. Until he formed the Border Patrol. All of a sudden it was cool to be ethnic. As long as it was the right kind of ethnic."

Rocky was combing her fingers through the back of her long hair and arranging her side-parted bangs so the hairs covered her scar. She'd never explained the origin of the scar on her face, and April hadn't yet worked up enough nerve to ask Mitch about it.

Was it a childhood accident? Something more recent? An abusive boyfriend? That would explain her clinging to Mitch. And her reluctance to let Mitch enter into a relationship.

Was anyone in this town what they said they were?

April turned and walked out of the closet. As she passed the big bed in the main part of the bedroom, something caught her eye. Hair. There was hair spread out on the pillow. She let her gaze trace the position of the bedding and realized she was looking at a human shape. Trish was here, taking a nap.

An involuntary yip flew out of April's mouth, loud in the empty space. She clamped a hand over her mouth and waited for Trish's reaction.

April swallowed hard. Her feet felt rooted to the spot. As though the pink carpet was actually made of bubble gum and was holding her down.

Trish wasn't moving. April stared. She couldn't see the rise and fall of the blankets.

She considered the bed again. It didn't

look so much unmade as it did thrashed about in. A very energetic sex partner could make the covers come out of the end of the bed. Someone could have gotten tangled in the sheets. April had the sense that someone else had left the room not long before she and Rocky showed up.

But why wasn't Trish waking up?

She called Trish's name as a clamminess started in her belly and crawled up her throat. Her spine tingled as though someone stood behind her.

CHAPTER 21

April whirled. Rocky was standing there, in her stocking feet. She was carrying her shoes.

She stage-whispered, "Ready to go?"

She couldn't stand the idea of telling Rocky what she thought was going on. She couldn't form the words. Trish was not napping. Not going to wake up.

She had to be sure. Before she could think any further, she strode to the bedside.

Trish was lying face up, her eyes wide open and bulging. Her fingers had frozen, clawing at the tie cinched tightly around her neck. She was naked, her body twisted in the pale pink sheets. The bottom of her feet were white.

April's hand flew to her mouth, and she turned back to Rocky.

"She's dead. Call the police."

"Shit!" Rocky said. "You didn't have to kill her. She would have been mad that we were in here without her permission, but she'd have gotten over it."

"Are you crazy? Me kill her? We've been together the whole time we were in the house."

"No, we kinda were not. Like right now. You were alone in here," Rocky said. "You *were* pretty shocked when I came up behind you."

"Of course I was shocked. I just found a dead body," April shouted. She glanced over at Trish's still body and lowered her voice. "You scared me to death."

"You knew I was in the closet, for crying out loud."

April had heard enough. "I didn't kill her. You didn't kill her. We don't know who killed her. Just call the flipping police and let them sort it out."

Rocky said, "I think maybe we should get out of here and then call. You know, anonymously. I guess we'd have to use a pay phone. Does the IGA still have a pay phone?"

Rocky continued talking, but April tuned her out while she thought about that scenario. She wouldn't have to be questioned by the police for hours and hours. Yost would never have to know she'd been here. That part would be good.

"Are you sure she's dead?" Rocky said. She'd moved closer to the bed and was craning her neck to get a better view. Her hair swung forward, covering her face completely and blocking April's view of Trish's face.

"Her lips are blue," April said. "Her chest isn't moving."

"Maybe you should try CPR," Rocky said.

"Do you know CPR? I don't," April said.

April had to stay. She'd left a crime scene earlier this week and the state police investigators had not been happy with her. She wasn't going to go through that again.

"Leave her be," April said. "Let's get out of here. My cell is in the car. I'm going to call this in." If the cellular reception gods smiled on her.

"Suit yourself," Rocky said.

April ran through the house, with Rocky following. The door from the kitchen into the garage slammed against the drywall as April pushed through. She didn't stop to see if she'd left a hole.

She opened her car door and got out her phone. Rocky headed for her own car, a small red Mercedes coupe.

"I'll call it in," April said, opening her phone.

"You bet you will," Rocky said. "You

found her."

April lowered her phone. "Why didn't you see her?"

Rocky stood, balancing on one foot, the other snaking inside her car. "I just stayed in the closet. I didn't even go into her room."

April stopped dialing. Rocky was behind the wheel of her car. In the split second it took to start the engine, April knew Rocky was going to abandon her. She was already halfway into her driver's seat when Rocky pulled away from the curb, leaving April alone to handle the murder scene.

April jumped out of her car, as if she were going to chase Rocky on foot. She stood in the middle of the street, her mouth open, watching as Rocky drove off. Her fingers were on her phone. They had already pushed 9-1-1. She hit the speaker function and jumped into her own car. She rolled down the window and laid the phone on the console. She started her car, pulled out of the driveway and followed Rocky's tail-lights. There was no way she was doing this alone.

The 9-1-1 operator asked for her emergency. April reached over and pressed the end-call button.

She followed Rocky past the empty guardhouse.

April heard Rocky grind her gears as she turned out of the development and down the hill toward town. April punched her accelerator, but her old Subaru was no match for Rocky's five-speed coupe.

The road forked. April had to slow. She strained but couldn't see Rocky's taillights up ahead on either road. One led to town, the other deeper into the valley.

April read the street sign. Mountain Road. Mitch's home was five miles up the road to the right. Her heart lifted as she turned right and sped down the wet road. She was confident Rocky had headed to Mitch's. If Mitch were her brother, that's what she'd do. In fact, she'd like to do that anyway.

Rocky must have really put the pedal to the metal. She was nowhere in sight, nor were there any other cars on the road. April strained to see through the dark. Streetlights weren't common out here. She passed weird looking shapes that turned out to be old silos and barns in near disrepair.

The darkness was so complete. She hadn't experienced this kind of night in a long time. In San Francisco, the city lights never went out. Here, the summer nights had been filled with fireflies and patio lights, but now it was nearing the onset of winter, and people were huddled inside. Daylight was short and night came early. She blinked, trying to open her eyes wider. Nothing helped.

She had to brake hard when the road took a ninety-degree turn. Her car shuddered with the effort of holding the pavement. She felt herself expel a breath. She didn't need a repeat of her earlier accident. She took her foot off the gas and let the car slow. The last two miles to Mitch's house took forever.

But it didn't matter. Rocky was not at Mitch's. The A-frame was locked up tight. The front porch light was on, but nothing else.

April felt panic rise in her. She'd walked away from Trish because of Rocky, and now she couldn't find her. The cops would not be happy with her.

Where else would Rocky be? Her other main haunt was the country club. April drove back into town and out to the country club. She trolled the parking lot but didn't see Rocky's car there, either.

She was out of time. She had to go back and face the police.

Witnesses could put her at Trish's. The guard knew she'd been out there several times. Whoever nearly ran her off the road might have recognized her car. If she didn't talk to the police and let them know what she knew, she could become a suspect. She started to pull out of the parking lot.

Light spilled out as a door leading to one of the small private rooms of the club opened. Her heart leaped to her throat and she threw her car into park.

Mitch. It felt like forever since she'd seen him. She would throw herself in his arms and tell him what she'd been through tonight. A stroke of his hand on her hair would give her the strength to face the police.

He was talking to someone. They'd stopped just outside the door. The other person lit up a cigarette and leaned in close to Mitch as he shook the match and extinguished the flame. A deep draw on the cigarette made a bright glow.

She peered out over the steering wheel. The smoking man had his head down. Who was Mitch with?

The door opened again and a figure dressed in a skirt stepped through.

April got out of her car, shutting the door quietly. She could hear Mitch's voice, low but insistent. She moved closer, still in the shadows.

Not a skirt, a kilt. Ferguson. They were

probably celebrating the telethon. April was a little hurt that they hadn't invited her. Dang these men anyway. Always the boys' club. No girls allowed.

"I'm glad I could bring you two together," Ferguson said, slapping the smoker on the back and reaching for Mitch's arm and pumping it. "This was a very productive dinner." He had a toothpick in his mouth, and his tongue worked it from side to side as he finished his sentence.

April stepped forward into the light. "Hello," she said.

The smoker turned to her voice, curious to see who had greeted them. His smile was lascivious. He probably figured that would make the perfect end to their evening. A good dinner, a back room deal and a pretty woman.

He blew a cloud of smoke, obscuring his features. She took another few steps toward him.

The light was stronger and the smoke cleared. She recognized the face just as Mitch and Ferguson caught sight of her.

"April?"

"Ms. Buchert, just the lady we need to see," Ferguson said. "I was just telling Ted here about your extraordinary fund-raising techniques."

The smoker was Traczewski, Trish's husband.

CHAPTER 22

April drew closer. She resisted Ferguson's arm, which was snaking around her back, pulling her close to him. She ducked away from him and stepped up to Traczewski.

"April, have you ever met Mr. Traczewski?" Mitch was saying. April looked at him with dismay. Why was Mitch acting like the head of Border Patrol wasn't scum?

She would deal with that later. Right now, there was a much worse problem.

Traczewski turned to snuff out his cigarette, exhaling with a cough and crushing the butt with his shiny shoe.

April wasn't sure she could speak. She opened her mouth once, but nothing came out. She tried again.

"Mr. Traczewski, I've just come from your house. I had an appointment with Trish. She didn't answer, so I went inside. She gave me the garage code. You know how she does."

April stopped. She knew she was babbling. Ferguson was looking at her strangely. She didn't want to explain why she went inside. And she couldn't tell them Rocky had been there. Mitch was waiting for her to get to the point.

She concentrated on Traczewski. This man needed to know his wife was lying dead in their bed. Before she could get out another word, however, she was interrupted by another voice in her ear.

"Ms. Buchert, I believe you called 9-1-1."

She wheeled a round to find Yost coming out of nowhere. He had moved up on her silently. His car was behind hers, blocking her exit.

He planted a hand on either hip, near his gun on one side, his walkie-talkie on the other. "We had a 9-1-1 call come in. The caller didn't identify herself but the area code was California, 4-1-5, to be exact. I believe that would be San Fran."

April turned away from him. She heard him blow out his lips impatiently, like a big dumb horse.

"I was calling in to report an incident," April stalled, looking from Mitch to Yost to Traczewski. Ferguson's good-ole-boy smile was fixed on his face. Mitch questioned April with a cocked eyebrow.

"Ms. Buchert, let's go talk in my car. You can let me in on what you think you saw," Yost said.

Traczewski huffed impatiently. She really wanted to wipe that smirk off his face. He was odious.

"I saw a dead woman. Dead in her bed. In Trish's bed."

Yost stiffened. "And you came here?"

Mitch said, "She knew I was having dinner with Traczewski."

April's head jerked toward him. He lied. That was the nicest thing anyone had ever done for her. Mitch moved over to put an arm around April, shielding her from Yost.

"She came right here to tell him about his wife," Mitch said.

"My wife? Trish?" Traczewski said. "Dead?"

He reached in his pocket and pulled out a set of keys. Ferguson snatched them from his hand. "I've got to go home," Traczewski said. His voice was soft, pleading. He reached for his keys.

"I'll follow you," Ferguson said.

Yost said, "Wait, just a minute, you two. I need to call this into the state police. Ms. Buchert, you need to come with me, back to the scene so you can give your statement to them. Mr. Traczewski . . ."

But Traczewski and Ferguson were already moving across the parking lot toward Traczewski's silver sedan. A moment later, the sedan was followed by an SUV out of the lot.

Yost followed them at a run. He called back to her, "Ms. Buchert, you'd better be right behind me."

Traczewski drove past. He was alone in his car. April saw Ferguson follow him, but their cars went in two different directions when they got to the end of the drive. Ferguson went toward Lynwood and his office. Yost roared past.

Suddenly it was just Mitch and April. April didn't want to face him. She started to turn back toward her car, but Mitch caught her by the arm.

"Where are you headed?" he said.

"Away from you. If you didn't hang out with racist wife-killers, I might like you more."

"I wasn't hanging out with them. Ferguson brought Traczewski along without my knowledge."

April felt her heart rate slow a bit. "You weren't meeting with him?" She'd jumped to the wrong conclusion. Her only excuse was that she was upset.

"He did tell me something interesting,

322

though," Mitch said, scratching his chin. "Ferguson swears he has witnesses who saw Hector buying spray paint from Ernst Hardware."

"Did Traczewski know, too?" April asked.

Mitch shook his head. "It was news to him."

"I bet he knew, I bet he was in on it with Valdez," April said.

Mitch was startled. "What do you mean?"

"Think about it. You've been working on this project under the radar for months, so to speak. No one noticed. You organized the building, got the volunteers, set up your committee to pick the family. All without any help from anyone from Lynwood. Right?"

"Yeah . . ." Mitch said. "What's your point?"

"The point is that just because the family that you happened to pick was of Mexican heritage, Hector gets interested. He brings along his opposition, Traczewski, because you can't have one without the other, and suddenly, you're on television and you've got protesters and you're having meetings with slimeballs like Traczewski."

Mitch looked thoughtful. It was obvious that the parade of events had just swept him along. He really hadn't given any of it much thought. He wanted to give a family a new home. That was all.

"What if the family whose name you'd picked out hadn't been Latino? Ever think of that? You think Hector would be around if the Kelly or the Becker family was the one you'd picked out of the hat?"

Mitch walked away from her. "But that's not what happened. It was a lottery. I drew the Villarreal family. Fair and square."

April followed him "And you got Hector. Worse, you got Traczewski. And ever since those two have been involved, you've had nothing but trouble."

"Hector and Traczewski didn't cause Xenia's death, and Xenia's death is what's causing all the trouble."

"Is it? Think about it. The graffiti was done before we knew Xenia was dead. The protest the next day was planned well in advance. That was no spontaneous event."

"I can't believe Hector would do anything to jeopardize the house."

"Mitch, open your eyes. These guys are using you to serve their own causes. They don't care anything about Winchester Homes for Hope. You're trying to save four families. They're both out to promote their own agendas. You're just a cog, a cog with an interesting story that gets them on TV."

Mitch was quiet. April could see he didn't want to believe it. She tried one more time. "Look at the facts. The anti-immigration feelings had died down. With no new legislation in the works, Hector and Traczewski were out of a job."

"Hector hates Traczewski," Mitch said.

"Maybe, but he needs him. They need each other. And they're both using you."

Mitch's eyes darkened. "Let's just agree to disagree, shall we?"

April could see she'd hit a dead end. "Sure. Did you at least get your money from Ferguson?"

"No. Ferguson said he's done a bank transfer online, but I haven't seen money yet. I'm going to run over to my sister's and use her computer to check."

Cripes. Rocky. She'd forgotten about her. She pulled away from Mitch. "I gotta go," she said.

Mitch said, "What are you doing? Let me drive you back to Pine's End."

She shook her head, fumbling for her keys. "I've got to go find Rocky first. She was there, at the Traczewski house, with me."

Mitch's brow furrowed. "My sister was there?"

"Yes. She saw Trish, too. In fact, I think she saw her before I did. She was up in the bedroom . . ."

"What were you doing there?"

"I had an appointment with Trish." April opened the door and sat on the seat, her feet on the ground. Mitch leaned on the open door.

"What was Rocky doing there?"

Good question. She looked up at Mitch. "Did you know she was buying the Stamping Sisters line from Trish?"

To her surprise, Mitch nodded. "I helped her with the finances. My sister never has a penny when she needs it. I was fronting her the money. I'm hoping the business will provide her with a steady income. You have no idea how many times I've had to bail her out of trouble."

"But you don't have any money," April said, standing up again. Mitch had to back up to get out of her way.

"What are you talking about, April? I still have my trust and my investments."

"But you're always talking about running out of money."

"Meet my brother, the tightwad," a voice in the dark said. Rocky came out from the side of the building. "You never have to worry about him. He's always got money. He's probably got the first dollar he ever made. Certainly has the first allowance Dad ever gave him."

"Rocky, this isn't the time," Mitch said. "You need to go talk to the police, both of you."

"That's more April's thing than mine. She's been through this before."

"So have I," Mitch said. "And it's important. I'll drive you both back. Leave your cars here."

He walked back and got his car. April and Rocky stood in awkward silence until Rocky leaned over to April.

"Want to know why I give you such a hard time about Mitch?"

April nodded.

"You didn't include me," Rocky said petulantly.

"Excuse me? How exactly does that work?"

April regretted her flip words as she saw a hurt look pass over Rocky's face. There was an undercurrent that April nearly missed. Rocky was hurt.

"Well, not like that. You guys need your alone time. I'm okay with that. But the Winchester Homes? I wanted to work on them, too."

"Mitch's been swamped," April said, still floundering. She wasn't sure if she could trust this new side of Rocky. Still wary that she was being punked somehow. That the real Rocky, strong, sassy and sarcastic, was hiding just beneath.

"Mitch asked you to design the interiors of the Villarreal house," Rocky said.

April saw the problem now. Before she'd arrived on the scene, Rocky had been the resident artist, the go-to gal for all things decorative and pretty. April had taken her place.

"There's plenty of work to go around," April said. "I'm sorry if it seemed like we shut you out. We didn't mean to."

April looked at this woman and recognized her vulnerability for the first time. She had me fooled, April thought. With the tough exterior and the constant teasing, she'd really thought Rocky needed no one. Instead, it was just the opposite.

And, if April hadn't been around, she'd be working with her brother more closely. Rocky missed her big brother.

April pulled Rocky in for a hug. "How about you paint the kitchen?" she said.

April felt Rocky stroke her back. "As long as you do the baseboards. I hate cutting in."

The two laughed and broke apart.

Rocky got in the front seat. April leaned in Mitch's window.

"I'm going to drive myself. See you there,"

she said, moving quickly before he had a chance to react.

She wasn't going to let Ferguson get away with stealing Mitch's money. She was going to his office and find out what was going on.

CHAPTER 23

Ferguson was running some kind of scheme, taking money from people like the Campbells and doing who knows what with it. April wasn't going to let him do that with the Homes for Hope money.

She pulled up to the studio. The retail store was dark, closed for business. She didn't see Ferguson's Porsche in the lot, but she decided to knock, just in case.

No answer. She walked around the building, peering in the windows. She tried the front door again. It pulled slightly but didn't budge. The handle rattled briefly. She glanced back at the road. Traffic was light at this hour, but Route 309 was a busy road and cars were whizzing by at fifty miles an hour. She was way too visible.

She went around the back, remembering the door Ferguson had taken her to that led directly into his office.

It was locked up tight.

Then, suddenly, the door opened. April nearly fell off the small concrete stoop. She caught herself on the iron railing and straightened.

"Looking for me?" Scott Ferguson was silhouetted in the doorway. He was the picture of relaxation, but he looked very different.

"As a matter of fact, I am," April said. She forced air into her lungs. She didn't want to sound weak or scared. All she wanted was what she'd been promised. He had money that belonged to Homes for Hope, money that would benefit the Villarreal kids, and she wasn't going to leave without it.

"Come in," he said.

She hesitated. They would be alone in his office.

She stayed in the doorway. "I just want to see that you transferred money into the foundation account," she said quietly. "Mitch believes you. I want the proof."

"You doubt me?" Ferguson crossed his arms and leaned in the jamb. He wasn't wearing the kilt she'd seen him in earlier. He was dressed in lightweight linen pants and a Hawaiian print shirt. Nothing like his usual attire. It was astonishing how different he looked.

"No problem. I'll print you a copy."

April was stuck now. She had to go in.

He held the door open.

She walked in. He busied himself at his desk, moving papers around.

"I didn't see your car out there. Your family not expecting you?"

"I always work this late."

She turned her attention to his credenza. He had the usual pictures of family. But one made her take a step closer for a better look. Trish and Ferguson grinning into the camera. The picture was clearly taken on a tropical beach. Ferguson was dressed in a Hawaiian shirt much like the one he was wearing now.

"You must be so upset about Trish," April said, an idea forming. "Her death."

"Excuse me?" Ferguson responded, closing a file drawer sharply.

April pointed to the picture. "I see your families vacationed together. Is this near your condo in Florida?"

He looked blankly as though wondering how much she knew about him. "No, that's the Bahamas."

Convenient. A place where banks didn't care where the deposits came from. He probably had money stashed. For all she knew, the beachfront property in the picture that the Campbells had hung so proudly could have belonged to anyone. Or no one.

"Why did you pay for Xenia's line of Bonita cosmetics?" April asked.

"An investment," he said. "I'm in charge of a lot of people's monies. I'm always looking for good investments."

"Trish probably wasn't too happy when she found out."

"She never knew," he said.

April moved down the wall, stumbling slightly when her toe caught on a small plaid suitcase that was in the corner of the room. She understood.

He was leaving town with the money he'd promised Mitch. Maybe that's why Trish got killed. She was supposed to go with him until her husband found out. And he killed her.

She turned back to Ferguson, to plead with him to give her Mitch's money, but it was too late.

Ferguson swooped a tie around her neck and pulled tight. She remembered how Xenia and Trish had died, strangled. April got one hand under the tie, keeping the pressure off her throat. She gasped for air.

Ferguson lost his balance trying to walk backward, momentarily letting go of her and the tie around her neck. April had a split second to get out from his grasp. She spun around, and the tie dangled innocently in his hand.

Using his foot, he slammed the door shut and pushed April up against it. He tried to push on her neck with his forearm. She squirmed away, stomping on his instep with all of her weight.

He took her place against the door, blocking her way as he rubbed his foot.

"Women," he spat. "They're never satisfied. Trish thought I wanted her to leave her husband and come with me. I never wanted that."

So it wasn't Traczewski who had killed Trish. It was him. April's blood ran cold. She saw the eyes of a killer looking back at her. He killed Xenia first, and then Trish.

"It's your fault, you know. I was ready to leave town days ago. I wouldn't have stuck around so long if you hadn't come up with the brilliant idea of having Clive Pierce and that Villarreal girl sing on the telethon. The extra money was too good to pass up."

He lunged for her in a fluid motion. April screamed and jumped back, knocking over the jug of walking sticks. Ferguson stumbled on them, looking like an inept log roller. He fell to the floor. April grabbed a walking stick and stabbed him in the chest, pinning him to the ground.

His eyes were snakelike now, evil and calculating. She knew he was just biding his time, catching his breath, gathering his strength before he came after her again.

She pushed harder on the walking stick, feeling him expel his breath.

"What did Xenia do to you? Find out about your schemes? Try to blackmail you?" she asked, feeling the rage. Xenia had had a long life ahead of her. Her children would grow up without a mother. Why?

He moved again, and April shoved hard with everything she had. The walking stick slipped off his chest and he rolled. He lumbered to his feet. She grabbed for another and swung at his head as if it were a softball. He fell, clutching his forehead.

Rocky burst through the door, with Mitch right behind her. Ferguson's eyes fluttered. He was out cold.

Mitch gathered April in his arms.

"Good thing my brother didn't believe you," Rocky said. Then, poking at Ferguson's shorts, she added, "Dang. I was really hoping to look up his kilt."

The stampers were gathered in the Harcourt Room at the club. It was the day before Bonnie's wedding and they were decorating.

Suzi came in with a large bouquet of money plant. The dried seed pods had gone translucent. She planned to pair them with orange berries and red roses. The result would be enchanting.

She set those down and pushed a long box toward April. "I got the roses at the flower market in Philadelphia this morning. Aren't they beautiful?"

April glanced inside. The roses were deep red, mature and complex. April touched one of the flowers, amazed at how intricately the petals were entwined. By this time tomorrow, the outer edges would open, revealing the whorls of color. April thought about her mother, wound so tight. Clive had begun to unravel her. In a good way.

"Help," Deana said, her voice distant.

Rocky was on a ladder, draping the ceiling with what looked like a parachute. She held a staple gun and used it noisily. Mary Lou was steadying the ladder, and Deana was nearly hidden, holding the rest of the gathered fabric in her arms.

April rushed in to assist. She took some of Deana's burden. Dee smiled at her. Up close, April could see the material had been stamped with glittery stars and moons. She looked up at the ugly ceiling tile and imagined the ethereal look that Rocky was going for.

"Rocky, this is going to be amazing," she said, choking up.

"April, don't start crying now," Mary Lou warned. "Save your tears for the actual wedding."

April rubbed her sleeve across her cheeks, unable to let go of the parachute without causing Deana to tip over. "I know, I know. I'm just so happy."

Deana laughed. "Things turned out okay, didn't they?"

April nodded. "Most things. The Villarreals moved into their house yesterday. Mitch and I were up all night Sunday . . ."

April waited for Rocky's snide remark, but none came. Progress.

"I was stamping the walls in the bathroom while Mitch installed the carpet in the boys' bedroom. You should see the mural Vanesa painted in her room."

"I helped," Rocky said. She grinned down at April, who nodded.

Mitch and April had been joined by Rocky for several hours. Rocky had been a trouper, taking a bucket of sudsy water to all the washable surfaces and hanging curtains, making sure the house looked great for the family.

"How about Ferguson? Is he going to get what's coming to him?" Mary Lou asked, turning to April. The ladder tipped. Suzi ran over to right it.

"Watch what you're doing, please," Rocky called. Her voice was muffled, pillowed by the fabric.

"So-rry," Mary Lou sang out.

Suzi went back across the room, back to arranging flowers in vases. She said, "That creep says he's sorry, that he didn't intend things to get out of hand. He keeps saying if the police will let him out of jail, he could pay everyone back."

April said, "That's not going to happen."

The thought of elderly couples like the Campbells putting their trust in Ferguson angered April, and no one in this room disagreed with her.

"He has to pay for what he did," April insisted, unable to resist a final jab. "There are consequences."

"Like new roommates for you," Mary Lou said, one foot on the bottom rung. She laughed, trying to break the tension in the room.

April took a breath. Scott Ferguson was under arrest. Justice would be done.

"My new roommates are marvelous," she said in an exaggerated voice. "She's a wonderful cook, and he's a great handy-man."

Deana winked at her. She knew Deana was proud of her for adjusting to her new circumstances. Deana lifted the last bit of fabric to Rocky, leaving April free to move over to join Suzi.

April stuck a piece of baby's breath in a vase and then continued her description of the Campbells. "They only sleep four hours a night and watch Fox News incessantly. She snores louder than an eighteen-wheeler trying to get up the mountain, and he passes gas as though he's going for a gold medal."

Rocky snorted from atop the ladder. Mary Lou giggled. The ladder shook.

April went on. "The good news is that they scared Ken off. One look at the way I was living, with old folks sleeping in the living room and a booster seat on my toilet, and he signed the divorce papers and high-tailed it back to California."

The rest of the parachute billowed out of Deana's grasp as Rocky tacked the last bit. The result was amazing. The entire ceiling was covered in gauzy white folds.

Rocky climbed down, shaking her arms out. Holding them over her head for so long had taken its toll. She stood in front of April. "So it's official? You're divorced?"

April nodded. "I just need to file."

Rocky's eyes narrowed.

April held up her hands. "It's just a procedure. The lawyer has everything in place. I'm practically divorced. Really."

Rocky slung an arm around her shoulders and hugged her. "Welcome to the Winchesters. I don't know why you'd want to date a dweeb like my brother or join a family as crazy as ours, but I'm glad you're willing."

"You're scaring me," April said, laughing.

"Love ain't for the faint of heart," Rocky said.

Deana said, "And Rocky will be your new boss, too."

Rocky had taken over the Stamping Sisters line. Trish's husband wanted nothing to do with it.

April wasn't sure how that was going to work out. She and Rocky had very different styles. "When do we start production on my California Dreamin' line? And then the home dec stamps, and —"

"Slow down, April," Rocky said. "I need to get up to speed first."

April smiled and said no more. It better not take too long, though.

"Take a look," Mary Lou said.

She turned off the lights. The day was gray and rainy with a forecast of snow, so the room was as dark as it would be tomorrow night when Bonnie and Clive got married. The five women watched as the room transformed.

The silk parachute was backlit with bright white twinkle lights. The glitter on the stamps caught the light and tossed it around. Suzi's roses reflected red on the walls.

April looked around the room. The tables were still bare, but she knew these friends she had found would make them beautiful, too. That's what they did. Out of the ordinary, the mundane, with a little love and a lot of effort, came the marvelous. The kind of beauty that would make Bonnie's wedding extra special.

She hugged them all in turn and said thank you. She let the tears fall so they could see how much their work meant to her.

CHAPTER 24

"Mom," April began. She entered her mother's bedroom with her hands behind her back, her fingers turning the gloves around and around. She stopped her nervous act. She didn't want to hand her mother a crumpled ball of fabric.

Bonnie turned. "April, I'm glad you're here. I need help with this zipper. I think I gained weight since I bought this dress. Clive is marrying a sausage roll, I swear. I look like a pea in a pod, all bumpy."

April kissed her mother's cheek. Soft and yielding, April felt her mother's shoulders come down a notch.

"You look beautiful," April began.

Bonnie waved her off. "Good thing Clive likes his women with lots of meat on their bones."

"Stop. He likes you."

Bonnie's hands fluttered impatiently. April knew the nerves were not just about standing up and saying her vows in front of all of her friends.

"Zip me."

"Hang on." April came around in front of her mother. She put the gloves in one hand and rubbed Bonnie's arm with the other. Bonnie took a breath and smiled a half-smile at her daughter.

"Why am I so nervous?" she asked. "It's only a wedding."

April laughed. "Maybe it means a little more than you're willing to admit," she said.

Bonnie's forehead creased. "I love him, you know."

April nodded. "I do know. We all know. We can see it."

"Oh god, does Clive know? I'd die if he didn't know."

"He knows, Mom. He loves you back. And it's wonderful to see."

Bonnie took a deep breath. April brought the gloves from behind her back.

"Look what I have," she said, offering the pair.

"Oh my," Bonnie said. She took the gloves from April and ran her fingertip down the seam. "Grandma Grace's gloves."

"Third time's the charm?" April said, laughing.

"I don't know about you, but I'm not doing this again. This marriage is my last."

"So the gloves did work, after all. It just takes us a little longer than most."

April hurried into the Harcourt Room just before Clive and Bonnie made their entrance. The rest of the guests were already inside.

Ed and Vince sat with relatives of Clive. From the crease in Ed's forehead, he was having trouble understanding their accents.

The Stamping Sisters' table was the next one over, close to where Bonnie and Clive would sit at small table for two, under an arbor laced with vines that Suzi had dotted with fresh cymbidium orchids. Deana and Mark, Mary Lou and her husband, Suzi and Rocky had already taken their seats and raised a glass to April as she sat down, fresh from posing for family portraits. They were waiting for the bride and groom to make an appearance.

The wedding ceremony had taken place in the gazebo an hour earlier. Clive had insisted on it being held outside despite the fact that the November day was sunny but cold, the heat wave of two weeks ago all but forgotten. Most of the guests had headed straight for the bar. Ruddy cheeks were still on display, and Ed couldn't stop blowing

344

into his hands to warm them up.

A side table groaned with the weight of food cooked by Pedro. He and his coworkers had cooked all day yesterday, forbidding Bonnie access to the kitchen. April didn't have to ask him. He'd insisted on cooking for Bonnie.

"How's our bride doing?" Deana asked.

April sighed and took a sip of the wine someone had poured for her. "Still insisting she didn't want photos taken. Still insisting she didn't want to be fussed over. But she can't stop smiling, and neither can Clive. I swear, he's going to trip walking in here because he can't take his eyes off her."

The door opened. The guests stood. The justice of the peace who married them called for their attention.

"It's my pleasure to introduce to you the newest married couple in Aldenville," he said. "Mr. and Mrs. Clive Pierce."

They all cheered as Bonnie and Clive walked into the room, arm in arm. Clive was dapper in a three-piece suit. Bonnie had found the perfect dress for herself, a pink satin that gave her skin a warm glow. Of course, she was radiant from within today.

April was still thinking about the wedding vows her mother and Clive had written together. What had started out as a way to keep Clive in the country had morphed into a real wedding. The vows had reflected that.

Getting married meant having hope, they'd said. Hope and trust. Hope that marriage would make their lives better in some way. That being a couple was not just about being two people together but becoming a third entity, a married couple, that was better and stronger than just two alone.

April looked over at Mitch. He'd brought the entire Villarreal family and was entertaining the little ones by dangling spoons off his cheek. He winked at her, and she felt a flood of warmth rush through her. Was it love? She wasn't sure yet. They needed time to grow as a couple.

Vince and Ed came over to the table.

"You girls did a marvelous job decorating," Vince said.

Ed was scrutinizing the curtains. "Those look familiar."

"The windows were bare," Suzi explained. "We had to do something drastic."

"As God is my witness," Mary Lou said, channeling Scarlett O'Hara, "windows will never go undressed again."

The stampers laughed. Ed looked confused.

"Aunt Barbara donated the fabric," Rocky said.

"Does she know?" Vince teased.

Ed's eyes narrowed. "Those are the drawing room drapes," Ed said, horrified.

"I'll put them back where I found them tomorrow," Rocky said. "She'll never know."

April put her hand on her father's arm to steady him and shot him a look of warning. He'd be anxious about it if she let him. Vince grabbed him by the other arm. Ed relaxed a bit.

"No later than tomorrow," he said, unable to resist one last parry.

April left them to go sit with Mitch. She kissed him as she sat down.

"God, you're freezing," he said. He took her face in his hands and kissed her cheeks. "Better?"

"Yes, thank you."

Jonathan and Greg were making gagging noises across the table. Their spoons fell over their faces and they giggled.

"You look nice," April said to them. Jonathan, Greg and Tomas were dressed in matching blue dress shirts and dress pants. Erika crawled down from her father's lap and stood next to April so April could admire her red velvet dress. She fluffed out the full skirt, showing off the lace petticoat.

April bent down. "You are as pretty as a fairy princess," she said. Erika smiled at her.

April's heart hurt for the mother who didn't get to see her daughter looking so sweet and lovely.

Vanesa caught her eye. April wondered what would happen to her Hollywood dreams now. April would bet she'd stick around to see Erika grow up.

Mitch turned his chair away from the table. April pulled up a chair so she was facing him. "Look at this."

April shot him a questioning glance.

"The state police gave Xenia's things to Pedro. In her purse was this, for me."

Mitch handed April a piece of construction paper, folded in half. April took her eyes off his ravaged face and opened it up. It was a child's drawing, of a house and seven sunflowers, ranging in height. Each flower face was grinning and had a name printed above it, naming all the Villarreals. The sun was shining brightly. A dialog bubble ran from the tallest figure. The words in childish crooked printing read: "Thank you, Mr. Mitch Winchester, for giving us our new home."

April's throat swelled. Mitch had tears in his eyes.

"This is what Xenia wanted to give me the day of the maze."

"Mitch . . ."

They leaned into each other, letting their bodies absorb their tears. "Those kids have a home because of you," she said.

"And they have justice because of you."

A tinkling noise cut through the chatter in the room. Clive was banging on his water glass with his knife. April wondered if he'd been tippling in the garden. His voice was high and squeaked. He cleared his throat and started again.

"A toast." Clive raised his glass, first to Bonnie, then to the group at large. "To Homeland Security!"

"To the chap who got my darling to do what all my cajoling, downright begging could not: get my luv to marry me. Cheers," he said.

Laughter rippled through the tables. But one person didn't see the joke. Bonnie said peevishly, "You know, it wasn't you. It was marriage."

Bonnie glanced at Ed. She held his gaze and April held her breath. Was her mother going to go there now?

April felt herself stiffen. She checked the exits. She had a clear path to French doors that led out to an empty patio. She pictured herself running across the frosty grass, her feet crunching the ice off the blades.

Bonnie took a deep breath and stood,

holding her glass in toast.

"I'm not much of a public speaker, so forgive me. But I do have something to say."

April's spine straightened.

Bonnie lowered her glass and tore her eyes away from Ed's face to gaze at her daughter. The room was quiet. April felt that Bonnie was speaking just to her.

Bonnie said, "I was married once to my best friend."

April's throat tightened. Would Bonnie bring up how Ed had disappointed her? April stole a glance at her father. His hands were tapping the table. Vince whispered to him and he stopped, but April could see he was struggling to stay composed.

"Mom," April said, starting out of her seat. Bonnie sat her back down with a look that April knew from a million dinner tables. She obeyed.

Bonnie continued. "It was a good marriage. We created a wonderful family."

She stopped again. April's stomach churned. The room was completely silent. April could hear the rustling as Greg jiggled in his seat.

Bonnie began again. "The marriage was so good in fact, I didn't think I would ever have anything like it again. I told myself I was lucky enough to have that once in my life."

Bonnie's eyes dipped to her hands. She'd taken off the gloves. No one moved. She raised her face again.

She was smiling, a huge smile that made her look like a young girl. "Somehow I got lucky twice and Clive found me. My reluctance to marry was about the institution, not about you. Never about you. I love you, Clive Pierce, and I'm proud to call myself your wife."

April felt an arm snake around her shoulders just as her tears threatened to dissolve her. She was sure she would have slid off the chair into a puddle if Mitch hadn't touched her just then.

The tears didn't fall, just stayed in her eyes making the world in front of her shimmery and glistening. She hugged Mitch's hand to her cheek.

Bonnie sat down, and Clive kissed her for a long time.

The crowd clapped. When they broke apart, Ed tapped his butter knife to his glass, signaling them to kiss again. Bonnie frowned but complied. Ed tried it again, but Bonnie shook her head. The rest of the crowd joined, and she gave in.

Clive broke the kiss. "One more thing,"

he said. "A musical interlude."

He pecked Bonnie's cheek and walked over to the keyboard that was set up in the corner.

"I'd like to introduce to you the vocal stylings of Vanesa Villarreal," he said with a flourish. He held his arm out, and Vanesa stood shyly. The group clapped. Mitch whistled his encouragement, and Rocky whooped-whooped.

Vanesa joined Clive on the bandstand, skillfully handling the microphone he gave her. She grinned at April.

Clive began to play some introductory notes. "Bonnie, my darling, I have one more surprise for you," he said.

Bonnie blushed. She was about at her limit for attention, April knew.

"I wrote a song just for you."

Clive sang. Vanesa provided lovely trills and background noises and joined him on the chorus. The song was upbeat, perky like a Kickapoos hit.

Love stepped in
And called my name
I wasn't listening
But I heard it just the same . . .

Mitch leaned in and whispered, "Quite a day."

His breath was soft on her neck, the promise of warmth on a winter's day.

April's heart was so full, she didn't have words to express herself. Her face felt tight, too strained to let her lips move.

"Nice when love triumphs," he said.

"Is that what happened?" she asked, searching his eyes for a deeper meaning.

"I think so, don't you?"

She did. She agreed with him. Love came when it was least expected, in all kinds of forms. Love came and it danced.

She picked up Mitch's hand and led him to the dance floor. She put his hands on her hips and let herself move to the music.

"Let's always remember to dance," she said.

Love stepped in
And now we're two happy chaps
And life is better than
I knew it could be.
Oh, Bonnie.

Bonnie was sobbing happily by the time he was finished. April's tears were flowing freely now. She ran to her mother.

One by one, the guests came up and

hugged Bonnie. By the time Clive came down from the stage, Ed and Vince were next in line.

"All the best," Ed said, his voice choked. Clive pumped his hand.

"Happiness," Vince said.

Bonnie hugged them both in turn and then hugged them together. Mitch called for a picture, and April gathered the four around her. She looked at Bonnie, Clive, Ed and Vince and smiled.

Her family.

STAMPING PROJECT

Supplies
- Pumpkin stamp
- Stamp pad(s)
- Cardstock
- Colored pencils or watercolors
- Scissors
- Scroll vine stamp
- Scrap paper
- Ribbon
- "Happy Fall" stamp

Directions

1. Use a stamp pad to ink the pumpkin stamp and then press stamp firmly to a piece of cardstock.
2. Using color pencils or watercolors, color in the pumpkin, and then trim the cardstock to square shape.
3. Take another cardstock and cut another, slightly larger, square.
4. Then, use the scroll vine stamp on the card background. To get a lighter color, you can use a lighter stamp pad or just ink the stamp and then stamp once on scrap paper before stamping the cardstock.
5. Next, take a piece of ribbon across the scroll vine background. Wrap the ribbon around the edges to give a finished look.
6. Mount the pumpkin square on top of the ribbon.
7. Finish by stamping the "Happy Fall" stamp underneath the pumpkin.

We hope you have enjoyed this Large Print book. Other Thorndike, Wheeler, Kennebec, and Chivers Press Large Print books are available at your library or directly from the publishers.

For information about current and upcoming titles, please call or write, without obligation, to:

Publisher
Thorndike Press
295 Kennedy Memorial Drive
Waterville, ME 04901
Tel. (800) 223-1244

or visit our Web site at:

http://gale.cengage.com/thorndike

OR

Chivers Large Print
published by BBC Audiobooks Ltd
St James House, The Square
Lower Bristol Road
Bath BA2 3SB
England
Tel. +44(0) 800 136919
email: bbcaudiobooks@bbc.co.uk
www.bbcaudiobooks.co.uk

All our Large Print titles are designed for easy reading, and all our books are made to last.